ENEMY DOWN

CATHRYN FOX

COPYRIGHT

Enemy Down
Copyright 2021 by Cathryn Fox
Published by Cathryn Fox

Discover other titles by Cathryn Fox at www.cathrynfox.com. Please sign up for Cathryn's Newsletter for freebies, ebooks, news and contests: https://app.mailerlite.com/webforms/landing/c1f8n1

ISBN 978-1-989374-34-4
ISBN Print 978-1-989374-33-7

1

MAIZE

"Hot, right?"

I glance to my left, to lane number four as fellow track star—and my very best friend—Kaitlyn Collins catches up to me. I lift my face to the sky to take in the late afternoon sun. It might be early fall, but it's always hot in Southern California this time of year. I swipe beads of moisture from my forehead and concentrate on my breathing and my pace. Our big meet is next week, and I need to take first in my category or...well, I can't think of the consequences.

"The sun is going down. It should cool off soon enough," I say, but before I get a chance to turn my focus back to my own lane, I catch her mischievous grin, and the wagging of her eyebrows.

"You know that's not what I'm talking about."

"Then what are you talking about?" I ask, instantly regretting the words spilling from my mouth. Stupid. Stupid. Stupid.

Honestly, I'd have to be a total idiot not to know she's talking about the football team, and their...oh, how does she describe them in their tight pants? Sexy, hot football butts. If you ask me, they all look like overstuffed sausages ready to burst wide open. I never did have a taste for sausages, except those flat breakfast sandwiches ones from my favorite fast-food restaurant.

"You don't want to tap dat ass?" she teases. I take a deep, fueling breath and focus straight ahead, putting an end to this conversation. I am not discussing butts with her, or any kind of sausage. But will she let it alone? Hell no. This is Kaitlyn we're talking about. She might want to work her way through the entire football team—bed every Falcon—but she can leave me out of it. I have more important things to think about than tapping any man's ass. Wait, is that even a thing?

"What about Christian?"

"What about him?" I grumble.

Her grin widens and yeah, I get it. She caught me staring at the quarterback as he called out the last play. I'd give just about anything to run track somewhere else, but no, Kingston had to efficiently build the track around the football field, forcing me to stare at cocky Christian Moore like it's my damn job. When it comes right down to it, I don't *have* to stare. I don't even want to stare. I hate that guy with the power of a thousand burning suns, and honestly, that might not even be enough sun to accurately describe the extent of my loathing.

Then why the hell were you staring, Maize?

Isn't that the question of the century. But there is one thing I know. It has nothing to do with his butt in those pants. Almost nothing, or maybe everything.

"Christian is looking even harder this year, don't you think?" She lifts her arm and flexes her impressive bicep.

I put on my best bored expression. "I wouldn't know."

I pick up my pace, hoping to leave my bestie behind, but she's not having any of that. I might be the school's top middle-distance runner, but she's the top long-distance girl, and there isn't a hurdle she can't jump. My stupid gaze slides to Christian again.

Speaking of jumping.

Come on, Maize!

Kaitlyn kicks out those long athletic legs of hers and catches up easily. Not that I really thought I could lose her. We're both attending Kingston College on sport scholarships. Most students here are on their parents' dime, but we're star athletes from the wrong side of the tracks. We met at Sweetwater High, an uber rich high school in So Cal. We both had to take three different busses to get there each morning, since it was outside our school districts. That's where I met Christian too. God, just thinking about him makes me want to hurl. The guy singlehandedly ruined my life in senior year.

I cast Kaitlyn a glance, and as if being pulled by some greater force, my gaze once again slides to Christian, only to find his eyes locked on me—like he could feel me staring, feel me thinking about him. Holy shit. I tear my gaze away fast and suck in air.

"We still on for the mall later?" I ask, trying not to sound winded. I could run for hours without losing my breath, but apparently, all it takes is one direct look from Christian to steal the air from my lungs.

Get it together, girl.

Her pace slows, as she finishes her run. "Yeah, but I can't be long. I have a group project meeting later."

I toss my words over my shoulders. "Okay, I have one lap left. After I shower, I'll meet you out front."

She nods and wanders off the track as I keep running. I pick up the pace, wanting to feel the burn in my legs—and expel images of Christian from my brain. My lungs expand, and I enjoy the rush of endorphins racing through my body. Nothing, and I mean nothing—sex included—feels as good as running. Not that I've had a lot of sex. I'm practically a virgin. A few years back, my buddy Ryan—the boy next door back home—and I, decided we didn't want to be virgins when we went off to college. So, we did the logical thing and had sex. It was awkward and fumbling, and it was over before it ever began. I'm not even sure I climaxed. Pretty sure I didn't. I can barely get myself off with my own hand. Usually, I have to switch to battery operated, which I hate to do in an old house with nothing but seaweed between the walls. I have four roommates, and I'd die of embarrassment if they ever heard.

Dear Mom, thanks for that strict Catholic upbringing and all the teachers who body shamed us. At Sweetwater, our uniforms were constantly assessed. I was told numerous times my skirt was too high. Um hello. Tall girl. Long legs. Capri pants on other girls are like shorts on me.

I'm about to slow my pace, but the next thing I know, something big and hard hits me in the side of the head, and I lose all sense of balance. The direct hit, combined with my speed, sends me flying forward, and the sound of bones popping, and skin ripping as I hit the ground hard, reverberates around me, over the ringing in my ears.

My jaw skids shut with an audible click as my face hits the track, and I skid. It takes forever for my body to stop moving and the world to stop spinning. When everything slows, I lay on the ground face down, too afraid to breathe...to move.

What the hell just happened?

"Are you okay?" I try to move, to check my limbs, but whoever is hovering over me puts his hands on my back to hold me down. "Don't move."

Move? I almost laugh, because I'm not sure I can move and that seriously freaks me out. I turn my head to the side, and that's when Christian puts his face down, right there, inches from mine.

"Maize, I'm so sorry."

What is he talking about?

"My football," he begins obviously reading the question in my eyes. "I don't know. I threw it, and Kyle missed it, and then you were right there, perfectly aligned for it to hit. You weren't there a second before. You must have picked up your pace."

"Oh, it's my fault, is it?" I manage to get out.

His brow furrows, and he shakes his head. "No, that's not what I mean."

Voices echo in my brain as everyone comes running, and embarrassment floods me. I need to get up, to move, to run all the way to Canada, never to be heard from again. I move my hand, and once again Christian presses down, to stop me.

"Can you stop doing that?" I whimper. "I'm fine. I don't feel anything."

His face twists. "Yeah, that's because of the adrenaline rush. Give it a second."

I swallow. Why do I get the feeling he knows something I don't? "Christian—"

"You're going to be okay," he says, but the strain in his voice tells another story.

A burst of panic floods my body, and I slide my hand and touch my forehead to find an egg-sized lump. It's possible I have a concussion. The world spins and my stomach lurches from the movement. Great, now I'm going to vomit in front of everyone. This ground might as well open up and swallow me whole.

"Here," he says, and slides his jersey under my head to cushion it from the ground. I sink into the soft material, heavy with the scent of soap and...Christian. Okay, I definitely have a concussion, because no way on the face of this earth would I be reveling in the stupid aroma of his shirt.

Damn him!

A siren sounds and I try to shake my head no. All I need to do is get up, throw a little dirt on my wounds, and I'll be okay. I give a very unladylike snort. That's what my Mom used to say to me when I was little and hurt myself. Throw a little dirt on it. Mom and me, we were a team. Just the two of us against the world. We did things on our own terms, and asked for nothing. We worked for everything, or we went without.

"Maize, please," Christian implores, his voice, heavy with worry, stills me. He drops to the ground, and lays on his side, his eyes locked on mine. Blue. My God, he has the most gorgeous blue eyes in the universe. I couldn't see them that night we were locked in the closet, playing seven minutes in heaven. I wanted so badly to fit in with the 'popular' girls at Sweetwater. When Chelsea Haverstock invited me to her party, I was thrilled. Of course, I had no idea it would ruin my reputation and leave me friendless, except for Kaitlyn. She had no desire to be a popular girl. She knew mean when she saw it. Now I see it everywhere.

"I think your ankle is broken," he says his voice low, like it will somehow soften the blow.

"No, it's not." I suck in a fast breath, determined to get up, but his big hand continues to push me down again and why the hell do I like that so much? What is wrong with me? I hate his face. I hate his touch, and I most definitely hate the way he's pinning me down, and making me wonder what it would be like if he were on top of me.

"The paramedics are almost here. Let's wait and see what they say."

"I'm not waiting for anything." No, I'm getting up, finishing my run, and meeting Kaitlyn for a fast trip to the mall for new laces. If I wait, they might tell me what I refuse to admit. If I refuse to admit it, then I won't be off the team, my scholarship won't be stripped from me, and I won't have to move back home, having made nothing of myself. I have big dreams, for God's sake. I want to be a lawyer, I want to right all the wrongs and help people.

His fingers splay on my back, teasing all my nerve endings until pleasure mingles with pain. I'm familiar with the sensations from running, and I have to admit, my body craves that rush. The next thing I know, I'm being checked out by two men, and nearly blinded by a flashlight. Everyone is moving, fussing about, and my head starts to pound so hard, nausea grips my stomach. If they would all just leave me alone, I'll be fine. The two paramedics move me, and shift me to a gurney. I briefly close my eyes, wishing I was an ostrich and could shove my head in the sand. I might be an athlete, but I don't love being the center of attention, and right now, every member of Kingston's football team is staring at me—so are their girlfriends, and all the cheerleaders.

It takes great effort to go up onto my elbows, to check out my body, and a sound that seems to scare everyone around me crawls out of my throat when I glance at my foot, which is twisted in an unnatural way.

"No…" I whisper. "No, no, no."

"Maize," Christian says, and I turn to him as tears burn behind my eyes. "It's going to be okay." He puts his hand on my shoulder.

I swallow against the pain in my throat. Christian is a rich kid, born with a silver spoon in his mouth. He has no idea that his wayward football just put an end to my scholarship. How the hell am I going to pay for next term's tuition?

"You have no idea what you're talking about," I shoot back, and he withdraws his big hand from my shoulder, worry and guilt all over his face. "You ruined high school for me, and…" a humorless laugh crawls out of my throat. "And now, not only have you ruined my senior year of college, but you might have ruined my future too." He rears back like I just slapped him. His mouth opens and closes, like my words have shocked him, but he knows what he did that day in the closet, what he's done now. I hold my skinned palm up to stop him. "Just go." He inches back, and I square my shoulders to pull myself together. No way, no how am I going down like this. I'm a fighter. A survivor. A girl who can stand on her own two feet —well, at the moment, on one good foot. As long as I can stand, I'll do whatever it takes—anything—to stay in college.

Well, just about anything…

2

CHRISTIAN

I pick my helmet up from the ground, and the coach comes over to me. He dips his head, and assesses me like he does after I've taken a hard hit on the field.

"You okay?" he asks.

"Not really," I respond as Maize's words beat against my gut. She blames me for ruining high school for her? Honestly, that's news to me. After our seven minutes in heaven, when she pulled my pants down to my ankles, and opened the doors so all the girls could get pictures, I never spoke to her again. Yeah, I get it, the mean girls were hazing the skinny new guy. I never paid Maize much attention after that, and even though she left me standing in my boxer shorts, the rumors about her being an easy lay never seemed to ring true. Then again, she did take my pants to my ankles. But how was that *me*, ruining school for her?

But the past is the past and what's happening now is far more serious than a stupid hazing prank. I might not like her as a person after that stunt—that doesn't mean I don't admire a beautiful girl when I see one—but I'd never forgive myself if she lost her spot on the track team because of my football.

Coach's voice pulls me back. "Why don't you go to the hospital, check on her."

I nod, tap my helmet against my leg and glance around. My best friend Linc, and his girlfriend Steph, slowly walk toward me.

"Okay, guys back on the field," Coach Meyers orders. He waves his hand and the guys all start back, and I nod as they check in with me.

"Fuck," I say to Linc. "Her ankle is shit."

He tears off his helmet and runs his fingers through his mess of dark hair. "That was Maize, right? From high school?"

"Yeah. That was Maize." I shake my head and stare at Linc, like he can somehow make this all better, even though I know he can't. He's a good guy, and back in high school took me under his wing, on and off the football field. We've been best friends ever since. I was sixteen when we moved to So Cal, and a skinny kid at that. It wasn't until eleventh grade that I filled out, and tried out for the football team. During my sophomore year, the girls might have teased me, splashed a picture of me with my pants at my ankles all over social media, but my status quickly changed when I excelled on the football field. Then I was moving in different circles, Maize's stunt long behind me, and the pictures from the closet became almost legendary, something to be admired instead of ridiculed. How fucked up is that?

I wasn't a fan of all the attention. I'm not one to flaunt or showboat around and as far as Maize goes, after the incident, she mostly kept to herself or hung out with Kaitlyn. I found out later she was a scholarship student. Maybe she had to focus on her running and classwork and didn't have time for parties. That doesn't change the fact that she was one of the mean girls—girls who never had anything to do with me until I was a baller. Of course, Chelsea Haverstock was a mean girl too and that didn't stop me from sleeping with her in my senior year of high school.

"She looks different," Linc says.

He's right. She does look different. She was a cute sixteen-year-old, now she's a tall, gorgeous college senior who excels in track. Impressive really, and now I might have taken it all away from her. Just because I don't like her doesn't mean I want bad things for her.

"Fuck," I say again. I'm responsible for the accident and I need to at least see what I can do to help. "Listen, I'm going to go to the hospital."

"I'll come with you," Linc says.

Steph slides her arm around Linc. "Me too."

"Hey, what's going on?" I glance up to see Kaitlyn coming toward me. Her ponytail bounces as she picks up her pace. "I was out front when I heard the ambulance. Who's hurt?" She glances around the track, and her face pales as worry moves into her eyes. "Wait, shit. Where's Maize?"

I jerk my thumb over my shoulder, to the street. "She, uh..."

"Oh my God, is Maize hurt?" she asks, her voice rising, bordering on hysteria as her gaze goes from me to Linc, to Steph, back to me again.

"It's her ankle. I think it might be broken."

"Holy shit." She starts toward the street.

"Where are you going?" I call out.

"To the hospital. Where do you think I'm going?"

"I'm going too. Come on. I'll drive you."

She keeps walking, and I guess if Maize hates me, her best friend does too. "It's too far to walk. Come on, Kaitlyn, I'll drive."

She slows and spins, her jaw tight. I don't miss the way Steph has her head lowered, like she's looking down her nose at Kaitlyn, because she's not dressed in the latest, most fashionable yoga clothes from that ridiculously overpriced store.

She yells out, "Fine."

"Meet me in the lot," I say and hand my keys to Steph. She takes them and doesn't even acknowledge Kaitlyn as she stalks off, not bothering to wait or make conversation. She could at least show concern for Kaitlyn's best friend.

I nod to Linc and we head to the locker rooms to change. A few minutes later, I'm behind the wheel of my Jeep, Kaitlyn beside me and Linc and Steph in the back as I maneuver through the campus and hit the street. Ten minutes later, I'm at the hospital and squeeze my Jeep between two cars. Linc pulls up his parking app to pay, as Kaitlyn and I both hurry inside.

Kaitlyn scans the waiting room. "They must have taken her in already."

"I'll go find out." I walk up to the nurse's station, and a pretty little blonde behind the counter offers me a big smile.

"Hi there." She smiles, and Kaitlyn snorts behind me.

"Seriously," she murmurs.

Ignoring her, because I am not flirting like she thinks, I ask about Maize and find out that she's been rushed to surgery. I thank the nurse and plop down into a chair next to Kaitlyn.

She turns to me, her face tight. "What the hell happened anyway?"

My stomach twists as I toss my car keys to Linc. "No sense in you both hanging out here. I'll give you a call when I know more and you can come get us then."

Linc catches the keys and nods, and I bend forward to brace my elbows on my knees.

"Are you going to answer me?" Before I can get a word out she continues. "It obviously has something to do with you, considering you're sitting here."

"It was an accident."

She snorts. "Oh, just like you pulling down your pants. Was that an accident too, Christian?" What the fuck is she talking about? I don't get the chance to ask before she blurts out, "Okay, tell me everything. Exactly what happened."

I let her earlier comment go, and exhale. "Kyle missed the ball, and it hit her. She went flying and landed hard." I steal a quick glance at Kaitlyn to find her shaking her head, and I can almost hear the wheels spinning.

"Fuck," she murmurs. "This is bad, so bad."

"Yeah, my sentiments exactly." I glance at Kaitlyn's ponytail, the glow on her cheeks, like she'd just been running herself. "What does this mean for her? You know, for track." I have no idea if she's a scholarship student here or not, but I can only assume she is, based on the fact that she told me I've probably ruined her future. I didn't want to come right out and ask, and make her feel, less, somehow.

Instead of answering, Kaitlyn pushes from the chair, and shoves her hands into her pockets, but her non-answer says it all. Shit. Kaitlyn paces for a few seconds and heads to the coffee machine. Coins plink as she drops them into the slot, followed by gurgling sounds. She surprises me by coming back with two paper cups.

"Thanks."

She doesn't respond. Instead, she sits down and loudly sips, like she's purposely trying to annoy me, but I'm already upset with myself as it is. I toss up a silent prayer, and tell myself that it's nothing serious and that after minor surgery she'll be back on her feet in no time. My gut however, doesn't quite believe it.

"Should we call her parents or something?" I ask.

"No."

I shift on the hard plastic chair, as more people enter and fill the seats. "Don't you think they should know?"

"No." Kaitlyn pulls her phone out and starts texting.

"Her parents should know. I mean she might want a family member here for when she gets out of surgery, and their insurance—"

"No."

I let loose a frustrated sigh and tug on my hair. "Can you say something other than no?"

"Yes."

"So you can, you just won't to me."

She gives me a humorless grin. I shake my head and I flick the plastic lid on the coffee as I push to my feet. My phone pings, and I pull it from my pocket. I read a message from Tamara, telling me there's a fun new band at the pub this weekend. That will get me out of Wolf House for the night, and I always try to be out of the frat house when the monthly 'ceremony' takes place. I shake my head. Jesus Christ. It's fucking crazy. My father is a goddamn Supreme Court judge, and what's taking place in the basement of Wolf House is fucking corrupt. Sure, it's a secret society, and we've all taken a vow of silence, but I don't want anything to do with it. Just like I didn't want anything to do with the hazing when I arrived. I am not going to 'bag' any virgins, for Christ's sake. I'd like to think I'm above that kind of disgusting misogyny. Women are not sex objects, put on this earth for my pleasure.

While I believe that, and respect women, it doesn't mean I want or am ready for a committed relationship. If my parents' marriage was anything to go by—she trapped him by getting pregnant with me—I'd steer clear of women altogether. But hey, I'm a red-blooded male. So, while I'm all about the sex, women know I have nothing more to offer.

I stop pacing. Maybe...this weekend, the 'ceremony' that takes place in our basement might just be the way to make up for taking Maize to the ground. Then again...I'm not sure it's something she'd ever do.

I spend the next little bit checking social media, and pacing. I head outside for a breath of fresh air, and the cute nurse eventually follows me out. She puts her hand on me and turns me her way.

"You don't remember me, do you?"

I narrow my eyes. Shit, did I sleep with her at some frat party and forget? "Sorry, no."

"I'm Fiona Witherspoon." She gives a little laugh. "I was a senior at Sweetwater when you moved to town." She nibbles her bottom lip in that flirty way women do. "I was there at Chelsea's party the night you sort of lost your pants."

"Yeah, great night."

She chuckles and nudges me playfully. "It was just a prank, put the new kids in the closet, and have some fun."

"It really wasn't fun." I narrow my eyes and inch back. "Was it fun for you?"

She waves her hand. "Actually yeah, it was a good laugh." I just stare at her and she shifts a bit uncomfortable under my scrutiny. Bullying is anything but funny. "It was harmless."

"I'm not sure I would agree with you."

"Come on. You got over it, big time, and Maize was a big nerd at our school on scholarship." She blows out a breathy sigh. "Did she really think she could be one of us?" A tsking sound is followed by a hard eye roll, and everything inside me tightens.

"One of us?"

"You know." She puts her hand on my chest. "One of us." Her voice is flirty, playful as she touches me. "People like you and me."

I shake my head as the pieces fall into place. "Oh, one of the popular kids, you mean?"

"Yeah, you know. Cool and popular and not on a sports scholarship. She should have stayed on her side of town."

"Okay, let me get this straight. You guys were out to prank *both* of us?"

"Yeah, but then..." Her gaze moves down my body, and her fingers follow, stopping when they reach my pants. "This happened, and then you fit in quite nicely, didn't you? No hard feelings?"

One of her hands goes to her hair, and in a flirty gesture she curls a strand around her finger. I jerk back, away from her touch. "If you'll excuse me, I need to get back inside to check on my friend."

"But—"

I don't want to hear what she says. I go through the doors as they open, my stomach tight at what I just heard. I honestly had no idea the prank was on Maize, too. Did they tell her to pull my pants down? Then make fun of her for doing it? She did stop hanging with those girls, because they turned her reputation to shit. She never seemed like she was an easy lay, as the guys used to say. In the hallway one day, I heard someone call out 'corn on the cob' when she passed, and I'd have to be an idiot not to get it—although I'm beginning to believe a lot of things went over my head in high school. But her name is Maize, which in French is loosely related to corn, and a guy's dick obviously represents the cob.

Those rumors must have evolved from that incident. Something the mean girls started to put her in her place, show her she didn't belong. Did she think I was in on it? Holy fuck, she must have, but had I known what was really going on, that she'd been set up too, I would have beat the crap out of everyone responsible—although most of them were the mean girls.

I drop down into the uncomfortable chair and Kaitlyn stares at me like I might have something on my face. Other than regret and worry, I'm pretty sure I'm clean. I swipe at my nose anyway.

"Christian?"

I stiffen, and brace myself because she looks like she has something very important on her mind. I lower my voice to match hers. "Yeah?"

"What goes on in the basement of Wolf House?"

3

MAIZE

I slowly open one eye, and then the other, and when my bedroom walls come into view, and reality comes racing back, I groan and roll over, the stupid boot on my foot a heavy reminder that I might never run again. It's been five days since they did the ankle surgery, and for five days I've been lying here trying to figure out how to pay for it, along with my next term's tuition. I run my tongue over my front tooth. It's been a bit wiggly since I fell. Maybe the tooth fairy would give me a large sum if I tucked it under my pillow. I mean, an adult front tooth must be worth something, right?

God, what am I even saying? I must still be concussed, because I'm clearly not thinking straight. The tooth fairy only collects kids' teeth. Sheesh. I laugh, almost manically at that last thought. My phone pings, and I sober as I reach for it. I put on my best happy voice when I see it's my mom calling. Then I wonder why she's calling at ten in the morning on a Saturday. I slide my finger across the phone, digging deep for my chirpy voice.

"Hey Mom, what's up?"

"What do you mean what's up? Can't a mother check in on her daughter?"

Okay, it's true. I haven't called or texted and that's not like me. It's just, well, I worried that if I heard her voice I'd burst into tears, and have to confess that I'm going to lose my scholarship. Mom is a nurse's assistant and can't afford to help me, even though I know she'd go without heat and food to try. But still, I'm an adult, and I need to find my own way out of this mess.

"Sorry. Just crazy busy with the upcoming meet," I say, and cringe as the lie spills from my lips. I hate to lie to my mother but under the circumstances, I have no choice.

"I thought that was today," she says, as dishes clang in the background and her tea kettle sings.

"Oh, yeah, no. I made a mistake. It's next week." I'm glad I don't have pants on, because yeah, they'd be on fire.

"That's not like you. Making a mistake on your meets."

"Fourth year, applying for grad schools." I have the grades to get into Harvard Law, I just won't have the funds if I can't get a scholarship, and with this broken ankle... "I have a lot on my mind." Time to change the subject. "How are you?"

"I'm good. Maybe I can drive up tomorrow, we can grab lunch—"

"No," I bark out quickly, too quickly judging by the way she just fell silent. "I'm sorry, Mom. I'm just crazy busy. I'll see you at Thanksgiving, okay?" Hopefully in two months, my ankle will be better, and I can get back to running. If not... Nope, not going to go there.

"I have a study group, so I have to go." Pretty much the first thing I said that was true.

"Okay, love. You have a great day. I'm looking forward to seeing you for Thanksgiving." A pause and then, "Will you be bringing anyone with you?"

I shake my head and silently laugh. "No. You know I don't have time for guys right now." I don't have the time, patience, or trust needed for a boyfriend. I've seen the way the guys here go from one bed to the next. My own father cheated on Mom right after I was born, then he screwed off, never to be heard from again. So no, I'm not about to put my heart in any man's hands only for him to crush it. "All my focus goes into my work."

She makes a tsking sound. "All work and no play—"

"Is what's going to get me into Harvard," I say, cutting her off. Mom knows my plans, and I get that she wants me to enjoy college and come out well-rounded. She wants better for me than she had, and I don't want to disappoint her, but I will not be bringing any guy home. I'll be bringing good grades home instead.

She laughs, and it mingles with the sound of her spoon in her teacup. I smile, missing my tea and honey moments at home. "Okay, love. If you change your mind."

I end the call, push from the bed, and about to head to the hall bathroom when a knock comes on my bedroom door. "Maize, you up?"

"Yeah, come in."

The door pushes open and in walks Kaitlyn. I instantly notice the tightness in her shoulders.

"What's wrong?" I steal a glance at the clock. "Shouldn't you be at the meet?"

"I just finished warming up. Headed back in a second. I wanted to talk to you."

I shift on the bed, to make room for her. "What's up?" I ask, my stomach tight. She's going to deliver bad news. I just know it.

"I was talking to Coach today. She uh...she's going to replace you. Janice is going to take your spot."

I grip the sheets and squeeze. Of course, she's going to replace me. I never thought for a moment she wouldn't, but it stings nonetheless. "Janice will do great."

She glances at my boot. "I'm worried about your tuition."

"Me too."

"There's a way..." Her voice falls off and my gaze jerks to hers, and from the way her eyes are wide, her head dipped a little, I'm not sure I want to hear what it is she's about to say.

"What?"

She picks at an imaginary piece of lint on my bed. "Remember those whispers we used to hear, you know about the secret society some of the athletes and scholars belong to, you know the Wolf Pack, at Wolf House?"

"First that's a stupid name and second it can't be true, Kait-lyn. Men can't buy and own women, it's the twenty-first century, and illegal." She slides her hand behind her back, and produces a card. I eye it carefully. "What's that."

"It's an invitation." She pushes it toward me. "It's for you, and only you. You have to turn it in tonight."

I take the card from her, and all it says is a time and a place, and that time is nine tonight. "What am I looking at?"

"In the basement of Wolf House. It's an auction of sorts. You'll belong to the highest bidder."

Forgetting all about my foot, I jump up, hardly able to believe what I'm hearing. "You've got to be kidding me."

"I wish I was, but..."

My heart crashes in my chest as my brain races to catch up. The Wolf Pack at Wolf House is real? "Where did you get this?"

She hesitates for a brief second. "I can't tell you."

"Kaitlyn," I warn.

She stands and puts her hands on my arms. "Just trust me on this." She takes the card and holds it up. "This...right here...is your ticket to Harvard, Maize. You might never run again, but as long as you can stay at Kingston and keep your grades up, you'll get that scholarship to Harvard. This will help you afford it."

I glare at her, unable to wrap my brain around this. "How long have you known about this?"

"A little bit now, why?"

"Why are you just telling me now?" I practically shriek.

She exhales and makes a groaning sound. "I was hoping you'd miraculously recover, and two, I wanted to wait until the last minute so you couldn't overthink it."

"Overthink it? I'm not going to overthink it. In fact, I'm not going to spend one more second thinking about it." Kaitlyn frowns. "Look, I can't..." My words fall off as I actually take a second to think—okay maybe overthink—all this, and what selling myself could mean for my future. The fact of the matter is, I'm a fighter, a survivor who will do whatever it takes to succeed. But would I sell myself, become some rich asshole's plaything? That's insane, right?

She blinks dark lashes over hopeful blue eyes. "It's a means to an end, that's all it is."

"I...I..." I sink back onto the bed. "What would I have to do?"

She shrugs. "I don't know. You just show up, and well, the guys bid, and you become their...I guess like maybe their servant or something. It can't be that bad. Maybe you just cook and do their homework or something..."

"Or something, something like sleep with them."

She glances down and frowns. "I don't know if that's true. But if it was so bad, why would girls agree to do it? I don't know much, but I know this happens once a month, on the last Saturday of the month, and these cards are not given out lightly, they're given out to—"

"Girls who are desperate!"

A door slams down the hall, and I jump. We live in a very rundown old house with three other girls, someone is always coming and going, and the place is always creaking—pipes always breaking—so I don't know why I'm on edge, or maybe I do. Am I really considering this?

I take the card from her and toss it onto my bed. "I need coffee," I say, and hobble to the door. "And you need to get to the meet. One of us needs to keep her scholarship."

"I'm going. I'm going. And I put a whole pot of coffee on for you. I figured you'd need it after..." She glances at the card I tossed to my bed.

"Maybe what I need is a stiff drink."

She gives a humorless laugh and walks into the hall with me. "You know, maybe Christian will bid on you. He does feel responsible. He actually seemed really nice at the hospital, once I started talking to him."

"He's not nice, and he *is* responsible, and he's the last guy on the face of this earth that I'd want to be serving." My stupid mind takes that moment to roam. If Christian bid on me, he'd likely make me clean his toilet, or something equally disgusting...like sleep with him.

My heart jumps into my throat as images of me in his bed, his big body next to mine, his callused hands holding me down, while he does dirty things to me. "Oh my God," I whisper.

"What?" Kaitlyn asks as we head downstairs.

I shake my head. "I can't do this. I can't sleep with some guy for payment. I'm not a prostitute."

"Christi...uh, I mean, the person I talked to, the one who gave me the card—"

I roll my eyes. "Christian, obviously." When did she start thinking I was an idiot, and when don't we tell each other everything? I guess whatever depraved activities take place in that basement really are shrouded in secrecy, because it's not like my best friend to keep anything from me. Maybe once you know about it, you're a part of it, and down the road, this ridiculous secret society offers protection or favors or something. Or maybe it's off with the head if you snitch. Okay, time to cut back on watching thrillers.

"I never said that." She puckers her lips. "Anyway, that person who gave me the card said the cards are actually coveted, and you'd never have to do anything you don't want to do, and come to think of it, you don't have to worry about Christian bidding on you. A little birdy told me he doesn't participate."

My God, what is with the heavy disappointment sitting in my gut.

I am all kinds of messed up, that's for sure.

You hate him, Maize. HATE HIM!

"His father is a Supreme Court judge, I sure as hell hope he doesn't participate," I shoot back, hating that I know more about him than I should. It was just curiosity that sent me to his social media a time or two. He doesn't post much. He mostly comes up in photos he's tagged in. "Not that I care about him or anything." I catch the smirk on Kaitlyn's face. "What? I hate him. You know what he did to me."

"To be honest, taking his pants to his knees and getting you expelled from the mean girls' club..." She pauses to do air quotes around the word mean girls. "Was the best thing that ever happened. I don't know why you ever wanted to be a part of that clique."

I frown, a heavy sensation building right around the vicinity of my heart. "I was trying to fit in and what he did was wrong, no matter how you look at it. Making fun of me because I wasn't rich enough... it's just cruel, and they can all go screw themselves. I'd rather be alone than hang out with people who could do that."

"Then I guess you were lucky I came along."

"You've always had my back."

We reach the kitchen, and she puts her hand on my shoulder to turn me to face her. "I do now, too. I wouldn't have suggested this if I thought there was any other way. No one talks about what goes on, but I'm thinking if it was bad, everyone would hear about it. Look, I'll go with you. If we don't like what we see, we leave, simple as that. But we do have to go, to return the card if nothing else. It's part of the agreement, and I agreed on your behalf."

"How kind of you, and I don't think there is going to be anything simple about it."

"You're not going to do it then?"

I give her a resounding, "No." With that, I hobble to the coffee maker and pour a big mug full. Kaitlyn hands me the milk from the fridge. "Who would bid on me anyway?" I wave my hand down my body. "I'm tall, with barely there curves, and if they want me to run errands, broken ankle, remember? I look like...like..."

"You're sexy as fuck, Maize. You just don't know it. You're tall, thin, have a great rack despite your low body fat, and I'd kill to have full lips like yours. Plus, your name is Maize Malone. If that doesn't scream sex kitten, I don't know what does."

Sex kitten?

I stand there for a second and stare at Kaitlyn, waiting for her to break out into a fit of laughter but instead she just raises her brow, daring me to challenge her views on me.

"Who are you and what have you done with my best friend?"

She checks her watch. "I never said any of those things to you before, because you never needed to hear them. Now you do. Okay, I gotta go. I'll be back by eight. Text me to let me know if you've changed your mind about going through with it."

"Not going to happen."

She gives me a big hug and I take a mouthful of coffee. I swallow it, and lean against the kitchen counter. My gaze goes to the hallway, my mind on the card sitting on my bed. My stupid brain takes that moment to wander again, back to the night Christian and I were in that closet. He was thinner then, but I was crushing on him hard.

My body tingles as I recall the way he put his hands on my hips. His skin was hot as his fingers bit into my flesh, and if I try really hard, I can almost still feel the imprint. We were both breathing a little heavy and when he shifted closer, his tall body crowding mine, I wet my lips, prepared them for him, but the stupid jerk took his hands off my body, pulled his pants down and threw open the door, making me look like a fool. I took off after the mean girls laughed and made fun of me, and don't even get me started on the rumors about me afterward. Christian came out on top after that, and I almost quit and went back to my own district, but I'm not a quitter. I fight for what I want and need and would do just about anything to achieve my goals.

Will you do this, Maize?

4

CHRISTIAN

The last time I felt this nervous was when I was locked in a closet with Maize back in high school. Fuck. *You're a grown-ass man, dude, get yourself together.* I run my hand through my hair, and pace my room, the robe I'm wearing heavy on my shoulders, despite the fact that it's lightweight.

I shouldn't have given the card to Kaitlyn. Hell, I never should have answered her question about what goes on in the basement of our frat house, even though moments before she asked, I was thinking about it, looking at it as a way to help out Maize. She obviously hates me, judging by the way she's always glaring at me—and likely thinks I was responsible for the prank too—and now, after my pass caused her to fall and ruined her ankle, I'm sure she's out for blood.

I pace around my bedroom, and steal a glance at the clock. Night has fallen over the campus and the auction will begin in fifteen minutes or so. My throat tightens at that thought. Stepping up to the mirror, I check out my long hooded ceremonial robe that hides our identities.

Am I really doing this?

I have never been a part of the bidding, never had any inclination to participate, but none of those girls were Maize—who I can't really hate anymore now that I know she was being pranked too. Plus, I *am* responsible for her circumstances. *Is that the only reason you're doing this, Christian?* I shake my head, not wanting to delve too deeply into my motivations. I walk to my window and stare out at the dark street below. The truth is, this is all just a game, and the women who are given cards are carefully vetted. They want this. They get to be adored, treated extremely well in exchange for favors, and no, I'm not talking sexual ones. If that happens, it has to be consensual, no pressure on anyone, but these girls are basically sugar babies, and we're their daddies. When I put it that way it sounds really bad.

Fuck me.

Maize though, she's not the kind of girl to take. From what I knew of her, she'd worked her way through high school on scholarship, and is here at Kingston on one as well—up until I hit her in the head with my football. She works hard to get what she needs, and really, if she becomes a sugar baby, and is doing chores, homework, and whatever else needs to be done, that's working hard to get what she needs too, right? I'm not sure I'm buying that logic either. I thought about straight up offering her money, but I appreciate my nuts between my legs, not shoved down my throat.

My door flies open and I spin around to see Theodore, also known as Thor because of his size and longish blond hair, come racing into my room. He looks a little like a superhero in his robe. He practically skids to a halt when he sees me in mine.

"What the fuck, dude?"

I'm tall, but I still have to lift my gaze to meet his eyes. I square my shoulders. "You've got a problem."

"Fuck no, but you never play. What's going on?" He backs up and leans against my doorjamb, blocking all light in the hall-way. "Wait, does this have something to do with that girl you ruined?"

I cringed. "Ruined? I didn't ruin her." My gaze goes to my bed. If I had her on the mattress, beneath me... then I might ruin her. My cock takes that moment to thicken. Not that it takes much when I'm thinking about Maize. Jesus, she's so fit, so tight everywhere, and those fucking kissable lips. I almost tasted them in high school. Almost had my tongue in her mouth, but she had to go and ruin things by pantsing me. Yeah, she's the one who ruined things, not me.

Thor frowns. "Well, she's never going to run again, you know that, right?"

"I thought you were a psych major. I had no idea you were getting a medical degree on the side."

He bursts out laughing, pushes off the wall and slaps me on the shoulder. "You need to relax, my man. Get your ass down there, get a bid in on the hottest girl, and do yourself a favor and get laid."

"Yeah, okay," is all I say, even though I have no intention of sleeping with Maize. He moves and I step around him, the knot in my stomach growing tighter and tighter as I adjust my robe and make my way to the basement. My brothers are all standing around, waiting for the invites to enter. I stand back a bit, and question my sanity. I can't do this. I just can't.

I'm about to bolt, never to set foot in the basement again, when the large solid brass bell rings.

Thor throws his arm around my shoulders and walks me to a chair. I tuck my hood around my head and drop into a chair. Thor sinks into the chair beside me, and while he's in his robe, I think he just likes attending, and right now is enjoying my nervousness. He's already got a girl, and from what I've seen, the two are getting along just fine. The other day, he put a gorgeous diamond on her neck, a thank you for doing his homework. It's a win/win, right? Not that I'd let anyone do my homework. I'm not risking expulsion from campus, and how would that look for my dad. Nope, I have to stay on the straight and narrow.

Then what the hell are you doing here, dude?

I take a deep breath as the first girl is led to the stage. She's dressed cute, flirty lingerie as she flaunts herself in front of the guys, and in no time at all, the bidding begins. I shift in my chair, restless, not really expecting Maize to show up, yet on some ridiculous level hoping she does. I glance at the door, which is locked and closed now and guarded by Andrew. Maybe she gave him the card and bolted. Heck, maybe Kaitlyn did it for her. She is in a boot for a busted ankle, and probably can't walk too far. As the time slowly ticks by I become more restless by the minute and I pull my phone out to scroll through social media. Thor nudges me when the last girl takes the stage.

"Doesn't look like she's coming," he points out.

I can't tell whether I'm happy or disappointed that she never showed up. I push to my feet, ready to go back to my room and get out of the ridiculous robe. "Just as well," I say. In the dark room, I maneuver around a long oaken table and tall marble columns, when a noise on the stage pulls my attention. I spin, and when my heart leaps into my throat, I'm able to answer my earlier question. It was disappointment, pure unadulterated disappointment that I wasn't going to get a chance to bid on the girl that's been in my fantasies a time or two—even when I hated her. I go perfectly still, take in the gorgeous brunette standing on stage, unsure, vulnerable. My pulse picks up as my protective instincts kick in full force, and one word bounces around inside my brain.

Mine.

I silently walk back to Thor, and without looking or speaking to him, quietly drop down into my chair. On the stage, James starts the bidding, and I raise my hand, and in a low, disguised voice—yeah, she'll probably run if she knows it's me—I shout out a ridiculous number that will more than cover her tuition. No fucking way is she going home with anyone but me tonight. Chairs scrape the marble floor as my brothers shift in their seats, trying to get a look at whoever started the bidding at such an unusually high price. I square my shoulders, my eyes on Maize as she tries to see into the crowd.

One of the guys challenges me, and ups the bid, and a noise, that sounds like an angry bear awakening from hibernation, climbs out of my throat. Oh hell no. I up the bid a couple more grand, and as the room falls silent, Maize's audible gasp whispers through the quiet and settles between my legs.

James points to me. "She's yours," he says.

"Fucking right she is," I murmur under my breath. We stand, and those who lost their bids exit the room, leaving the rest of us to collect our new purchases. The women come off the stage, and what I noticed tonight was that most of them were dressed skimpily, whereas Maize is in a dress, one she almost looked uncomfortable in. I guess she prefers running shorts and yoga pants.

Did she get dressed up for me?

That thought brings a chuckle to my lips. Honestly, when she finds out it's me, she's going to bolt. I'd best cover my nuts when I remove my hood. I walk up to Maize as she glances around nervously, not that she can see much in the dark basement, the lights low on purpose. No cameras are to be used, and this place is locked up tight every day of the month but one.

Her head lifts, and in the dark and quiet room, I can almost hear the pulse pounding at the base of her neck, right where I want to put my lips. Everything in me stiffens as I work to purify my thoughts, but with Maize here, all sweet and vulnerable, out of her comfort zone, makes it fucking hard, literally. Yeah, all I want to do is take her to my bed and kiss the worry from her body and mind, and tell her everything is going to be okay. Although I'm not sure it will be.

"Are you my..." She pauses, like she can't quite figure out what word to use.

"I'm your sponsor," I say, and that wording seems to relax her. Best to leave sugar baby and sugar daddy out of it. That's not what this matchup is, anyway. I don't want anything from her, other than to pay for the accident.

Is that entirely true, Christian?

I shut that inner voice down, and take her hand in mind. At first it's stiff, but I give it a gentle, reassuring squeeze. "Are you okay to walk, or should I carry you?"

She lifts her chin, and my cock swells as those plump lips pucker in defiance. "I can walk." She begins to move, and I keep her hand in mine as we go up the steep basement staircase. When we reach the top, her steps slow, and she angles her body, turning in to me.

"Where are we going?"

"I'm taking you to my room, where we'll go over the rules of our arrangement."

"I'm not sleeping with you," she blurts out, and my lips quirk. Even though she's nervous, I like her strength and convictions.

"I never said I wanted to sleep with you."

Of course, I'm not saying I don't want to, either.

A pause and then, "Good."

"Come then." I give a little tug and she falls into step beside me. I lead her through the big house, and up the stairs to my large bedroom. Inside, I shut and lock the door behind us, and when I walk further into the room, she stays back, and presses against the door.

"Who are you?"

"Stand over there," I say, and point to the television mounted on my wall. A small gasp catches in her throat. What, does she like being bossed around? Is there a side to Maize that she doesn't show the world?

"Why?" She angles her head, her eyes moving over me, trying to discover my identity.

The truth is, I want her away from the door so she can't run. But instead I say, "I'm not going to hurt you, Maize."

"Why did you bid on me?"

"We'll get to that."

When she doesn't move, I look at the boot on her foot. "If it's causing you too much pain to walk, I can carry you."

She pushes off the door, and I grin, knowing that would get her moving. She does not like to show weakness, that's for sure. She slowly crosses the room, each step determined as she walks by my small table for two, and stands by my comfy recliner, which faces my television. She turns to me, and crosses her arms over her chest in a protective move.

"What exactly do you want from me?"

"I don't want anything from you."

"Why did you bid on me then?" She glances around. "What really goes on after these auctions?"

I reach up, and she goes quiet, still, as I grip my hood and slide it off. Her big brown eyes go wide when she sees it's me, but that shock quickly morphs into anger.

"No, no way," she seethes between clenched teeth. "Not you. I was told you didn't participate in these auctions." She makes a move to go, headed straight for the door, when I block her path and put my hands on her shoulders. A hard quiver makes its way through her body and if I didn't know better, I could be convinced that she likes my hands on her. The other day when I held her down on the ground, the flush on her cheeks hadn't gone unnoticed. I assumed it was from her injury, now...maybe it was from something else.

Then again, I could just be projecting my own desires, and the only thing this girl wants from me is my nuts in a vice.

"Maize, you're mine," I whisper and as soon as the words slip from my lips, my body reacts, eager for her to be mine, to take her any way I'd like, over and over again. Her eyes grow wide again, and it snaps me back to reality. "Wait, I don't mean it like that."

"I'm leaving."

"Can you please just hear me out?"

She hesitates and I can almost hear the wheels spinning as she tries to figure a way out of this, and a way to stay in school. That's my angle right there.

"All I want is to help you stay in school. That's it." I hold my hands out, palms facing her. "It's my fault you were hurt, and I feel shitty about that."

Her eyes narrow to slits. "This is about high school, isn't it? You want to finish what you started when you pulled your pants down, and tried to fuck me in that closet."

I shake my head. "I didn't pull my pants down, Maize. You pulled them down."

Her mouth drops open and pink crawls into her cheeks. "No, I didn't. Why would I do that?"

"You tell me."

"Oh, I get it." She shakes her head and lets loose a humorless laugh. "You decided to make fun of the new girl. Was it you who started the rumors that I was an easy lay? Did you call me corn on the cob?"

"No, I didn't, and I didn't do what you think I did." I honestly don't know why she's saying I pulled my own pants down, and I'll examine that later. Right now, we have more important things to discuss. "Look, let's forget about what happened in the past and focus on the now."

She shifts and I instinctively cover my nut sack. Her eyes drop. "What are you doing?"

"Protecting myself from your knee."

She exhales. "You ruined high school for me, and now college, but I'm not going to hurt you."

I back up an inch. "Then let me explain. I'm not asking anything from you. You say I ruined you, then let me fix that." I wave my hand between us. "Us...there isn't an us. I just want you to live your own life, and I don't know...get your ankle healed, get running again. Consider me your benefactor, and you're the beneficiary."

She puts one hand on her hip and glares at me, and that's when I notice the pretty gold flecks in her eyes. Jesus, she really is gorgeous. "I'm not taking money from you, and not giving you anything in return. What's fair is fair, and I don't take without giving. Just tell me what you want." This time she waves her hand back and forth between the two of us. "There might not be any 'us,' but that's the only way this beneficiary thing works for me."

My cock twitches, dying for me to hand over the mic, to let him tell her what I really want. I shut those thoughts down, and try not to visualize her legs spread wide, my tongue bringing her to climax. I shift, and tug the robe away from my body.

"What do you want to do for me, Maize?" I ask, my voice a little low, a little rougher.

She glances at her feet. "I...I...guess I could do your laundry or something..."

"Or something?" I ask, hating where I'm taking this but unable to stop myself. "What do you mean by that?"

Her sexy lips thin. "Not sex," she blurts out.

"We've already established sex was off the table."

But maybe it could be on the bed, or the floor, in the shower...

"Do...do sponsors have sex with the women?"

If she's so against it, why does she sound like she's interested?

I give a casual shrug. "It's not so bad, Maize. Most women are honored to be chosen. Who wouldn't want to be pampered, put on a pedestal, or love being taken care of?"

She squares her shoulders, and her lush breasts press against the buttoned-up front of her dress. "I take care of myself."

My gaze drops to her boot. "I'm well aware of that, but now, with your foot, you might just have to rely on someone else. Would that be so bad?"

"You didn't answer the question, Christian."

My dick twitches as my name dances on her soft pink tongue. I shrug. "I suppose sometimes they sleep together. If it's mutual."

"Oh."

"But it's not mutual for us, because neither of us want that, right?" I point out, testing her, because these mixed signals I'm picking up from her are messing with my head and my dick.

Her chin inches up. "That's right."

"If another guy had bid higher, and you went home with him, would you have let him take care of you, maybe even considered sex?"

"I don't know. It's possible. You're the only guy who ruined high school for me."

"Yeah, so you keep telling me," I say, and while I didn't ruin her in high school, since she's misremembering what happened, I can't help but think about all the delicious ways I could ruin her tonight, right here in my room, now that I'm her sugar daddy.

5

MAIZE

I slide from Christian's car, and he opens his door and circles the front to meet me. I lift my head and glare at him. "I can get into my house just fine," I tell him, but there is this totally weird part of me that likes his attention. Ridiculous, I know, considering I can't stand him. But I also can't stop thinking about what he said to me, about being cared for. For as long as I can remember Mom and I have been taking care of ourselves. I wouldn't know the first thing about handing myself over to someone.

But you want to, don't you, Maize?

"Yes, you can, but I can help you get to the door, too," he responds.

I just shake my head. Kaitlyn had said she heard Christian never participated in the auctions. A stupid thrill goes through me and I quickly shut it down. He feels guilty. He's only my 'benefactor' because he's responsible for my fall. He does not want to sleep with me, a point he has made a few times, and I'm perfectly fine with that. Perfectly!

I try to slip away when he puts his hand on the small of my back, partly because I can walk without his help and partly because it's arousing things inside me, things that are foreign —things that are settling deep between my legs. Gawd... What the hell is wrong with me?

Oh, just that you would like to have some good sex, just once in your life, and God's gift to women here has a reputation a mile long.

"Are you going to be this annoying all semester?" I ask.

"Probably."

"Lucky me."

"That is entirely up to you," he says and when I hear what almost sounds like want in his voice, my gaze flies to his. The corners of his mouth twitch. What exactly is he saying to me? That getting lucky—with him—is up to me. Yeah, okay, I'm clearly still concussed. Or not.

We climb my front steps and he when opens the door, I turn to him. "So are you going to tell me what I need to do?"

"I'm thinking on it."

"I am not taking money that isn't earned."

He steps closer, crowding me, and my pulse jumps in my neck. His gaze drops like he can see the steady throb in my neck and he wets his mouth. Does he want to kiss me or something? God, there I go with the 'something' again.

"How about I text you later, with a list."

"Fine," I say. "I'll be waiting for that." He holds his hand out, and I stare at it. "Phone."

"What for?"

"Do you always have to question everything?"

"Yes."

"Good to know. I want your phone so I can put my contact information in."

I nod and fish it from my pocket. His hand touches mine, his skin warm and rough against my wrist, and once again my mind wanders. What would his hand feel like on my naked body? I clear my throat, and his lids lift, those mesmerizing blue eyes full of curiosity.

"Something the matter?" he asks.

"No."

I stare at his big hands as he puts information into my phone. A second later, his pings. We stand there staring at each other for an awkward moment. For some unknown reason, I can't seem to step away. He's like a big magnet, and I'm a scrap of metal drawn by his force.

He breaks the quiet. "See you later, Maize."

The slow sexy way he says my name sends tingles down my spine and I resist the urge to say, not if I see you first, because I will be seeing him. "Bye, Christian."

I step into the house and shut the door. I press my forehead against it, and put my hand on the wood, sensing he's still standing there. Pull yourself together, girl. I shake my head, push off the door, and hobble up the stairs. I head down the hall, and there's no tiptoeing and trying not to wake Kaitlyn when my boot makes more noise than a pirate with a peg leg. I have no idea why that makes me chuckle, madly, like a woman who escaped an asylum. Maybe it's my way of letting the stress of the night go.

Did I really go to an auction and sell myself to Christian Moore?

Yeah, I sure did, and I wish to hell I regretted it more than I actually do. Ugh.

Kaitlyn's door opens and she looks at me like I might have grown a second head as I try to stifle my laughter. "I guess tonight went well, then?"

I sober quickly. "It was horrible."

Her gaze goes up and down the length of me and she grins. "Maybe I should have stayed and watched."

She walked me to the frat house, but left after I entered. "It went fast, and so much for Christian not bidding."

Her mouth falls open, and she grabs me by the shoulders. "You're Christian's?"

"I'm not *his*," I snap, but yeah, I kind of am. Bought and paid for. "He's my benefactor, and I will do things for him to earn the money."

"Oh, what kind of things?" she asks with a wag of her eyebrow.

"Sex isn't on the table, if that's what you're getting at." Her head angles, her gaze moving over my face. "What?"

"You sound disappointed about that."

"I'm not a prostitute, and I do not sound disappointed. I'm just tired. It's been a long day and going up on that stage was beyond stressful."

Maybe I should have stayed, let Christian massage my tight muscles.

"Well now you're a sugar baby, a kept woman." She frowns. "I wish I'd gotten a card. It's kind of a sweet deal."

My jaw drops open. "You can't be serious."

"As serious as a damn ankle injury, Maize."

"Maybe you'll get lucky and get a football to the head."

She laughs, and covers her mouth, not wanting to wake our roommates. "Get some sleep," I tell her.

I hobble to the bathroom, get ready for bed, and then walk to my room. I tug on a night shirt, crawl into bed, and pull the covers up. Even though I'm exhausted, I'm too keyed up to fall asleep. I grab my cell, and a wave of disappointment curls through me when I don't find a message from Christian. I toss it aside, but as soon as I do, it pings. I snatch it up far too quickly, and try to calm my racing heart as I read the text from Christian.

How are your culinary skills?

I run my fingers over the words as a goofy smile crosses my lips as I text back. *"I'm a pretty good cook."*

Breakfast tomorrow?

I guess I can make you breakfast. My place or yours?

Mine.

Would this be breakfast in bed?

Dammit, why oh, why did I have to bring up his bed?

Yes.

I drop my phone like it's on fire, and peek at it over the covers.

Nine okay?

I snatch my phone and text back. *That's not much of a list.*

Still working on it. I'll have it ready in the morning.

I let him know nine is fine and I wait to see if he's going to respond and when no message comes through, a ridiculous sound catches in my throat. I close my eyes, and toss restlessly. I'm sure my body has never been so alive. God, when I walked onto that stage tonight, and heard Christian bid on me, although at the time, I had no idea it was him, I was both nervous and shocked. I couldn't understand why any guy would bid so high. Of course, I quickly learned why. Christian feels responsible for my ankle. But I can't deny there was something in his eyes when he removed the hood of his robe, something that looked like desire. He assured me he wasn't looking to finish what he started in that closet and I'm happy about that.

If I'm so happy about that, why are my fingers inching downward, sliding between my widening legs? Normally when I fall into bed, I crash hard. Training will do that to you, but I suspect I'm not going to get any sleep tonight until I take the edge off, and not even sure if I can with my fingers, but dammit, I'm sure going to try.

I let my knees fall open, and slide my finger over my clit. I imagine it's Christian's hand between my legs, his mouth working the nub that's swelling beneath the pad of my finger. I groan and envision him in his bed right now, his cock in his hand as he strokes himself while he pictures me on my knees, his cock in my mouth. I rub myself harder, my mind on an erotic journey like never before. I've fantasized a time or two, but tonight the vision behind my eyes is vivid, real. Maybe it had something to do with the way he held me down the other day, or the way he looked at me tonight. I swear to God there was something that resembled hunger in his eyes. I slide a finger into my body and crush my clit beneath the heel of my hand, and just like that, a powerful orgasm grips me hard, and I try to stifle a moan as I grow slicker between my legs.

I stay like that until the spasms stop. I go quiet as wind picks up outside, beating against the old house and rattling the windows. I try to breathe, to refill my collapsed lungs as I revel in the post-orgasm bliss. My God, I have never, in my entire life, climaxed so fast or so hard. What is going on with my body?

Maybe it just really wants to be touched by Christian.

No, no, no. I hate him, but that doesn't mean I can't admire a work of art when I see it, right? Still, I'm not going to sleep with him. This exchange is me helping him, and him paying for it. It can't be about anything else. When I can finally move again, I grab a few tissues, clean myself up, and fall into a restless sleep filled with dreams of Christian.

My alarm goes off, and I peel one eye open, and when thoughts of seeing Christian this morning race through my sleep-deprived brain, I sit up, wishing I wasn't quite so excited. I push to my feet, the stupid boot heavy and awkward as I grab my robe and throw it over my shoulders. I can't wait until I no longer have to wear the boot while sleeping.

My roommates are still asleep, although I don't know how with the rain pelting against the window. I glance at the rotten wood around my window, wet from the downpour. I can't even imagine the mold we're all breathing in on a daily basis, living in this run-down place, but it's all we can afford and our landlord is a deadbeat. My gaze lifts to the gray and dreary sky and the need to go for a long run physically pulls at me. I can feel it deep in my gut. But I can't run, and the only way I can pay my bills is to get my ass over to Christian's and cook breakfast for him, which is ridiculous. But far better than sleeping with him. Right?

My thoughts go to my mother and my stomach tightens. What would she think if she knew I was basically a sugar baby, minus the sex? I don't know and I can't think about that. All I know is I have to do what I have to do to get to where I want in this world. It's a means to an end that will help me become a lawyer, so I can use my knowledge to help others.

Just focus on that, girl, and you'll be just fine.

I tug off my robe and nighty and remove my boot. I shower quickly and once done, I pull on my underthings, my favorite yoga pants, T-shirt and a light raincoat, then put my boot back on and cover it with a plastic bag. I snatch up my purse, but the second I open the door and step out onto the stoop, and find Christian walking toward me with that sexy swagger that squeezes my damn ovaries, I know in an instant, I'm not going to be just fine.

Not going to be just fine at all.

6

CHRISTIAN

I catch the way her eyes widen, and her mouth drops open, but before she can say anything, I hurry up to her and put my umbrella over her head to keep her dry. Dark brown eyes narrow to slits as she looks up at me, a mixture of anger, and perhaps pleasure on her face.

Her ponytail swishes as she turns toward my vehicle, then zeroes in on me again. "What...what are you doing here?"

I shrug and even though it's obvious, I say, "It's raining, and you're in a boot. I didn't want you to get wet."

As soon as the word wet leaves my lips, her cheeks flush with color, and my cock thickens, because it has its own ideas regarding Maize getting wet. Lots of ideas played out in my head last night—none of them PG—forcing me to take my cock into my hand as I pictured it deep in her throat, her pretty pink lips wrapped tight around my girth. Did she touch herself, and think of me? I snort, because if she was thinking of me, she was probably dreaming up all the ways she wanted to neuter me.

"I'm fine," she says, her chin inching up a bit more. "I have a raincoat and I covered my boot. I could have walked."

"And I can drive you. Besides, shouldn't you be resting it more?" She opens her mouth like she's going to protest, and I shake my head. "Might as well get used to me doing things for you, Maize. You're mine, remember."

"I remember," she says putting a scowl on her face, but there's something beneath it, just below the surface, and I can't help but wonder if there is a part of her that likes the idea of being mine. A little sound catches in my throat. Maybe I'm the one with the concussion. Maize does not like me much. "But it's not like that with us. This is about me earning my tuition, and that doesn't mean you get to boss me around."

"I get it, you don't like to be told what to do." I pull her close, and don't miss the tightening of her body as I guide her down the steps to the passenger side of my Jeep. I open the door, and wave my hand. "But that probably isn't going to stop me from trying." Her gaze jerks to me. "Hop in."

She stands there for a second, the pink stain on her cheeks growing brighter, her anger thick in the air. "I'm getting in because it's raining, not because you just told me to."

I laugh at that. "Maize, you're killing me."

"Good," she says and lifts her head high and sets her purse on the floor at her feet. I shut her door, and keep my eye on her as I circle the front and climb in.

I buckle in and note the way she's shifting, trying to get her foot situated on the floor. "Comfortable?"

She nods. "Not really. Hard to get comfortable with this thing on. I'll be glad to get it off my foot. It's itchy."

I start the vehicle, and turn on the wipers. "How much longer do you have to wear it?"

She crinkles her nose. "I have an appointment in a couple of weeks to have my ankle checked." Her head tilts and she glances out the window, but I don't need to see her face to know she's upset by all this. Why the hell wouldn't she be, and I don't think the word upset is strong enough to describe what she has to be feeling. Guilt prowls through my blood, as I glance over my shoulder and back out of her driveway.

"I really am sorry," I say. "I'll take you to that appointment."

"You don't have to do that." Her head swivels my way, and her brow arches. "It's not like you did it on purpose."

I eye her, take in her raised brows. "Why did that sound like a question?"

She exhales. "It wasn't. I don't think."

"I'd never take you down on purpose, Maize."

She swallows and the sound is loud in the Jeep, barely drowned out by the swishing wipers. "Yeah, I guess."

I catch the fast flicker of her eyelashes. Jesus, she won't even look at me. Is there a part of her that thinks I did it on purpose, as some ploy to get her to be my sugar baby? I don't want this any more than she does. I shake my head and concentrate on the wet road. It's obvious she doesn't trust me, and why would she? There is a part of her that thinks I was behind the incident in the closet that got her bounced from the mean girl club—clearly, she was never going to be a part of it. Truthfully, I hate that she went through any of the pain that went with their pranks, and the resulting rumors. Those girls weren't nice then, and they're not nice now, and whether she knows it or not, she's undoubtedly a much better person for not hanging with them. I could tell her that, but there is no way she'd believe me—and does it matter? We're adults now, and she's going to believe what she wants, and nothing I say or do is going to change that.

Onward and upward we go.

I come to the intersection, and take a right, instead of a left, and she looks around. "Did you forget your way home?"

"Nope."

She reaches into her backpack, and pulls out a tube. The scent of vanilla fills the vehicle as she swipes it over those lush lips of hers. "Then where are we going?"

"Out for breakfast."

She recaps her lip balm, and tosses it into her purse. "I thought you wanted me to cook for you."

I gesture toward her foot. "With that ankle?"

"Christian," she says, her eyes dark and fiery. "I thought we were going to treat this like a job. I'm not just taking money from you. If that's what you think, pull over." She reaches for the handle of the door, stubborn as hell, but I like that she's not a pampered princess like the girls who hang out with us ballers.

"I know. I know." I hold one hand up, palm out to calm her. "I made a list, but I have been craving eggs benedict."

She squares her shoulders, but her hand drops from the handle. "I could have made them, you know."

"Yeah, I know but Julep Café is the best." I turn the radio down, and press defog to keep the windows clear as the rain falls harder and her anger steams up the inside of the vehicle.

"Well, mine probably wouldn't have been as good," she admits. "I've never made them before, but I could have tried."

I like that about her, that she's not afraid to try new things, and no, I am not going to spend a second thinking about some of the things I could try with her. I flick on my signal light, and go up the ramp to get on the expressway. "Have you ever eaten at Julep?"

"Nope, never even heard of it. Where is it?"

"Over in Oceanside Park."

Her brows bunch. "That's two towns over. I'm sure we could have found a place near the college."

"You wait and see. It's worth the drive. I found it one day when I just needed to escape the frat house."

"I never took you for a loner."

I shrug. "Sometimes. The frat can be a little much. Guys and their girls coming and going from the place all hours."

"I wouldn't know anything about that," she says, and I don't miss the hitch in her voice.

"Believe me, it's not a place you want to hang out."

"I never said it was. The only reason I was going there this morning was to cook your breakfast."

I take a moment to digest her words, the little lost look on her face. What is going on in that pretty head of hers?

"Speaking of your breakfast." She stares out the window, and doesn't look at me when she says, "Did you bring your list?"

I reach into my team jacket and hand over a crumpled sheet of paper. She smooths it out, and I cringe. "Sorry about the messy handwriting."

"So cooking, tidying your room, washing your Jeep..." Her gaze lifts to mine, like she's totally unimpressed so far.

"When your ankle is better, of course."

"Of course," she says all sassy like. She continues to read. "Make your bed every morning. Are you serious? I have early morning classes."

"Doesn't have to be first thing in the morning. You can come after classes."

"How kind of you." She rolls her eyes. "I guess I'm your maid." She drops her hand, the sheet of paper on her lap. "I am not wearing a French maid outfit or anything stupid like that."

"You can wear what you want."

She glares at me for another second and goes back to reading. "You want us to do our homework together? This is ridiculous, Christian. Why would we do homework together?"

"I'm not asking you to do it, like some of the guys do, but we should do it together in case I need help. You're smart, aren't you?"

"Yeah, you are too, so don't pretend you're just another dumb jock. You're anything but."

I cock my brow. "How do you know that?"

She stiffens. "I just do." When I stare at her, wanting her to expand on that knowledge, she says, "Girls talk about stuff."

"Yeah, or maybe you've been checking me out." I have no idea why I enjoy rattling her. Maybe because it pulls her out of her comfort zone, and gets her to loosen up a little. She's always so serious, so on the straight and narrow—like I should be.

"As if. God, you have such a big ego."

"Is that what you heard?"

"It's what I know. Look, I hear things okay. I'm going into law school, and you're doing a degree in sports management. You're going to be a professional football player. We don't have any of the same courses, or anything in common. It's ridiculous for us to study together, and I couldn't do your homework even if I wanted to. I know nothing about sports science. I'm not even good in science."

"I think there might have been a compliment in there," I laugh.

She shrugs. "Science is hard and we wouldn't study well together."

I lean into her, and her chest rapidly rises as she sucks in air, and lets it out quickly, like my closeness somehow affects her. "How would you know that when we know nothing about each other."

"I just do, and for the record, I hate football."

Tension arcs between us, and rattles my dick. I lean back, putting a measure of distance between us. "That's a surprise, considering how much you watch the practices when you run."

"I do not," she shoots back. "Wait, if you know that, then it would imply that you watch me." She puckers her lips and does a little bobblehead thing, looking at me like I'm a rat backed into a corner.

I simply answer with, "Maybe I do," which totally makes her jaw drop open.

I grin at her and she quickly pulls herself together and gives an unladylike snort. "You've got me all wrong. I'm not watching any practices."

"Because you don't like football, or because you don't like me."

She folds her arms. "Exactly."

I can't help but laugh out loud, and I swear to God, every-thing in me wants to change her mind. But to what end? She's a good girl who wants to go on to law school, and we live very different lives. I'm not about to pull out all the stops to get her to like me, only to fuck off once college is over, because I'm not a guy who could give her more. Not that she's looking for more. No, Maize Malone is a girl on a mission, and I don't think a man, children, or any picket fence play into her future plans, so best I keep things the way they are and let her hate me. I can't help but wonder what made her all work and no play, though.

We fall quiet, and I tap my thumb on the steering wheel as I listen to the music. Forty-five minutes later, my stomach is grumbling loudly as I pull into the parking lot of Julep Café. I can almost taste the eggs benny now. I unbuckle and she seems a bit hesitant.

"Everything okay?"

"Christian..." she begins and nervously wraps her purse strap around her fingers, and that's when it hits me.

Shit, making her feel poor, like she's in a place where she doesn't belong is the last thing I meant to do. Christ, sometimes I can be a real dick. "This one is on me. I want you to taste the best eggs benny in the world so you'll be able to replicate them." She eyes me like she doesn't believe that for a minute. "This really is about me, and not you. I'm kind of self-centered sometimes."

That brings a smile to her face. "As long as you know it."

I laugh and it lightens the tension between us. The rain has let up a bit by the time we step out of the vehicle, so I leave the umbrella and circle the Jeep to meet Maize. I put my hand on the small of her back to lead her to the café, and don't miss the way my body reacts, or the way hers quivers beneath my touch. Is that repulsion, or something else entirely?

Doesn't matter, dude, you're keeping your hands to yourself with this one.

"I know you can walk by yourself, but believe it or not my mother raised a gentleman." More like my grandmother. My mother didn't spend a whole lot of time with me.

She lets out a loud 'hmph' sound and casts me a disbelieving stare. Right, she thinks I pulled my pants down in the closet to get with her, and made her the laughing stock of Sweetwater High.

I open the door to the café and lead her in. A few minutes later, we're seated by the window, with a nice view of the back garden where they grow their fresh herbs. She glances around, a small smile on her face, and for some weird reason, I'm glad

I was able to put it there. I don't think this girl has had an easy go at life, and I made things worse for her.

"This place is really nice. How did you discover it again?"

"I needed a break from the frat house." I stretch out, and my leg touches hers. She sits up a bit straighter, a look on her face that speaks of agony. "Shoot, sorry, did I hurt your foot."

She takes a fast sip on her water. "No, it was my other one. So, you were saying…"

"The house has fifteen guys, and it's always noisy and there are parties going on." I rake my hand through my hair. "Sometimes it's all just too much, you know."

"My house is pretty quiet. Of course, it's off-campus living, and most of the girls work part time jobs. With my track, and the time it takes, I'm not able to work."

"You like it there?"

She curls her ponytail around her fingers. "It'd be great if the landlord wasn't a deadbeat. The pipes break all the time, and the windows leak. In the winter, it's freezing. I'd plug in my electric blanket, but only half my outlets work and I'm afraid to plug in an extension cord. Last year, there was a small electrical fire that woke us, but we were lucky to put it out before the place burned down and we went with it."

My heart thumps in my chest. "Jesus, are you serious?" She nods and my mind races as I ask, "Who is your landlord?"

She leans forward and puts her chin in her palm. The flecks of yellow in her eyes are bright beneath the overhead light. "He owns a lot of the houses in the area actually, and never answers any of our calls."

Anger burns through my blood. No one deserves to live like that. He's putting lives at risk here. "You need to sue his ass."

She shrugs, and shakes her head, like the effort would prove futile. "I have one year left, and once I become a lawyer, maybe I will."

"Give me his name. I'll have a talk with him."

"I'm not going to do that, Christian." She shakes her head, like the idea is ludicrous, and maybe even a little amusing. "My problems are mine, not yours."

I lean in. "Are you forgetting that you're mine now, Maize? I plan to take care of you. That's how this works."

"That's not how it's going to work for us, remember? Tit for tat." She shakes her head. "I mean..."

Her voice falls off when the waitress comes, and she smiles when she sees me. "Christian, nice to see you. It's been a while."

"Nice to see you too, Nancy. Back for my fourth year, and have been dying to get back here," I say to the elderly lady with short silver hair who treats me like the grandson she never had. I know that because she told me all about her daughters, and granddaughters.

"And who do you have with you today?" she asks, and adjusts her glasses as she takes in Maize with a wide smile.

"This is my friend Maize." I put my hand by my head and mimic an explosion. "We're going to blow her mind today."

"I take it two orders of eggs benny, then?"

"You know it."

She winks at Maize who smiles back as she collects the menus. "Right back with some coffee for you both." She tosses me a wink before leaving and I get it. She thinks Maize is my girl. In a sense, I guess she is, sort of.

Her eyes dance with questions. "You must really be a regular."

I shrug it off. "Like I said, it's my spot to come to when I need some quiet time."

"You bring all your girlfriends here?" As soon as that question leaves her mouth, she puts her hands up. "I'm sorry, that's none of my business. I don't know why I asked. Ignore me. I don't think I've had enough coffee yet."

"No, I don't bring any girlfriends here. I don't really have girl-friends," I admit honestly.

"Yeah, right." she shoots back. "I've seen the way the girls look at you, and the way the cheerleaders are all over you, getting piggybacks after every game."

"So what was that you said about not watching me?" Her face turns red, and I grin, letting her know I'm simply teasing her. "It's okay, I know why you do it, Maize."

"Why?" she asks, "And again, for the record, I don't watch you."

"You do it because you're still trying to figure out how to get me back from the closet incident."

She stares at me for a moment, and the corners of her mouth twitch. "I'm not much into revenge, but for the record, I guess there was a time or two in high school I considered running you over with my friend Ryan's car."

"For the record," I say in return, feeling a strange wave of possession as she talks about this guy named Ryan that she clearly knows well enough to borrow his car, "I don't have girlfriends, and I don't date, but I do fuck."

My crassness totally takes her off guard. She looks down, considers it for a moment and nods. "I guess there's nothing wrong with that, and at least you're honest about it with the girls, right?"

Just then, I glance up and see a couple of guys from a different fraternity enter. I lean forward and duck my head.

"What's wrong?" Maize asks.

"I don't know what those assholes are doing here."

She turns and sees the guys taking a seat, two tables over. "You don't like them."

"I like my privacy," I say.

"Oh, right." Her shoulders round, as she sinks into herself. Jesus, does she think I don't want to be seen with her.

"This is about me, not you," I quickly tell her. She nods but I'm not one-hundred percent sure she believes me.

Just then, Brad Kennedy lifts his head and looks right at me. I nod, and he jumps up, comes over and takes the seat across from me, his big body crowding Maize in her chair. His gaze turns to her and he smiles.

"Hey," he says.

She returns his smile. "Hi."

Goddammit, I do not like the way he's looking at her, or the way she's looking at him. He's not part of the Wolf Pack, at Wolf House, but if he was, and had won Maize, would she have slept with him? I really don't like the idea of that, even though she can sleep with whoever she wants.

My insides take that moment to burn, and it's all I can do not to pick him up by the scruff and shove him out of our booth.

I said I wasn't going to try to get her to like me; that it was best to keep things the way they are and let her hate me. But maybe I'm revising that plan.

7

MAIZE

I can't understand the scowl on Christian's face or why he's staring at Brad like he wants to take him to the ground—with his fist, not a football. They must have some private feud that I don't know about, or Christian really doesn't like being seen with me. We are, after all, two towns over for breakfast. Perhaps I'm an embarrassment. But as soon as that thought goes through my mind, another one shuts it down. Christian didn't have to break his rules and bid on me. He didn't have to give Kaitlyn that coveted card. He did it because he felt responsible, and I guess that's kind of nice, and shows he's a man who owns up to his mistakes. He might not have owned up to the one in high school, but we're not teenagers anymore. Maybe he's no longer a jerk. Maybe he's grown up a lot, and I'm a girl who just assumes every rich kid is mean. Am I being too harsh? Should I give him a second chance at friendship?

Nancy comes back with our coffees and sets them down. "I didn't realize you were having a third," she says as she focuses in on Brad.

Brad nudges me, his elbow sharp against my side. "Ooh, a three-way," he says with a bark of laughter, and neither Nancy nor Christian seem impressed.

"He was just leaving," Christian tells her through clenched teeth. Brad abruptly stops laughing. His glance goes to Christian, and if he was a smart man—if he could read a room—he'd get up and get out while he still could.

He pushes from his chair and steps back. With his head down, he says, "Yeah, I'll see you later, man."

Once he's gone, Christian physically relaxes and reaches for his mug of coffee. "Thanks Nancy, and if he gives you any trouble, let me know."

She gives a laugh, and a wink. "Son, I've been doing this a long time. That boy knows better than to give this old lady any trouble." She's still laughing as she saunters off.

I lean across the table conspiratorially, wanting to lighten Christian's mood. "Do you think she does something to the food?" I ask.

"Like spit in it or something?"

"Yes."

A quiver goes through him. "Jesus, that's disgusting."

I shrug. "I know, but I had this friend from back home who worked in the industry and the stories she told." I give a low, slow whistle. "Just don't ever be mean to a server and never send your food back."

He laughs out loud, and my girly parts flutter. As I revel in the sound, I wonder why I wanted to make him laugh. "Duly noted." He rips into a sugar packet and dumps it into his coffee, while I add a splash of milk to mine. "Where is home, Maize?" His laughter falls and his voice turns serious.

I shift, suddenly a little uncomfortable. "I lived in Cumberland, but I was on a scholarship at Sweetwater." He nods, and takes a sip, like he's absorbing all that. "What about you?"

"I moved to Sweetwater in high school, as you know. We used to live in D.C. Dad's a Supreme Court judge but maybe you know that."

I nod. "Why did you move to So Cal?"

"It's where my parents are from and Dad worked so much. Mom wanted to be closer to family."

"That's nice, I think. Do you have any siblings?"

I don't miss the tightening of his fingers around his mug as he fiddles with it. "No, just me. I'm not really close to my parents, but I have a cousin I'm close to and I'm really close to my grandmother on my father's side."

"That's really nice. My grandparents are gone, and no cousins to speak of."

"You're an only child too, I take it."

"That's right."

He slaps his palms on the table, "Well, that settles it then," he says teasingly. "We can never marry."

I laugh. "Not that I'm ever getting married, but I get what you're saying, only child syndrome. We're both too independent, ambitious, and obsessive. We'd kill each other."

He leans into me, his smile gone as his tongue brushes his bottom lips. "Obsessive. That's a good word."

Holy. Crap. What is going on with him right now? My brain might not know; I've not had a whole lot of experience with guys, but my body is reacting all on its own—nature completely taking its course.

"Are you saying you're obsessive?" I ask, and wish my voice wasn't so damn shaky.

"I guess we'll see."

"What is that supposed to mean?"

Over the rim of his cup, he asks, "You want to be a lawyer, huh? Here in California?"

Alrighty then, way to change the subject. I shrug. "I don't know where. My mom is here so I don't want to be too far from her. We're close."

I take a sip of the strong coffee and decide it needs sugar. I reach for the bowl with the sugar packets at the exact same time he does, and just like in the movies, our hands brush. I always thought that move was so darn corny, so contrived, and their reaction from a simple hand touch was totally over the top. You know what I think now, as my heart beats a little faster and I come alive deep between my legs.

I was wrong.

God, how can an innocent, barely-there touch awaken me, set off fireworks between us?

"Sorry about that," he says, and I note the way the blue in his eyes seems to darken. "Go ahead."

I put my hands on my lap, as my traitorous body continues to tingle. "No, you go."

He gestures with a nod. "It's okay, you go."

I give a fast shake of my head. "No, you."

As if we both want to put a stop to this stupid back and forth banter, not to mention the sudden burst of electricity between us—although I could be the only one feeling it—we both reach for it again, touch hands, and boom, my ovaries clench so hard, I'm worried I might have just climaxed. We both snatch our hands back.

"We are both so stubborn." He laughs and sits back. "I think I'm going to drink this with just one sugar."

"Yeah, I don't need any sugar either." I snort. "Now that I'm not running every day, who needs the extra calories, right?"

"You're perfect," he whispers, his voice low, and filled with such sincerity that a weird little thrill goes through me, but I push it down. He's just being nice. I've seen the cheerleaders he goes out with—or rather fucks—as he so bluntly put it, and I appreciate his honesty. Why lead a girl on only to dump her and leave her broken?

"I'm not perfect," I tell him. Wait, am I fishing for a compliment? I stifle a groan, because I think I might be.

"You're an athlete. You need to eat, whether you're currently running or not." I look down and he slides his hand across the table, this time his rough fingers purposely caress mine, a scrape of a touch that makes me forget I don't like this guy. My gaze flies to his. "You'll run again, Maize."

He looks so sad, the need to soothe his worries compels me to say, "I love running, and I'm grateful that I'm good at it, but it's just a means to an end."

Someone clears their throat and we both turn to see Nancy standing there. Jeez, how long has she been standing there, and how did we not even know?

She has a knowing grin on her face as we push back to give her the room to set our food down. I almost open my mouth to tell her it's not what she thinks, then change my mind. What's the point? I can't afford to eat at a quaint place like this, and won't ever see her again.

She leans forward. "If you two need anything else, just shout."

We both mumble our thanks, and I stare at the beautiful display of eggs benedicts and home fries. "Yeah, I don't think I'm going to be able to replicate this, Christian. You might have bid on the wrong girl."

"No, I didn't." My gaze goes to his, but he's busy stabbing one of his home fries. With the way he's focused on his food, I'm not even sure he realizes what he said.

I reach for my fork, and begin to eat, digging into my eggs benny first. A moan catches in my throat, and I briefly close my eyes. When my eyes open again, I find him staring at me. The intensity in his eyes as he gazes at my mouth dries my mouth and turns me inside out. I set my fork down.

"Christian?"

"Yeah."

"Are you okay?"

His brow furrows, and he glances down like he's fighting some internal war. "Yeah," he says. "I'm just glad you're enjoying your meal."

"It's delicious. Thank you for bringing me here."

"See, not so bad, huh?" He winks, and I get what he's asking. Not so bad that I'm his 'sugar baby.'

"It's still early in the game," I say and we both chuckle, things a little lighter between us.

We talk about classes as we finish our meal, and when we're done, he helps me to my feet, my boot feeling extra heavy this morning. He walks slow, like he knows I might be in agony, then opens the Jeep door for me. His brow is furrowed as he circles the vehicle and climbs in.

"Do you have to wear it twenty-four-seven?"

"Not really. I'm just the kind of girl who thinks if you're going to do it, then overdo it, moderation is for pussies."

He sits there staring at me for what feels like a full minute, then he bursts out laughing. I laugh with him and he shakes his head. "I can't believe you just said that."

"What?"

"I think there is a whole side of Maize Malone that no one sees," he says and grins at me as he backs out of the parking lot.

I take in the hard, handsome angles of his face, as I consider that. Maybe he's right. All I know is I've been so focused on succeeding in life, I've not stopped to think about who I really am, other than an ambitious girl from the wrong side of the tracks with something to prove. That's not a bad thing, but is that the only thing?

"What are your plans for the day?" he asks.

"To cook you breakfast, then homework."

He smiles. "Let's go get your books."

"What for? I can do homework at my place."

"From the sounds of it, your place isn't even safe. You'll be staying with me."

I grip the rail above the door, and turn to him. "I'm not staying with you."

"Yeah, you are."

"Christian, you can't tell me what to do. I have a room in a house, and that's where I'll be staying."

Okay, this is ridiculous. As my brain says one thing, my 'eggs Benedict Arnold' body is screaming something completely different.

Ignoring me, he pulls onto the freeway, and jacks the music. Like hell he's going to drown me out. I turn the radio down and glare at him and all he does is cast me a quick glance and raises his brow.

"Don't like that song?"

"I am not staying with you."

"Until the repairs are done on your house and it's safe, you're staying with me."

"I told you the landlord is a deadbeat. He won't even answer my calls."

"Which is why I'm going to pay him a visit, once you tell me his name."

Frustration seeps through my blood. "You can't do that."

"Why not?"

I open my mouth, but can't think of a good reason so I say, "You don't need to involve yourself in my business."

His head turns slowly, and those blue eyes lock on mine. I swear, being the sole focus of this guy's attention is as disturbing as it is exciting. My breath stalls in my lungs, and my head spins a little when he says, "A little too late for that now, isn't it?"

8

CHRISTIAN

Instead of answering, she just stares straight ahead and I quietly pat myself on the shoulder, figuring I've won this argument. She's mine, not in every sense of the word, but enough for me to be protective. Now that I know the truth about her, and about what happened that night in high school, I plan to take care of her—because goddammit, this girl needs a fucking break.

I go quiet for a long time, giving her time to process her thoughts and I don't want to press my luck. After a long time, we both turn to each other and speak at the same time. We laugh, and I say, "You first, and don't argue, I mean it."

"I was just wondering if other girls stay at the house with... whoever bid on them."

It's always a choice—which I'm not really giving her—and, worried she might be able to twist this on me, I say, "They usually want to."

She nods. "Because it's...nice."

"They're treated well, Maize."

She fiddles with the strap on her purse. "But your place is noisy, right? Will I be able to get any sleep? I don't do well without a decent night's sleep."

If she's in my bed, and willing to do what I want, chances are she won't be getting any sleep, but it's best I don't tell her that. "Good point. The parties are on the weekends, and we can make alternate plans then, unless of course you want to go to one."

She gives a hard shake of her head. "No thanks…" She looks down. "Unless you want me to go to one."

"I don't," I say quickly. I'm not sure what's going on with me, but ever since that douchebag Brad sat down beside her—since she mentioned this Ryan guy—it made me want to take her somewhere private, keep her all to myself. Which is strange, considering sex is off the table. I can't touch her. I won't. Thor was right, I did ruin her, and I'm not going to make things worse by taking her to my bed. Christ, I wouldn't doubt it if she was a virgin. She kept to herself at Sweetwater, and I haven't seen her with a guy since we started college.

She shifts to face me and rubs her knee, right where her boot ends. "What were you going to say?"

"Pack a bag when we get to your place.""

She crinkles her nose. "Christian—"

"Just until the landlord gets your place fixed, okay?"

She shifts, and I sense her struggle. She's a girl who does everything on her own, and I don't know why, maybe because I hurt her, I don't want to see her struggle anymore—maybe it's because I like her. Nevertheless, I want to help her out, show her it's okay to put herself in someone's hands once in a while.

As long as those hands are mine, of course.

"I'm not sleeping with you."

"I didn't ask you to."

Her shoulders sag a bit. "Right. Fine then. If the landlord doesn't start repairs in a week, then I move back home."

I laugh. "I knew if I gave you time to think about it, you'd figure out a way to take back control."

"I like being in control."

"You don't have to tell me that."

We drive a little longer, and I pull into her driveway. She reaches for the handle. "I'll be right back."

"I'm coming in to help you."

"No," she blurts out, and puts her hand on my arm. "I need to talk to my roommates. Kaitlyn knows, but the others will wonder what I'm doing with someone like you and it's hard to explain."

"Someone like me?"

She angles her head. "Come on, Christian, you're smarter than that. You don't need me to spell it out."

"You're right, I get it. But we're not so different, Maize."

"If that's what you think, then you've never been on my side of the fence, Christian."

She leaves the vehicle, and I tap the steering wheel. She's right. I was born with a silver spoon, but that doesn't mean I don't know what it's like to be bullied or picked on. Back in D.C. I was a skinny kid who often got pushed to the ground. My dad was a US senator but that meant nothing. The other kids also came from well-established families, with parents more important than mine. Kids from all classes target and bully anyone who is different.

I listen to the radio as I wait for her, finding it hard to sit tight. It's in my nature to help, and while she doesn't want it, that's not going to stop me once she's living with me. A curtain moves in the living room window, and I spot a couple of girls who don't look familiar peeking out. Maize grabs the curtain and yanks it shut and I can't help but laugh. I also can't help but wonder what she's saying about me, or the names she's calling me.

She finally comes out with a big bag, and a backpack. I jump from the Jeep, take them from her, and toss them into the back. Inside the vehicle, I turn to her. "Everything okay?"

"Fine," she says and hands me a manila envelope.

"What's this."

"My rental agreement. Good luck getting anything done."

I nod and lean over her to put it into my glovebox. My arm lands on her legs, and her sweet scent washes over me. My dick instantly hardens and I marshal him into submission.

Not going there, buddy.

"Sorry about that," I tell her. "Just don't want to lose this."

I shove the envelope into the box for safekeeping, with plans to personally visit the address on the agreement. Her landlord might be able to bully five college girls, but let's see how he fares against me and half my team. It also doesn't hurt that my dad is a Supreme Court judge.

We drive back to my frat house, and instead of parking in my spot, I go around to the back door. I park and I'm about to get out, when she asks, "Why are we parked around back?"

I gesture to the door. "No outside steps, and with your boot, I thought it would be easier. You were hobbling when you left your place."

"I've been on it too long. I need to get it elevated."

She exits the vehicle and I gather up her bags. I follow her, and open the door. She steps inside. "This is a really nice frat house," she says.

"I'd give you a tour, but you need to be off your feet." I gesture to the back steps leading upstairs. "How about I take your things to my room, and I'll come back for you."

"I can walk."

I drop her bags and put my hands on her shoulders. "Any more pressure on your foot today is just going to slow recovery. Wait here, and I'll be right back for you and help you up the stairs, Okay?"

"What if...someone comes along and thinks I'm breaking in the back door or something?"

I grin. "It's funny where your mind goes."

"I watch too many legal thrillers. Must be the lawyer-wannabe in me."

"Wait here."

She sits on the steps as I hurry up the stairs and drop her bags in my room. When I return to her, she's sitting in the exact same position.

"Excuse me," I say in a deep voice as I descend the stairs. "Do you have permission to be here?"

Her shoulders stiffen and she stands, spinning to face me. My God, if looks could kill. "Christian, that's not funny."

"I'm sorry." I quickly put my hands on her shoulders. She relaxes beneath my touch. "I thought that would be funny, but it's not."

"Then why are you smirking?" she challenges.

"Not smirking. This is just my serious face." Before she can say anything, I scoop her up and a little yelp catches in her throat. Her hands go around my neck, her thumbs right at the base of my hairline.

"You could have given me a warning."

"Knowing you, you'd probably protest."

She opens her mouth, but as I start to carry her, she falls silent, her body soft and pliable against mine while I carry her up the long flight of stairs and into my room. I quietly kick the door shut behind us and set her on my bed. I sink down to the floor in front of her, going to one knee as I take her boot and set it on my thigh.

"What are you doing?" she asks, her voice low and breathy.

"You've been in this too long. How about we take it off and get this ankle elevated."

She nods and reaches down, but I capture her hand. Her gaze flies to mine as I put her hand on the bed. "I got this."

"You don't know—"

I laugh. "I'm a baller, Maize. Trust me, I've been injured before and know how a boot works." I deflate the balloon inside, and release the straps. She exhales as the pressure is released. I set the boot aside, and she exhales.

"That feels so much better."

"Good, now lay back, and let's get some pillows under it."

She shimmies back on my king-sized bed, positioning herself in the middle, and I prop one pillow behind her and grab the others to get her leg up. I carefully cup her long, strong calf and lift, sliding the pillows under. She releases her hair from the ponytail and it fans out as her eyes fall shut.

"That feels so good," she murmurs, and my cock stands up to take notice. I'd do almost anything to hear her say those exact words while I was moving inside her. I scrub my face as my stupid brain takes a moment to visualize it.

"Christian."

My head jerks up. "Yeah."

"You look like you're in agony too. Do you need to elevate something?" As soon as the words leave her mouth, a pink flush crawling into her cheeks. "I mean...it's just...does something hurt?" She lifts her arms and lets them fall, hitting the bed with a thump. "You had a game the other day, did you get hurt, is something swollen?" A garbled sound of agony comes out of her throat, as she covers her face with one hand, and I stand there and grin at her, enjoying her babbling way too much. "None of this is coming out right." My heart pinches, I move around the bed, and take her palm from her face. She blinks up at me. "I'm going to shut up now."

"It's okay," I tease, to ease her worries and cut her some slack. "I know what you mean and I'm fine. I wasn't hurt in the game." I don't tell her nothing is swollen; that would be a big fucking lie. "How about you rest, and I'll get some ice."

She takes a deep breath and lets it out slowly as I hand over the remote. "You're right. I need this ankle to be better before Thanksgiving."

"Why is that?"

She looks at the remote and for a second I think she's not going to tell me but then she says, "I don't want my mother to know."

I stare at her, recall the things Kaitlyn said to me back at the hospital when I asked if we should call someone. She straight up said no.

"Would this upset her?" I ask, and sit on the bed as she runs her fingers over the buttons on the remote.

"One, she's a mom and nurse's assistant, so she'd be putting me to bed and fussing all over me." She glances at me, and the corners of her mouth twitch. "Kind of like you're doing."

"And you don't like that, I get it. What's number two?"

Confusion moves over her face for a second, then she blinks and answers with, "I don't want her to worry about me."

"It's what mothers do, but you mean financially, don't you?"

She curls into herself. "Yeah, I'm an adult. I need to be responsible for myself and find my own way to pay my hospital bill."

I nudge her chin. "I have faith in you. You found a way to pay your tuition, didn't you?"

"I honestly still can't believe that I allowed Kaitlyn to talk me into going to the auction, or that I'm with you right now."

"With the right motivation, a person will do just about anything. I had an English teacher say that to me once when we were reading an assigned novel. It really stuck with me."

"And now I'm stuck with you because I had the right motivation."

"It's not so bad though, right?" I question.

She gives a humorless laugh. "You're right not so bad. I could have gone back home with my tail between my legs."

"That's not your style." I push from the bed, rather pleased with myself. "I'll be right back with that ice. Don't go anywhere."

Air leaves her lungs as she huffs. "It's not like I can escape, Christian. Not with this ankle."

It's really insane how much I love hearing my name on her lips. I reach out and lightly trace my finger down her warm calf, stopping when I reach the support sock she wears under her boot.

"Even if it wasn't broken," I begin. "I wouldn't let you escape, and if you tried, I might just tie you to the bed."

What the fuck am I saying?

I don't know, but from the way a quiver just traveled the length of her body, from the top of her head to the tips of her toes, I'm not sure she's so opposed to the idea.

Get it together, Christian. You can't touch her. You've done enough already.

Right?

9

MAIZE

I flick through the stations as doors bang and guys shuffle in the hall. I guess they'd all slept in on this rainy Sunday. With my body still tingling from the way Christian had touched me, I sink further into his cushiony mattress. What the hell is his bed made out of? I'd never get up if I had this kind of luxury.

A yawn pulls at me as I aimlessly go through the channels. I don't normally watch TV and especially not on a Sunday. Sundays are for running hard and studying even harder. I turn my gaze and it lands on my backpack as a yawn pulls at me. My God, why am I so tired? Probably because I've not been exercising, and last night, I had a hard time falling asleep, even after touching myself while I thought about Mr. Quarterback. Star player, and star of my dreams.

You are so screwed, girl.

I'm not and that could be the problem. Maybe if I did sleep with Christian, I'd get over this crazy infatuation. Sex is sex and what I experienced with Ryan is probably what it's like with all guys. I think girls just make stuff up, to make themselves and the jocks look good. I'd probably be disappointed if he touched me in a sexual way, although every single innocent caress feels erotic when it comes from him.

I shut my eyes as the rain once again picks up outside, the drone against the window pulling me under—that and the monotone delivery on the news station I settled for. The cozy mattress shapes my body and I reach down and pull up a blanket from the end of the bed. My heart slows and I swear I've never been so warm or comfortable in my life.

The next thing I know, my eyes are opening, and I glance around. Where the hell am I? I blink, trying to orient myself, and go up on my elbows as my vision clears. "What's going on?" I ask when I find Christian sitting in a big comfy recliner, tapping away on his laptop. As soon as I speak, he shuts it and jumps to his feet.

"Hey," he whispers, and the soft sound goes through me, awakens a deep need inside me and in that instant, I want Christian to touch me, I want to feel his hands and mouth on my body. I want...him. "How did you sleep?"

I give a slow shake of my head, and note the stack of blankets on me. Did Christian tuck me in? "I'm sorry, I didn't realize I was so tired."

"It's okay, I was just working on my assignment."

He sits next to me, and as the bed dips, I slightly roll toward him. I try to remove my foot from the stack of pillows so I can sit up, but he puts his hand on my stomach, fingers splayed, and holds me down.

Dear God, I wish I didn't like that so much.

"Where do you think you're going?"

I blink. "Home."

His grin does incredibly strange things to me. "You're staying here now, remember?"

My brain fills in all the missing pieces as it wakes. "Oh, right."

"And we didn't ice your ankle. I didn't want to do it while you were asleep. You looked adorable, and the snoring..." He holds up his phone. "It's blackmail."

He recorded me snoring! "Christian—"

"Kidding. Kidding. Relax, Maize." He sets the phone on his nightstand, and holds his hands up in surrender. "It's all good. I would never do that to you."

I give him a look that suggests he's done worse, and instead of commenting, he glances at the clock and frowns.

"Am I keeping you from something?"

He gives a slow nod. "Yeah, sort of."

"I can leave."

His nod turns to a fast shake. "No, I want you to stay put. Consider my room your room now. I just have to run out, but before I do, I want to ice your ankle. Give me a second." Before I can say anything, he rushes from the room, tightly closing the door behind him and the sound of his boots pounding on the wooden stairs reverberate through me. I sit in silence, noting the house is quiet now. I guess the guys are up and gone, or in their rooms studying...or doing something maybe a little more pleasurable.

I touch the bedding. God, how many women have been in this bed and spread their legs for Christian? He might have bought and paid for me, but that doesn't mean he can't be with other girls, even if I'm not putting out.

Oh, but how I want to.

I quickly shut that thought down as he comes back into the room, a cloth covered plastic bag filled with ice in his hands. His smile is soft and warm as he sits at the foot of the bed, puts my leg on his lap, and removes the sock.

He puts the cloth on my ankle. "This okay?" he asks, those piercing blue eyes gazing at me with a hint of worry.

"Fine."

He lightly runs his fingers over my scar. "Does it hurt a lot?"

Oh, something is hurting. A lot. Right now, however, it's not my damn ankle.

"It's getting better."

"Warrior wounds," he says. "Something to tell the grandkids about."

I laugh. "No kids or grandkids in my future."

He nods, like he understands. "Ditto. But why don't you want kids?"

I look at him like he might be insane. "This world is too cruel to bring kids into it." But as I look at him, take in the frown on his face, I realize I might sound bitter. I'm not, it's just that I know firsthand how unaccepting people are if you're different.

"Maybe one day you'll fall in love, get married, and see things differently."

"Maybe. What about you, though?"

He moves the ice to another spot on my ankle and I wince a little. He glances up to check in on me, and I really appreciate the gesture. I nod to let him know I'm good. He falls silent for a long time and I don't think he's going to answer me when he finally breaks the quiet.

"I don't know, Maize. I guess I'm influenced by my past."

I stare at him, completely dumfounded. "What happened in your past?"

"When I said we had more in common than you think, I wasn't kidding." He glances down and shakes his head. "Never mind. Let's talk about something else. What do you do in your spare time?" He chuckles. "What am I saying? You don't have spare time. I barely have any. But now you have spare time." Sadness invades his eyes as he moves the ice along my ankle, and for the first time, I wish he didn't feel so guilty. "Are you going to take up any hobbies?"

"I'll just study harder."

I take in his posture, the tenseness in his shoulders, and while I wasn't interested in getting to know him better, I really can't help but want to know what it was he was going to say—what's so painful for him to tell me. I want to ask, I actually open my mouth to ask, but he cuts me off.

"Shit, I have to go." He takes my hand in his, his big palm practically swallowing mine whole, and puts it over the bag of ice. "I'll be gone for a couple of hours. Just dump this in the sink when you're done." He jerks his head toward a closed door.

"You have a sink in your closet?"

His bark of laughter trickles through me. "No, there's a bathroom in there."

I roll my eyes. "Of course, there is."

"Feel free to use it." He pushes to his feet, snatches up a backpack, and stands over me. "You'll be okay?"

"I'm a big girl, Christian." I tug the blankets tighter around me, feeling oddly exposed, and aroused, and dizzy, and aroused. Oh wait, did I say that already? His gaze moves down my body, sending sparks through me. "Been taking care of myself for a long time."

"Now I'm going to take care of you."

"While I always appreciate your honesty, nothing is going to change."

He grins at me. "That's where you're wrong."

I want to protest, but can't quite give voice to the words in my head. Why? Because I want to be wrong, want someone— Christian—to just once take care of me for a minute, or maybe two. But hasn't he been doing that? Putting me in his bed because my house is falling down around me, and just now, icing my ankle. He has, but maybe I'm thinking of other ways—sexual ways. He's such a contradiction. One minute he looks at me like he wants to eat me alive, touching my skin like I'm a prize possession, and the next he's saying this isn't about sex.

I hate, hate, hate that I want it to be.

"Make yourself at home, and if you want to lock the door go ahead. I'll be back in a couple of hours," he says and disappears through the door, closing it tightly behind him, without telling me where he's going. I sit there for a minute, my brain racing, trying to figure out what's going on, when my phone pings.

I slide off the bed, grab my backpack, and fish it out to find a text from Kaitlyn.

Call me when you get a chance. I want all the deets on his room, mainly his bed.

I can't help but expel a somewhat nervous laugh as I hit the video contact for a face-to-face chat. She comes into view, her eyes wide, excited.

"Tell me everything. Actually, show me."

I grin at her enthusiasm, and while I should be mad, I'm in this predicament because of her—and Christian—I can't seem to muster up the anger.

"There's nothing to tell," I say casually. "I came here, fell asleep for a bit, and then iced my ankle." I set the phone beside me, and tug on my sock. I reach for my boot, pull open the liner, and pump the balloon to the proper tension. Once it's secure, I snatch my phone back up. "Christian isn't even here." I'd never hear the end of it if I told her Christian iced my ankle, or describe in detail what his touch did to my body.

"Did Hot Stuff nap with you?"

"Really, Kaitlyn, we're going there?"

Her face goes serious. "Are you okay, Maize? You look...I don't know...upset about something." She puckers her lips, her eyes narrowing as she brings the phone closer to her face.

I frown at her. "Of course I'm upset. I can't run anymore. Broken ankle, remember?"

She goes quiet, pensive, and I almost reverse the camera because I don't like the way she's studying me. "No, there's something else. You and I both know running was a means to an end, and that's been taken away, but with Christian, your tuition is covered, so what's up?" She taps her chin, and continues to study me.

"I'm not used to such luxury," I tell her. "This place is posh with a capital P. I don't think I belong here."

"I've been in Wolf House before, but I've never been upstairs. Never say you don't belong. You belong in a castle, my friend." I grin, loving how she always has my back.

"I'm not Cinderella, Christian is no Prince Charming, and this is no fairy tale."

She shrugs me off. "Show me around his room."

"No, I'm not snooping."

She makes an irritated tsking sound. "How is it snooping if he brought you to his place and left you there to fend for yourself?"

"Fend for myself? I haven't been taken to the forest and left to survive on my own."

"Like Snow White?"

"You need to live in this reality, my friend."

"Still, he left you in a house full of wolves. You're prey, Maize."

I laugh. "No worries, I'm tucked in his room. It's not kill or be killed."

"Do you mean eat or be eaten, like Little Red Riding Hood," she says with a sassy smirk that makes me laugh out loud.

I cover my mouth, hoping no one burst in to see what the excitement is all about. "Do you have to make everything about sex?"

She angles her head. "Ooh, who says I was?" She points a finger at me. "I was simply making a point, you're the one who put a sexual spin on it."

Maybe she's right. Maybe my brain is thinking about sex because I'm in Christian's bedroom, and the scent from his blankets on my skin, turning me into a hormonal teenager lusting after the star of the football team. "Goodbye, Kaitlyn."

"No, wait," she says quickly. "I want to see around." I glare at her, and she hurries on with, "Look at it like you're on a familiarization quest of his space because you're going to be staying there, nothing more."

"Only for a week. I doubt he'll get the landlord to do anything."

"So that's a yes?"

I hesitate and glance around. "Fine," I say, and reverse the screen so she can see what I see.

I do a slow circle to show her the entirety of the room. "Big, huh?" I say, and instantly regret my word choice. I shake my head and brace myself for a sexual response.

"You make it too easy, girlfriend," she laughs.

"Yeah, yeah, I know. Maybe because I'm not always thinking about sex like you are." Okay, that's a lie, I've been thinking about sex ever since Christian brought me to this room last night, removed his robe and put his hand on my shoulder.

I walk along one wall, cataloging his dresser and closet, which are beside the door to the hall. The wall behind the bed has a shelf with numerous medals and trophies. Across from me is a great big window with the curtains drawn for privacy and the fourth wall to my right has a door to the bathroom, a big comfy chair, a small two-seat table and a TV on the wall. It's quite nice and comfy.

"Not much blackmail material here," Kaitlyn says, and I laugh, hard, remembering how he teased me about my snoring. "It wasn't that funny."

"Yeah, I know. I think I'm nervous. This feels like snooping." I glance over my shoulder. Maybe I should have locked the door.

"Open his nightstand."

"No," I say in a hushed voice. "That's his private space."

"Do it," she insists. "You have to make sure you're not sharing a room with a serial killer who keeps weapons or body parts in his nightstand." I cock my head, and stare at her, incredulously. "What?"

"Are you for real?"

"Yeah, do it."

I turn the screen back to me. "You'd say just about anything to get me to do it, wouldn't you?"

She blinks dark lashes over not so innocent eyes. "I only have your best interests at heart, Maize, you know that."

"Yeah, that's why I'm in Christian's room right now."

She stands and walks to her dresser. She casts a quick glance at me after grabbing her yoga pants. "Is it that bad?

"Yes!" I blurt out, a straight up lie, and reverse the camera so she can't see my face. Wanting her attention off me, and how I kind of enjoy being here in luxury, I pull open the nightstand drawer, and come face to face with a mega box of condoms—for her pleasure.

"Dear God," Kaitlyn says. "Does that say magnum size? Bring me closer."

I stifle a laugh, and slam the drawer shut, then glance over my shoulder again when I hear footsteps in the hall. I hold my breath, but they move down the hall.

"He even has his own bathroom," I whisper.

"Ooh, fancy. Take me in."

I tiptoe across the room, being careful in my boot, and push open the door. I do a quick scan and revel in the big tub and separate shower. "A girl could get used to this."

"I would do anything for a bubble bath in that tub."

"Me too."

"Go for it," she tells me.

"I'm not getting in his tub."

"Why not?"

I shrug. "I don't know. Then again, he did say his place was my place." I walk across the room and pick up a plastic bottle to examine the contents. "Grapefruit body wash." I laugh. "No wonder he always smells like citrus."

"You always did like grapefruit."

I set the body wash back down, and take a big, rejuvenating breath, reminding myself who I am and who I'm not. One thing is for certain. I do not belong here, with Christian none the less, and I'd be wise to remember that.

"One week," I say under my breath. "Then I'll be back."

"Oh, I forgot to tell you something," Kaitlyn says her face twisted.

"What?"

She looks a bit sheepish when she says, "Your room kind of flooded."

"You're kidding!"

"Nope, we had all that rain, and you know the shingles are bad. Water dripped all over your bed and floor. Looks like you won't be coming back here for a while."

Son of a bitch.

10

CHRISTIAN

I shouldn't be nervous, or excited, as I park my Jeep and head back inside Wolf House. But no matter how many times I try to convince myself that I'm just helping Maize out, the thought of her in my room, my bed, does the strangest things to me. Watching her nap earlier, hearing her soft breathing sounds, her little sleep murmurs was enough to make me want to crawl in there, wake her with a hot kiss, and bury my face between her long, gorgeous legs.

Fuck me sideways.

I take the steps to the front stoop two at a time, and push the front door open harder than necessary. I catch it before it bangs against the wall, and shake my head to get myself together as I shut it quietly behind me.

Rumblings from the kitchen, along with light, breezy laughter from the girls who stayed over last night fill the front hallway. Honestly, I'll be glad when I can get my own place and have a bit of privacy. I suppose I could have done it before now, but there was no pressing need, no girl like Maize that I wanted to keep in my bedroom all to myself. Obsessive and posses-sive, which isn't really like me. Wanting to get straight to Maize and avoid small talk with my brothers, I head to the stairs, but Andrew comes from the kitchen, a bowl of cereal in his hands.

"Hey," he says, around a mouthful of food as his spoon clinks against the ceramic bowl. He glances at his watch. "You're back early."

"Yeah, I cut out a bit early." Volunteer work is important to me. Not just to look good on paper, but because I like putting a smile on the faces of sick kids, and tossing a ball around with those who can. It's just something private I do for them and for me. I don't want glory, and I guess it's not totally altruistic, because I get something out of it too. I might have been born with a silver spoon in my mouth, and a nice trust fund, but I have values and morals—I did until I bought Maize—and try to give back as much as I can. I won't always have football, and when my career is over, I want to be a well-rounded guy.

"Where have you been hiding?"

I stop on the first step and turn to him. "Not hiding, just busy."

"I was surprised to see you in the...basement."

I shrug and take another step. "Yeah, well. Surprise."

He shoves a spoonful of sugary cereal into his mouth. "Who's the girl? She's kind of cute."

My stomach tightens with possession. "Yeah, I'm helping her out. I injured her, so now I'm doing the right thing."

"Thor said something about that. She's staying here, then?"

He has a grin on his face as he questions me, and I get it. This is out of character for me. They know it, and I know it, but I'm doing this to right a wrong. My father is a Supreme Court judge, he's all about justice, which has rubbed off on me. While that's all true, and no matter how hard I try I still can't ignore the fact that she intrigues me, and I like talking to her.

"Just until she gets on her feet." He nods, and I rush up the steps. My heart pounds a little harder as I head down the long hall to my room. I knock, and when no answer comes, I try the knob, half expecting it to be locked. I turn the handle and push it open, and disappointment sits heavy in my gut when I find my room empty.

She's gone.

Fuck, of course she is. I probably scared her off when I told her I planned to take care of her. I drop my backpack as my gaze goes to my bed, which is now neatly made. I'm about to head back out, go to her place, put her over my shoulder caveman style and drag her back here with me, when there's a noise sounds in the bathroom, a whine of sorts. Shit, is she in there hurt? I hurry across the room and without giving a second thought to anything but her safety, I swing the door open, and find her in the tub, singing off tune with her ear buds in, and eyes closed. My throat tightens and my entire world tilts on its axis.

Here's the thing, I've seen plenty of naked women. Plenty. The sight of Maize in my tub, her bad ankle lifted and braced on the edge of the tub, as grapefruit bubbles tease her pretty pink nipples, shouldn't rock my world quite so violently. But it does. There's no explanation. Other than the fact that maybe I want what I can't have.

I breathe in the scent of my body wash. In the mornings, it pulls my brain awake and rejuvenates me, but right now, it's pulling something else awake, something that lives a little further south. I stand there for a second, immobilized, not knowing what to do. Do I run and pretend I was never here, or do I make a sound letting her know I'm home, watching her?

The choice is taken from me when her eyes open, and her head turns my way. I back up as her mouth opens, and she jackknifes up into a sitting position, her foot falling from the edge and splashing in the tub.

"Ow," she cries, and I cringe.

"Maize, I'm sorry," I say quickly. "I didn't mean to scare you." She covers her lush breasts, although it's far too late. The sight is burned into my memory and I'll be putting that show on repeat as I take my cock into my hand tonight.

"What are you doing?"

"I came home, heard a noise, and thought you were in here, hurt."

"I was singing."

"Yeah, okay," I say, and when I realize I'm still staring, I grab a towel, spread it wide and block my view as I open it for her. "Here."

Water splashes, and her grunts and groans as she tries to climb from the slippery tub fill the room. "Stupid tub. So wet and slippery."

Wet and slippery.

Jesus fuck, does she have any idea what kind of torture this is for me?

"I can't get up," she grumbles.

Sadly, I can.

I take a step toward her. "Let me help you."

"I don't need your help," she barks out and my steps still.

"Okay." I stand there, and listen to her struggles, but she's too damn stubborn to let me lift her out. Seconds tick by, and my arms grow tired of holding the towel. She finally lets loose a frustrated sigh.

"Christian."

"Yeah?"

"Can you...help me?"

"Yeah."

"Just don't look."

"That's going to be hard."

Good God, what am I saying? At least the big towel is blocking the sight of my raging erection.

"Just feel your way around."

Jesus Christ, she's killing me.

I take slow steps and stop when my foot hits the tub. I let the towel go with one hand and reach for her. She puts her hand in mine, and her warmth seeps through my skin, arousing me even more.

"If I tug, I'm going to hurt you. I need to put my arms around you." I set the towel on the edge of the tub, feel my way around her body, nearly swallowing my damn tongue as my hands slide along the swell of her breasts, until I have both hands under her arms. "Ready?"

"Yes," she says, and it comes out sounding torturous, full of heated desire. Unable to help myself, I open one eye to find her staring at me, her cheeks a sexy shade of pink, her lips full, parted, like they're waiting for my mouth.

"No peeking," she says in a whisper full of need and want. Am I reading her right, or am I misconstruing embarrassment for desire?

I close my eyes. "What were you thinking, Maize?"

"I don't know. Your tub is so big, and we only have a shower at my place. I didn't think you'd be home so fast, or that I'd get stuck."

"Next time you want a bath, I'll help you."

"I don't need—"

"Clearly you do need my help," I correct her, completely frustrated in so many ways as I lift her out, and wrap the towel securely around her. I open my eyes. Her breasts have left two damp marks on the towel, and a groan full of want crawls out of my throat.

"What?" she asks.

I shake my head. "Really, Maize? You have to ask what?"

"I..." She glances down. Does she not know how hot she is? That I've laid in bed and beat off to the image of her far more times than I would like to admit? That in a few minutes, I plan to do it again, because I can't—won't—ruin her any more than I already have?

I shake my head, scoop her up and carry her to my bed. After I deposit her on the mattress, I stand back and work to recapture my breath, not because she's heavy—she's not—but because I'm losing my shit big time here.

"Get dressed," I say, much harsher than I intended. I scrub my face, and turn a bit so she can't see my dick.

"Um, okay. Can you at least turn around?"

I turn, and head to the bathroom. Once there, I drain the tub and as water gurgles away, I rip into my pants, and throw my head back as I take my dick into my hands. I pull from the base to tip, and stifle the moan in my throat. Eyes closed, I visualize sweet, yet sexy Maize on her knees before me, her mouth open, waiting for me to feed her my cock. I tug, and reach down to grab my balls, giving them a squeeze as my breath comes faster.

"Yes," I say quietly, the draining tub drowning any sounds as I think about putting my cock in her mouth, and spilling my load down her throat. "Fuck," I say and just like that, I come. I lean back, and before I can get my T-shirt up, I soak it. I lean against the bathroom counter, my breath coming in labored bursts as my gaze goes to the door. Shit, I was so keyed up, I didn't even lock it. I snort. If she'd walked in here and saw me like this, it would send her running back to her run-down apartment.

Or would it?

Fuck, it doesn't matter. I'm not going to touch her. I tear my T-shirt off, drop it into the hamper, and grab a cloth from the sliver of a linen closet. I wash up quickly, do up my pants, and step into the other room. I can't tell whether I'm happy or not, when I see that she's fully dressed.

"What...what happened to your shirt?" she asks, her gaze latched on to my chest. It slides lower, and I swear to fuck her breathing has changed as her gaze moves over my abs, coming to rest on the button to my jeans.

"Got it wet," I say and her gaze flies back to mine. I reach over my head and rub the muscle at the base of my neck. "Do you want me to help you with your boot?" I ask, as she struggles with it, her hands a bit shaky.

"No, I got it." She finishes fastening it, and opens her mouth like she wants to say something.

"What?" I ask.

"Where...where are you going to sleep?"

"There's a cot in the basement, I'll bring it up."

She nods. "Is there anything on your list that you'd like me to do?"

Oh, there was a lot of things I'd like for her to do, but none of them are on my list. My phone pings, and I pull it from my back pocket. I text Kyle back.

"I have to go," I tell her.

"Christian, if you want to bring someone back here, you know to...fuck...I can...I don't know, go downstairs or something."

Hearing the word fuck on her lips just about does me in. I take a fast breath, clear my throat and say, "The guys want to pull together a practice."

"Oh, okay."

"If I want to fuck, you'll be the first to know." Wait, that didn't come out right. "I mean, I won't put you out. I'll fuck elsewhere."

"Right, okay," she says and swallows hard.

I jerk my thumb over my shoulder. "Do you...want to come watch?" Shit, why would I ask that. If she's watching when I'm on the field, she'll be a distraction I don't need and she's tortured me enough already.

She snatches up her backpack. "I think I'll get some homework done. Besides, I know how bad Kyle is at catching and don't want to risk another ball to the head."

"Suit yourself." I turn from her, a little brusque—even though she's trying to lighten the mood—and I don't mean to be a dick. I'm the one who brought her here.

"Christian."

"Yeah?" I say without turning back to her.

"I...I really appreciate what you're doing for me. I know it doesn't come across that way, but I am, and I know it was an accident and you didn't have to do this." I peek at her. She waves her hands as she looks around my room. "Maybe someday, I can make it up to you. Maybe you could, I don't know... just let me know how I could do that."

Jesus fuck, please tell me she didn't put that on the table.

11

MAIZE

Two long weeks have passed since Christian first brought me to his impressive bedroom in Wolf House. Two long, agonizing, sexually frustrated weeks, that is. Why again did I tell him right from the start this wasn't about sex? That I wouldn't have sex? He might be sleeping on a cot, but watching him walk out of the bathroom every morning with nothing but a towel wrapped around his waist is torture to the utmost extreme. I'm beginning to question whether he's doing it on purpose. Maybe he knows what it does to me, and this is about finishing what he started in the closet all those years ago.

Oh, how I wish.

"You okay?" he asks, from the hard plastic seat beside me as I wait for my doctor's appointment.

I shift uncomfortably, shake off my musings and nod. "Yeah, just thinking."

He reaches out and gives my hand a squeeze. We're friends now, and that's what friends do, right? They give reassuring squeezes, that shouldn't be tugging me deep in my core. I shouldn't be feeling anything other than warm friendship. I guess the needy spot between my legs didn't get the memo.

"I know you're worried about running again." His eyes hold a measure of hope and comfort as they move over my face. "It will happen. I'll help any way I can."

I nod and glance at our joined hands as he continues to hold mine. "It's not as important now, thanks to your help."

"I was responsible, which is why you're staying with me until you heal completely," he says, quietly, solemnly, and it's yet another reminder that I'm at his place, not because he wants me, but because he feels responsible for me. I know a way he can pay off that debt.

Don't go there again, Maize.

"Besides, you can't go home. Not with the flooding."

I sigh. "True."

He nudges me, and turning playful, he says. "It's not so bad, is it?"

"It's been tolerable," I say with a sarcastic twist of my lips. "Except for last weekend, and the partying."

"Yeah, I was thinking about that. My buddy has a place off campus. We can stay there if you want."

I give a fast shake of my head and my ponytail bounces. "No, I'm not putting anyone else out," I say, lowering my voice as someone takes a seat beside me. "I'll deal with the noise."

He gives my hair a playful tug. "I don't mind putting out." My gaze flies to his. Was that sexual, or is that just my wishful thinking?

I bite the inside of my cheek to pull myself together and redirect the conversation, but I have to say, these last couple of weeks, being with him has been easy, our conversations natural—when I can stop thinking about sex for one second. I almost think he enjoys my company as much as I enjoy his. "I still can't believe you paid the landlord a visit."

"I told you I would, and I did. I keep my word."

I nod, secretly liking that about him. He's been honest about everything so far—even the part of fucking and not having girlfriends—and he's a guy who stands behind his word. "I guess I'll believe it when I see it."

"I dropped my Dad's name, Maize." He grins at me. "It goes a long way."

"Someday I'd love to be on the supreme court," I tell him with a sigh, and I'm not ruling it out. " I need to get myself into Harvard. I want to be the next RBG."

He laughs. "You could do it. You know my dad went to Harvard. He has connections."

"Really?"

He nods. "Yeah, he knows the Dean of the law department quite well. He's the guy with all the power and if he likes you, he can get you great internship opportunities. I met him a few times myself."

Wow, it's nice to have connections, but I'm not about to ask for an introduction. None of that feels right to me. "Maybe you should have thought about law, then."

"Nah, it was never for me, much to my father's disappointment."

"He can't be disappointed that you're a football star, Christian."

"You wouldn't think," he says with a smirk that holds a hint of remorse. I take it he doesn't like disappointing his father.

"Wait until you make it in the NFL."

He shrugs. "Maybe then he'll come see a game."

My heart stalls, and I don't want to make too big a deal of it, but it upsets me that in all his years playing, his father never once went to see one of his games. That's not right on so many levels. He's not looking for pity. He's telling me something very private, and probably something hard for him to say, so I stay silent, and give his hand a squeeze, saying everything I need to through touch, and from his smile, he clearly appreciates that.

"About the music and partying," he says. "We won't have to worry about it over the Thanksgiving weekend. After our Friday night game, most ballers go home, so the place is quiet."

"Are you going home after the game?"

He shakes his head and I don't miss the hint of sadness in his eyes. "No, that's Mom's big shopping weekend with her friends and Dad won't be there, so there's no point."

"Oh." I pause, unsure what to say. "I'll be going home." My throat tightens at the thoughts of him being here alone and Mom's words ping in my head.

Will you be bringing anyone with you?

I open my mouth, not sure whether to ask. That's crossing a boundary, and I'd be so embarrassed if he said no or laughed at me.

He nods, and looks across the room, but his thoughts suddenly seem a million miles away. "I guess I'll do the usual and go skiing in Aspen."

I've never been to Aspen. I've never even been skiing. "That's sounds amazing, Christian."

He gives a shrug, like he's indifferent about it. "Why don't you...come," he says. "Come to think of it, the Dean of the law department spends time in Aspen. I've skied with his daughter many times over the years."

I wince like I'd just been stabbed with a hot poker. Now where did that crazy burst of jealousy come from? I've seen Christian with many girls. Not since we've been living together or whatever it is we're doing, but still.

"Wow, that is awesome. Maybe she'll be there again." I put on my best smile and hope he can't see the ridiculous cracks in it. I have no right to be jealous, like no right at all.

He nudges me. "Too bad you couldn't come. I could have introduced you to Dean Saunders."

I laugh. "I'm injured, Christian, and I've never been on skis. One concussion this semester is enough."

"You could be healed by then, or you could stay in the chalet and drink hot chocolate."

"While that all sounds tempting, I have plans with my mother that I just can't break." I kept her from coming to see me a couple of weekends ago, and she'd be devastated if I didn't come home for Thanksgiving, although she'd probably be all for me going to Aspen with a boy.

"I get it. Family is important." He turns away, but not before I catch the little lost boy look on his face. My throat tightens, pretty sure I'm reading him wrong—seeing things that aren't there. This is Christian Moore, star football player, every girl's fantasy come to life. No way is he lonely. He can't be, right?

His father doesn't go to his games, Maize.

As I consider that, the receptionist calls my name, and I lift my head to find two deep blue eyes staring at me with great concern. "Want me to come in with you?" he offers.

"No, I'm a big girl, Christian," I tease with a grin. "I can take care of myself."

"Right, I know. I'll be here waiting," he tells me and my stupid heart squeezes tight at his sweetness. I like the way he takes care of me and dotes on me at every turn. I love the way he always wants to be there for me, when really he bought me and I'm supposed to be doing things for him, but no, he's been cooking and cleaning and pampering me. I'm not used to it, and I wasn't even sure I wanted it at first, but dammit, he's proving to be so much more than a jock out for his own pleasure. Which really sucks, because when my apartment gets fixed, I'll be leaving his place for good.

Unless...

Unless what, Maize? Unless you seduce him and trick him into keeping you for a little longer? I almost snort at the idea as I walk to the examination room. The receptionist puts my file on the counter, and my stomach knots because I've yet to pay my bill. I was hoping once I got the boot off, and I could move around a little better, I'd apply for jobs on campus to help pay the medical costs. Christian's payment only covered tuition and room and board, and I still can't believe how this all turned out. The thing is though, when I become a successful lawyer, I plan to pay him back every cent. What happened was a freak accident, and while he was the one who threw the ball, an accident is an accident. The fault is not his, deep inside I know it, and I'm the one responsible for my own tuition.

"About payments," I say and twist the strap on my purse. "I was hoping I could make installments."

Her brow furrows like she has no idea what I'm talking about. Picking my file back up again, she flips through it. "Your bill has been paid, Maize. In full."

I shake my head. "There must be some kind of mistake."

She glances at the papers again, and shakes her head. "No, not a mistake."

My mind races. Mom has no idea about the accident, so it's not like she emptied her meager savings account and came to my rescue. Kaitlyn would have if she could have. She's a scholarship student like me, without two cents to rub together. No, there is only one person who could have paid it, and I'm honestly not sure how I feel about that. I have no time to think about that though, not when the doctor is here to examine me.

He gives me a grandfatherly sympathetic smile. "How are you doing today, Maize?"

"I'm doing well, thank you. How are you?"

"Just fine," he says. "How about you sit up here and let me have a look at your ankle." As I walk to the examination table, he dims the lights, puts my X-rays up, and goes quiet as he looks them over.

"You're healing quite nicely," he says.

"Will I be able to run again?" I ask. Even though I'm off the team, I'd like to be able to run again someday just for exercise.

"I'm sure you will. But in time, maybe three to four months. Right now, we need to give you some strengthening exercises." He turns the lights back on and I lay on the table as he removes my boot and feels around my ankle. "No swelling," he says. "You've been taking very good care of yourself."

I nod. I've had a very good caregiver. "Do I have to continue wearing the boot?"

"For at least a couple more weeks."

"Do you think I'll be better by Thanksgiving?"

"You should be pretty healed by then."

"Able to go skiing?" I ask and shake my head. Now why on earth would I ask that? I have absolutely no plans to go with Christian. I miss my mother, and want to see her.

He laughs. "I'm afraid not." He steps back and writes something in his file. "You don't want to push it and have lifelong trouble. So, stay off it, and keep that boot on for another few weeks. We'll set up another appointment."

I nod, and while I hate the idea of wearing the boot longer, there is a part of me that is a little excited about it. As long as I have the boot, Christian won't let me leave. Not that I can go back to my apartment. Not with the leaks and I'll believe a new roof is going on when I see it.

After the doctor leaves, I put my boot back on and Christian stands when I enter the waiting room. He hurries over to me, and a little flutter goes through my body as he slides a hand around my back, and looks at me with questioning eyes.

"It's healing nicely, and I should only have this thing on," I lift my leg to show him the boot, "for a few more weeks."

"That's not so bad." He leads me outside, helps me into his Jeep and I can't seem to take my eyes off him as he circles the vehicle and climbs in. He checks his watch.

"You're not going to be late, are you?" It's Friday night, and there's a home game he needs to get ready for, which is the only reason I'm not bringing up my bill. It will lead to an argument, especially when I'll insist on paying him back. I don't want him upset when he plays.

He reaches across and gives my hand a squeeze, and my sex muscles clench. Crawling into bed, with him on a cot beside me, has not left me with much privacy. Privacy to touch myself, while imagining it's Christian's hands on my body, on my breasts, and between my legs. Never in my life have I been so sexually frustrated.

"No, we're good," he says. "You going to stay in and study?"

I shrug. "I guess." He's not asked me to go to any games, and honestly, I'm not sure I want to hear all the girls screaming his name. He's not been 'fucking' as far as I know. When he's not at practice, games, classes or studying with me at the library, we're in his room. Although he does disappear on Sundays for a couple of hours at a time, and never tell me where he's going. I guess it's none of my business. That doesn't stop the curiosity though.

My phone pings and I fish it from my purse. He casts me a glance. "Kaitlyn," I tell him.

I read her text, asking me how my appointment went, and I text her back and tell her. I stare at the phone until her response comes in, and I put my hand over my face to stifle a laugh. I wish she'd give it up and stop asking me if I'd gotten a look at Christian's 'cob' yet. It's funny when she says it, but it wasn't so funny back in high school.

"Everything okay?" he asks.

"Yeah, just Kaitlyn being Kaitlyn." I drop my phone even though she's still texting, and let loose a sigh as I take in Christian's profile. A few minutes later, he pulls up to the back of Wolf House, and I climb out. He carries me up the stairs, per usual, and after depositing me on his bed, he grabs his backpack.

He eyes me, as I stretch out, and I'm almost certain I heard a groan in his throat as he takes me in. "Pizza after the game?"

"You know you don't have to come back here to keep me company. I know you guys like to celebrate at the Growler and I don't want to keep you from your teammates and the fans."

He hikes his backpack over his shoulder. "That's assuming we win."

"Are you going to win, Christian?"

He grins. "Fuck yeah, we're going to win. See you later, Maize, I'll bring pizza."

"No Christian, I am not keeping you from the party and I'm sure there are plenty of girls who've been missing you."

He opens his mouth, and for a second I think he's going to protest, but he doesn't. Instead he says, "Yeah, you're right."

He leaves, and I hate, HATE, the stupid disappointment settling in my gut. He should be with his teammates, the cheerleaders and his fans. I'm beginning to believe, despite what he says, I *am* putting him out. A goddamn burden, because he feels responsible for me. I should just pack up, and go back to my place, flood or not.

I glance around, and as I consider that, I get a text from Kaitlyn.

Meet me outside Wolf House. I'm here waiting for you.

I snort. She's good at reading me, and maybe she's thinking the same thing I am, despite her 'cob' comment earlier. Needing a breath of fresh air, I text back that I'll be there in a second, or as fast as my boot will allow me—because I suddenly need to be out of Christian's space. Maybe she'll come back in with me to help me pack up.

The house is silent when I open the bedroom door. Later tonight though, after the party, whether the Falcons win or not, it will be rocking. I go down the back stairs, as it's easier with my boot, and circle the building to find Kaitlyn standing there, scrolling on her phone.

"Hey."

She turns, and makes a face. "Where did you come from?"

"Back entrance. That's the way Christian always makes me come in and out."

"Okay." She frowns. "Not weird at all."

I laugh. "It's the boot. There are fewer stairs." At least that's what he says. A knot tightens in my stomach. Maybe it is weird, and maybe I'm overlooking the weirdness because I'm well, not seeing things clearly when I'm around Christian.

"That makes sense," she says, and I feel a measure of relief. "Come on," she says and tucks her arm in mine, dragging me along.

"Where are we going?"

"To the game, of course." She says it like I should know.

I dig my good heel in, but my heart takes that time to squeeze, a not so gentle reminder that Christian's father doesn't attend. "I don't like football."

"We're still going. It's your fourth year, and you haven't been to a single game. You can't graduate from Kingston with that black cloud hanging over your head."

I laugh. "It's not a black cloud."

"Maybe, maybe not. But don't you want to watch hot stuff play?"

I fold my arms, and lift my chin a notch. "No, I don't." Okay, well, maybe secretly I do, but he didn't ask me to come. Will he be upset? It's a big stadium, he'll never know.

She winks at me like she knows something I don't. "I bet he'll like having you there."

I give an unladylike snort as a car drives by on the street, the horns honking. Looks like everyone on campus is excited for the game—everyone but me, that is. "He won't even know." Wow, way to sound like a whiny baby. We're nothing more than friends—and yeah, I want to jump him—but I have no claim on him, no reason to be upset that he didn't ask me to come. Why would he? I told him I hated football. I hate myself for that now, because a good friend would go to support their friend whether they hated the game or not, right?

"If we scream loud enough, he'll know we're there."

"I'll leave that to the cheerleaders. Wait, why would you say he'll like having me there?"

She pokes my forehead. "For a smart girl, you're kind of dense."

"I am no—"

"Maize, he's totally into you. I've seen you two at the library. You're too lost in your textbooks to notice the way he looks at you."

Honestly, I'm too tenses when I'm around him to even concentrate on my textbooks. I read the same paragraph ten times last time we were at the library, which is so not good for my grades. "How does he look at me?"

"Like *you're* the corn on the cob and he wants to eat you."

I swallow as that visual dances in my mind's eye. Christian on his knees, his hands touching me as he parts my sex with his tongue and brings me to climax. Oh boy!

"Whatever," I say, ignoring the flutter inside me, and hating the high pitch of my voice. "Fine, I'll go, but promise me, no screaming. I don't like to draw attention to myself and you know that."

"I can't promise that. I get caught up in the game and things just spill from my lips."

I roll my eyes at her. "I need a new best friend."

She laughs, and drags me across campus and to the stadium. We finally find seats, and I can't seem to take my eyes off Christian throughout the game. Kaitlyn cheers beside me when the Falcons get a touchdown, she jumps, and I find myself screaming right along with her from my seat. Who knew I could get into the game so easily?

"Fun, huh?" Kaitlyn grins as she drops back down.

"Who knew."

"There's a whole world out there, my friend. You should have a look at it once in a while."

I laugh at that, but she's not wrong. I've always kept my head down and my mind focused. But now, I can't focus on anything, thanks to Christian. Maybe I should jump him, climb him like a damn tree, and have my way with him. Maybe that would help get me back on track, and yeah, living life a little.

"What's going through that mind of yours?" Kaitlyn asks.

"Oh, just thinking about having sex with Christian," I say honestly and her jaw drops. Her hands go to my shoulders.

"Do it. Tonight."

Nervous energy swirls through my stomach. "What if he doesn't want me?"

She lets loose a hysterical laugh that draws attention. "Shh," I say.

"Trust me on this. He wants you."

Could she be right? What if I take a chance and she's wrong and Christian laughs at me?

What if she's right and Christian takes me to his bed?

Neither one of us are thinking long term or a future. We are both on different paths, but why couldn't we have one night of pleasure?

Kaitlyn jumps up again, and I sit there wondering what happened. God, I was so lost in my own thoughts I didn't realize we just won the game.

"Come on," Kaitlyn says and grabs my arm. "Let's head to the Growler so we can get good seats."

We weave our way through the excited crowd as the cheerleaders jump on the players' backs and they carry them inside. My stomach is in knots. Does Christian have after-game party plans with one of those hot girls tonight? If he does, I'm going to have to see about changing that.

Whoa, where did this fierce Maize come from? I'm not sure, but I think I like her. We make our way to the Growler, which is totally packed, so we find seats at the bar. Minutes tick by and my anxiety peaks as I wait for Christian. Antsy and hardly able to sit still, I tell Kaitlyn I'm making a trip to the ladies' room, where I splash a bit of water on my face. As I come back down the hall, I hear the commotion and know the players and cheerleaders have arrived.

I reach the end of the long hall, and stop where I am as Christian walks in like he owns the damn place. I do love that man's confidence. There's a cheerleader on his back as he makes his way to the bar, and he goes completely still when his gaze lands on me. He shakes the girl off, says something to her, and with pouty lips, she saunters off.

His strides are long, determined, as he moves people out of his way, to get to me. He stops, and I try to breathe as I lift my chin to meet his eyes.

"You came," he says, an intensity about him that is both terrifying and exhilarating. Is this how he gets after a game? I'm not sure, and I'm also wondering why my fierceness from earlier has disappeared. I nod and he angles his head.

"Were you at the game too?" he asks.

"Yes." I glance around at all the girls vying for his attention. "Am I keeping you from your fucking?"

Taking me by surprise, his face goes hard, the blue in his eyes deepening as he backs me up into the long hallway and pushes me against the wall. "What do you know about fucking, Maize?"

12

MAIZE

I stand there staring at Christian, my gaze moving over the tightness in his jaw, as well as the fierceness in his eyes, as I try to process the question still lingering on his kissable lips.

He leans into me. "What do you know about fucking, Maize?" he growls into my ear, sending shivers of hot desire through my trembling body.

I swallow hard, and the sound gets drowned out in the rowdy crowd and for that, I'm grateful. But does it matter? I'm pretty sure the man who bought me a few weeks ago can feel the tension, the need emanating from my body as he hovers over me, his groin pressed against my body in a way that has shut down my ability to think with any sort of clarity. I might not be his regular type, but tonight, I think I'm going to be his everything. Or at least I hope so.

Is this really happening?

His head dips, his lips close to mine. "Answer me."

"Christian...I." What the hell do I say? I know nothing about fucking, other than how the moving parts fit together. I fumbled around in the dark with Ryan, for God's sake, and took no pleasure in the actual messy, painful act of sex.

His fingers tighten on my shoulders, and the rough pads of his thumbs are sure to leave a bruise, but what frightens me most is how much I like it, how much I like when he holds me in place...holds me down hard, like he did that day I was injured. Dear God, I can't even believe I'm admitting that to myself. Does that make me weak, feeble, a delicate little girl in need of a man's care? I pride myself on being capable, strong—unbreakable.

But I don't want to be any of those things right now. No, I want Christian to...break me. God, what am I saying? What am I admitting?

His gaze moves over my face, like he can see the internal struggle going on inside my brain, see exactly where my thoughts have strayed, and more importantly, exactly where they've settled. He nods, a slow movement of his head, like he's coming to some hard-earned conclusion himself and I can't help but think he too has been battling his own demons.

"Is this where we are, Maize?" I stare at him, and get what he's asking. This has nothing to do with being in the Growler, nothing to do with our location in the hallway. This has everything to do with this tug between us, one we're both clearly feeling. But what he's really asking is, are we going to act on it?

Do we really have a choice? I don't know about him, but if he doesn't touch me soon, I'm going to melt into a puddle at his feet.

"Christian," a high-pitched voice says from behind. "What are you doing in the hall? I've been looking everywhere for you." Annoyance spills from the pretty girl's lips as she grabs the back of his jacket and pulls. Without taking his eyes off me, he rolls his shoulder to shrug her off. An angry sound rises in her throat and she moves around him to glare at me with hate and disdain. I take in the scowl on her face, but my gaze is forced back to Christian's, when he cups my chin and bluntly moves me.

"Is this where we are, Maize?"

I take a breath, try to fill my constricted lungs, and as I let it out, I say, "Yes."

His pupils dilate even more, his pulse pounding at the base of his throat as he pulls me from the wall. "Home. Now."

Before I know what's happening, he has my hand and is tugging me through the crowd, his stride a bit slower than normal, and I chalk that up to my injured foot. I scan the bar and catch Kaitlyn smirking at me. She gives a little finger wave and a nod of approval as he drags me outside, the cooler night air falling around us.

Without a word, he takes off his team jacket, drapes it over my shoulders and scoops me up, setting me in the passenger side of his Jeep. I still can't quite get enough air as he circles the front, and climbs in beside me, his big presence eating up the space and completely overwhelming me. The smell of his freshly soaped skin reaches my nostrils and my girly parts tingle as I breathe him in.

Five agonizing minutes later, he carries me up the long flight of stairs at the back of Wolf House, and when we reach his bedroom, he steps inside, kicks his door shut with a hell of a lot of force, and sets the lock. The sound of the bolt sliding home sends shivers through my overheated body.

I stare at him as he sets me on my feet, shoves his jacket from my shoulders, and presses my back to the door. The fierce energy radiating off him glides over my skin. Is he always like this after a game, or does this have more to do with the tension that has been building between us?

His head dips, his lips a breath away from mine, and a whimper catches in my throat. My God, I don't think I've ever whimpered in my life. He cups my face, his thumb brushing over my lower lip.

"This fucking mouth." He shoves his thumb between my lips and I suck. "I can't stop thinking about fucking this mouth," he murmurs and draws his thumb out to put his hands on my ribcage, his thumbs touching the underside of my breasts. "I want to fuck you everywhere."

I gulp, and he stands back, his hands falling as he looks me over, like he's gauging my reaction to his crass words. I'm sure the quiver in my body is a dead giveaway—to him and me— how much I like it. Who knew I'd like dirty talk?

His gaze rakes over me, and something flashes in his eyes. Need, want...worry? For one quick second, I think he's changed his mind about going any further with me, but then his gaze jerks back up to mine, and like he's no longer in control of himself, he picks me up again like I weigh nothing, and carries me to his bed. He sets me down, drops to his knees, and with little effort removes my boot. He lightly runs his fingers along my ankle after he frees it from the binding, and the rest of my body aches for that kind of attention.

"Better?" he asks, his voice deep and labored as he stands, and I can't stop myself from staring at the huge bulge in his jeans.

Christian is aroused...because of me. That thought does the strangest things to the needy spot between my legs and my throat grows dry with desire.

"Yeah," I manage to get out, and I swipe my tongue over my bottom lip as I envision myself with his cock in my mouth. His growl pulls me back from my musings.

"Look at me, Maize." My head lifts as his commanding tone dampens my panties even more. What is it about his take-charge attitude that turns me on so much? I don't know but... please don't stop.

His fingers fist and relax again at his sides. I get the sense that it's taking all his effort to keep it together, and that thought turns me on even more.

"Been taking care of yourself for a long time huh?"

I grip the bedsheets, curl them in my fingers. "Yes."

He sinks to the floor, crawls toward me, and grips my knees. He widens my legs and slides one hand up my inner thigh, touching my sex through my clothes.

"So gorgeous." He widens my legs even more and the second he touches me, his rough finger caressing my swollen clit through my pants, my synapses stop firing and my body burns with an unfamiliar want.

He presses his finger a little harder against my clit, drawing my attention down. "Even here?" My God, no one has ever asked me such a personal question before. I stare at him, my mouth opening and closing. He cocks his head. "It's easy, Maize. Yes or no?"

"No...Yes, I mean...I don't know." With my Catholic upbringing kicking in, I try to slam my thighs shut, but he won't let me. I'm strong, but he's stronger. He sits there waiting for an answer, his hand still on my clit, as my brain races. Ryan and I fumbled around in the dark and it's far too bright in this room. When I touch myself, I do it without sound, fearful of anyone hearing in the dead of the night. How am I going to go through with this?

"I need to know, Maize."

"Yes, even...there." I glance around. "It's too bright in here."

Ignoring me, he goes back on his heels, his hands on my thighs. "So what do you know about fucking?"

My first reaction is to blurt out, "A lot."

He angles his head, and goes thoughtful for a moment. "You've done this before, then?"

"Yes. I've had sex. Ryan and I...well, we had sex," I blurt out, although he has no idea that my childhood friend and I deflowered each other, all with zero romance. What the hell am I even thinking? This isn't romance. This is about fucking. The one and only Christian Moore doesn't do romance or relationships. He fucks. Simple as that.

The muscles in his jaw tighten. "This isn't the first time you've mentioned Ryan. Who is he?" he asks through clenched teeth, and a wave of embarrassment moves through me. I'm not about to tell him the story. Although from the look on his face, I fear he might just drag it out of me.

I give a dismissive wave, and note how shaky my hands are. "Just a guy, from a long time ago."

His gaze narrows in on me. "Is he here, at Kingston?"

I shake my head. "No."

"Good, now I don't have to kill him."

I stiffen. "Why would you—"

"He obviously means something to you. You keep bringing him up."

"He's just a guy from back home. A friend I grew up with. The boy next door."

He stares at me long and hard, like he's trying to process. "You fucked a friend?"

"I don't date, Christian. I fuck," I say, with more bravado than I feel as I shoot his words back at him, and he grins.

"Is that right? So you and Ryan fuck, then?"

"We did once." I give a frustrated sigh and hit the bed with my fist. "We just...wanted to get rid of our virginity before college. Him more than me."

His fingers curl. "It was mutual?"

"Yes," I say quickly, and take in the anger in his eyes. What would he have done if it wasn't? "I was tired of being a virgin."

"You did it once, then." He nods and scrubs his face. "You know nothing about fucking, do you?"

"No, I don't," I admit. Will he leave now? Leave the inexperienced girl who knows nothing, to take the edge off herself while he goes and gets a seasoned girl who knows how to please a guy?

"Good."

His answer takes me by surprise. "Why is that good?"

"Because I get to be the guy to show you how good it can be. There won't be any fumbling in the dark," he says, pushing me down on the bed as he glances at his lamp. "The lights stay on. I want to see you."

He holds me immobile. A gasp I have zero control over crawls out of my throat and he stares at me so long, I swear he can see all my dirty secrets, read all the filthy thoughts that would have undoubtedly send my old Catholic teachers into a frenzy. Do I care? Hell no, and yeah... Hell. That's where I might be going. But right now, I suspect this man is going to take me to heaven and I'm ready for the ride because I want this.

I want him.

Consequences be damned.

He stands up, reaches over his back in typical guy fashion, grabs his shirt and pulls it over his head. Starting at his shoulders, my gaze drops, taking pleasure in every bump and valley. For the last few weeks, I've tried not to stare, but now I can look my fill.

"Sit up," he commands, and I do what he says. He steps up to me, takes my hand and puts it on his body.

"You've been staring for weeks, Maize. I thought maybe you'd like to touch."

I nod—no sense in denying it—and unable to find my words, I run my hands over his taut skin and hard muscles. My breathing changes, and when he rips into his jeans, I nearly collapse. He stands there, with the button open, and a measure of panic goes through me. Do I shove my hands in his pants? Do I take him into my mouth like he talked about?

"Relax, Maize." He runs the back of his hand over my cheek, his eyes full of understanding. "I'll walk you through this." I nod, and look down, but he touches my chin, bringing my eyes to his. "Tell me you want that."

I nod again.

"I need to hear it."

"I want that," I say, pushing those three words from the depths of my dry throat. "I want...you." The next thing I know he's on his knees, his hand cupping the back of my head as his mouth finds mine. His lips devour me, eat at me as he unceremoniously puts his tongue into my mouth, seeking mine. I give him what he wants, shutting my eyes against the intense pleasure sliding through my quivering body. My nipples harden and it teases every erogenous zone in my body, even a few I had no idea existed until now—until this man. There is only one word to describe what I'm currently feeling. Heaven.

"Sweet mother of God and all that is holy."

"Are you praying, Maize?" he murmurs, before going back to doing insane things to me. Tasting, teasing, licking...owning. This man is going to own my body tonight.

I work to form a coherent sentence as that thought circles my brain, warning I should probably be more frightened by that. "Oh, sorry. I didn't mean to say any of that out loud."

He inches back, his lips damp from our kiss. "Don't be. I want you to tell me everything. What feels good, what doesn't. I don't want you to hold anything back. That's what fucking is all about."

"Okay," I say. He takes my hands and puts them back on his body, and his muscles flex as I explore, touch him all over, reveling in the tightness of his skin as I run my palms around his back—wanting to touch every last inch of him. I slide upward and fist my fingers in his hair, deepening the kiss and his growls of encouragement fill me with bravado.

He breaks the kiss. "This is how it's going to work," he says, the intensity in his eyes letting me know he's calling the shots —because clearly, I know nothing about fucking. "I'm going to put my mouth, my hands and my tongue on every inch of your body..." His hand slides lower, going between my breasts until he reaches the juncture of my legs. "Even here."

"I've never..."

"Yeah, I get it. Ryan didn't do right by you, and while I might have mixed feelings on that, I'm totally going to give you everything you deserve."

While I don't understand what he means about mixed feel-ings, now is not the time to ask, not when he's tugging the elastic from my hair, letting it spill down my back.

"I get you like control," he begins. "But I told you before that's not going to stop me from telling you what to do." His grin is playful, but so damn needy I could weep with joy. Christian wants this as much as I do. Honestly, no matter how many times I tell myself that, I still can't quite wrap my brain around it. "Are you going to fight me on that tonight, Maize?"

"No," I say so quickly, the corners of his mouth turn up in a grin. I bite my lip to hide my own smile, but he can see right through me, see how excited I am, and what's the point of hiding it? He's being honest with me, and that's what I should give in return.

"That's my girl." He gives me another little shove, until I'm flat on my back. He stares at me again, the blue in his eyes deepening and sending more quivers through my body. He tears into his pants, the zipper hissing as it releases. A second later, he has his cock in his hand, and I nearly bite off my tongue. "Spread your legs," he commands and wraps one big palm around his thick cock.

I do as he asks, my breath coming quicker now. "Christian."

"Yeah?" I want to look at him, to meet his eyes, but I can't take my focus off the way he's stroking himself. "Something to say, Maize?"

I wet my lips. "I just…"

"I take it you've never seen a man fuck his palm while he admires a gorgeous woman sprawled on his bed."

Did he just call me gorgeous? I mentally roll my eyes so hard I nearly give myself a headache. Is that what I'm focusing on right now? And really, I'm sure he says that to every girl he's ever had in this bed.

"I've never," I answer honestly.

"Put your hands down your pants."

My brain stalls. He can't be serious. The second I look into his eyes, I know he is. "You see what I'm doing here, Maize."

"Uh huh."

"I've been doing this every morning in the shower. Fuck, knowing you're in this bed, all warm and soft and not being able to climb in here and taste you has been total fucking torture."

"I…I didn't know."

"Now you do." He falls quiet for a moment. "Now touch yourself."

I take a fast breath, hoping it fills me with bravado as I slide my hand down my stomach. He watches me, his gaze never faltering as I tuck into my yoga pants, and go lower, until my fingers connect with my swollen clit.

"Yes," I gasp unable to help myself.

"Yeah, just like that," he murmurs and runs his tongue all over his lips. "Get that pussy all nice and wet for my mouth."

I gulp and grow wetter as he talks dirty to me. "Christian, please..." I murmur even though I have no idea what I'm begging for.

"Is your pussy wet for me, Maize?" he asks, clearly understanding what I want, judging by his response. I nod and he continues. "Does it want my big fat cock?"

A little eeping sound catches in my throat and he chuckles. "Look at me."

My lids open, and my gaze goes directly to his cock. It's big and hard and is probably going to destroy me, but I just don't care.

"Want to touch me?"

My gaze flies to his, and I take in the question on his lips, the want in his eyes. I nod and sit up. He comes closer, and kicks his pants completely off. I resist the urge to pinch myself as he stands before me completely naked—so goddamn gorgeous I'm sure I won the man lottery. I must have done something right in this lifetime, to be here with him, like this.

He takes my hand, puts it around his cock, and closes his hand over it. "Yeah," he murmurs as he moves my hand up and down his shaft, squeezing my hand to show me how much pressure he likes. A bit of pre-cum drips from his slit, and unable to help myself, I lean forward and catch it on my tongue.

His entire body goes stiff, every muscle tight, and I straighten. Oh God, did he not like that?

"I...just couldn't help myself," I explain quickly. "If you didn't like—"

"You've got to be fucking kidding me right now."

His voice is harsh, his eyes brutally hard as he stares at me and I'm about to scurry backward when he captures my hand. "That's the hottest thing I've ever seen."

A thrill goes through me as his breathing changes, becomes labored, like standing now is too much of a chore. It must be, because he drops to his knees, grips my yoga pants and tugs on them. I fall back and lift my hips for him, giving him access to my most private parts. As he pulls my pants down to my ankles, a burst of unease goes through me and I turn toward the lamp.

"It stays on, Maize. I want to see you."

My lashes flutter, moving as quickly as my heart. "I just..."

"You're beautiful. Trust me, I don't lie."

Liking that he doesn't lie, and suddenly feeling beautiful—almost worshiped—under his watchful eye, I take in the way they shine with appreciation as he removes my pants, leaving me in my panties. He goes perfectly still and inches back when he sees my less than sexy, white cotton underwear. Oh,

God, why am I wearing my everyday white cotton panties that hold zero sex appeal? Not that I'd know sex appeal if it jumped up and bit me in the face.

Oh, because you didn't know you'd be having sex with a football star.

"I..." Once again, I try to scramble backwards, but he holds my leg and stops me.

"Jesus Christ," he swears, and slides his hand under the thick white elastic band. "Your panties."

"I know." I cover my face, once again wishing I was an ostrich.

"Maize."

His voice is so deep and hushed, I spread my fingers and peek at him, but he's not looking at my face. No, he's admiring my panties, touching the fabric and elastic like they belong on a Victoria's Secret model.

"Stand up."

He reaches for my hand, and helps me to my feet. Standing beside me, he hangs on to my arm to stabilize me. "Do you have any idea how sexy you are?"

"Not really," I whisper honestly.

"These panties. You're killing me, Maize."

"They're not lacy or sexy," I say.

"This is what I want." He kisses my mouth and puts his hand between my legs, running his fingers over the cotton. "This... so fucking innocent. I want you like this always, every time."

I gulp again. Does he mean we're going to do this more than once? God, I hope so.

"You have more of these?"

"Yes."

He sinks to the floor, presses his mouth to the cotton, and the heat of his breath stimulates my clit. I quiver, and rake my hands in his hair. "Then you should also know, I'm keeping these." He drags my panties down my hips, and tosses them onto the pile of his clothes.

No man has ever, in my entire life, made me feel the way this one has right now. My entire chest flutters, never having felt so important, so cherished before. I could definitely get used to this, and I don't even care if he makes every girl feel this way. Right now, I only care about the way he's admiring me, making me feel so comfortable in my own skin.

"Are you ready?

"Ready?" I ask.

"Ready to give yourself over to me?"

13

CHRISTIAN

My cock is so goddam hard as I glance up at Maize, it's a wonder I've not ruptured something by now. I honest to fuck can't remember the last time I needed any girl so badly. It's all I can do not to toss her on that bed and bury myself in her—balls deep—and stay there until morning a week from tomorrow.

But right now, Maize needs more from me. She needs to be treasured and guided—taken care of—and that's a pretty big deal, considering she's been taking care of herself for a very long time and hates to give up control. But she's handed herself over to me. That had to have been difficult for her, and I don't take it lightly. Not lightly at all.

I truly came so close to losing my shit when I stripped her. Her innocent look—white cotton panties, I swear to God they were nearly the death of me. How I've gone this long, fucked dozens of women, and didn't know simple, white cotton panties were the sexiest things on the face of the earth is beyond me. Then again, I've never seen underwear quite like hers. The women I've been with come dressed in silk and lace, what they assume is sexy and what they assume is my preference. They've all been wrong. Besides, I'm not sure any of them would look this good. The way that cotton covered her sweet ass, and came high over her hip bones. Christ, I'm not sure Maize has any idea just how perfect she is. But I'm about to show her.

I part her damp lips with my fingers and a growl crawls out of my throat when I glimpse her wet pinkness. So fucking flawless. Her sweet, aroused scent fills my senses and I lean in, tasting her from bottom to top, and back down again. Her entire body quivers and I fear her legs are going to go out from underneath her as her trembling hands grab onto me. She's been on her foot too long, already. I stand and guide her backward until her knees hit the bed.

I place my hands on her sides and grip her T-shirt. She lifts her hands above her head and once again her innocence overwhelms me. I peel her shirt off and take in her white bra. Total and utter perfection.

"I had no idea white cotton was my favorite," I say, as her breasts rise and fall with her quick intake of breath. "Pink, yes," I say and put one hand between her legs, "but white." I brush my other thumb over her nipples as they poke against her sensible bra. "Yeah, I love you in this." I stroke the side of her lush, covered breast. "But right now, I need my mouth here, or I might just die, Maize." I give a slight pinch to her nipple and she yelps. In one fluid movement, I slide my hand around her back and release the hook. Her bra falls, and I consider adding it to my new collection.

Dark lashes fall and a measure of her uncertainty comes back. "You're...good at that."

"Yeah, I know. I'm good at a lot of things, Maize."

"Confident, I like that," she says, her voice a low whisper that wraps around me and tugs at my balls.

"Hey, when you know, you know. You're good at a lot of things too," I say, wanting to soothe her concerns. She might not have much experience, but the experience we're going to have together is forever going to rock *my* world. Of that I have no doubt.

"Yeah," she murmurs her gaze lifting, a hopeful look on her face as I cup her breasts, admire the hell out of her fullness.

"Yeah, you're really good at making me hard, sweetness." I take her hand, and put it on my aching cock, and she smiles, liking the effect she has on me as she strokes me from base to crown. Fast fucking learner. Before she brings me to premature orgasm, I take a rejuvenating breath and with every ounce of effort I possess, I force myself to step back. Her hand falls, right along with her smile.

"I want—"

"Maize," I growl, cutting her off. "If you keep touching me like that and I'm going to lose it, and no shit like that ever happens to me."

She gives me a bashful look, but she likes it. She likes what she does to me, and I like her knowing. I take one long moment to admire her curves and beauty, and she stands there unabashed, letting me. I like that too. My head lifts, and the second I meet dark eyes full of need, I gesture with a nod to a spot on the mattress behind her.

"On the bed, legs spread wide open. Show me your pussy. Right. Fucking. Now."

She gulps and I love the way my dirty talk revs her up. She settles on the bed, and ever so slowly—is the innocent Maize teasing me?—she parts her long, lovely legs. I'd like to say I'm a patient guy, and usually I am, but this is Maize, who's been giving me blue balls, and my patience has pretty much reached its limit.

"So fucking sexy," I mutter and go to my knees on the bed. I put my hands on her knees and with little finesse and much greed, push them wide open and the breath that leaves her lungs washes over me in a whoosh. I slide my hands under her arms and reposition her. I lightly run my eager fingers up her quivering inner thighs, and pre-come drips from my aching cock. Fuck, when she stuck her tongue out and tasted me, I thought my head was going to explode—both of them.

"This hot little pussy needs so much attention, doesn't it, Maize?" Is that my voice?

"Yes," she whimpers and writhes beneath me, the last of her inhibitions disappearing, making way for need, and honesty.

"It's gone without touch for too long, huh?"

"Too long," she agrees as I stroke her, circling her engorged clit as it beckons my ravenous mouth. "Please, Christian."

It's insane how much I like to hear her beg, hear my name on her tongue.

"I'm not going to make you wait any longer, sweetness." I drop down, slide my hands under her ass and lift her pussy to my mouth. I bury my face in her folds, and moan as her flavor explodes on my tongue. As I eat at her, I know in an instant she's the sweetest thing I've ever tasted.

I want more.

I slide my tongue around her wet silkiness, soaking my nose, my cheeks and chin. God, I could stay here devouring her all day, and never get my fill. It's a bit disconcerting if I really think about it, which I'm not going to. No, I have more important things to think about—like her climax.

Her hips move instinctively, her pussy banging against my face, desperate for more—for everything, and I plan to give her everything. "So damn needy," I whisper, and slide one finger inside her as I take her clit gently between my teeth. Her muscles clench my finger tightly and my cock pulses, wanting to trade places. I take deep breaths to calm myself down as I work her clit, nibbling, sucking, biting gently until she's gripping my head and pulling my hair—going wild. I fucking love it. I take a quick glance up. Maize unleashed. That's the sexiest thing on the face of the earth.

"Yeah, just like that, babe. Show me how you like to be fucked."

She bucks harder, my words fraying something in her, and her moans of pleasure grow louder. Downstairs a door opens and closes, and I pray to fuck no one comes knocking on my door. If anyone interrupts this, upsets Maize, they're going to get a good pummeling from me.

I inch my finger in and out, and her hips lift. She's so hot and tight, she doesn't need a second finger, but I push one in anyway, wanting to prepare her for my cock. I glance up at her, and her head is rolling from side to side. My chest squeezes, my throat going tight at the pleasure on her face.

"You like this, sweetness?"

"Yes," she cries out.

"Your poor pussy. So desperate for pleasure."

She goes up on her elbows, and I angle my head so she can watch me lick her. "Good, so gooodddd," she cries out, and

I pick up the pace, change the rhythm as her muscles slowly start to spasm. I suck her clit back into my mouth, lave it with my tongue as I fuck her with my fingers, and she lets loose a small cry, her breath stalling as her body lets go, her muscles clenching so hard around my fingers I can feel it all the way to my dick.

"Jesus, fuck," I murmur and stay between her legs, to lap up her sweetness. She falls back onto the bed and goes completely still. As soon as her pussy stops spasming, I slide up her body, and cup her face. My gaze moves over her face, assessing her, and I press my forehead to hers as she struggles to get air. "Breathe, babe." I take a deep, even breath and she breathes with me.

"Christian...that was..."

"Just the beginning."

Her eyes light up. What, did she think we were done? Oh, sweet Maize I have so much—so many inches—to give you. "Yes, more..."

Spreading her legs, she wraps them around my back and moves. My damn cock is so hard and ready, so close to sliding in, but I need a fucking condom. I reach over to my night-stand and pull one from the box. I go back on my haunches ready to slide it on, but come to an abrupt stop when she shakes her head.

Holy fuck. Is she having second thoughts? If so, I'll respect them, but nothing, not even a million hand jobs, is going to take down this raging erection. No, the only thing that will help is getting inside her and fucking her until I can't breathe...can't think...can't feel.

"Maize?"

The corners of her mouth twitch as she stares at my throbbing cock. "Can I...put you in my mouth?" I exhale a relieved breath as she gives an almost bashful shrug. "I've just never done that before, and I thought..."

"You thought you could learn from me?"

Worry dances in her eyes. "Is that okay?"

I touch her face. "Yeah, it's okay," I say but my stomach tightens for a second at the thought of her taking this knowledge to another man's bed, which is ridiculous. We're not a couple. I don't do relationships—don't want to—and this is just fucking.

Yeah, just fucking.

She lightly touches my cock, and weighs it in her hand. "You're big," she says, her eyes wide, but then an adorable little laugh escapes her throat. "I don't really have much to compare it too."

"I won't hurt you," I say quietly and her gaze flies to mine.

"I know."

My heart misses a beat as she blinks at me, giving me all her trust. That's a fucking treasure, and I won't forget it.

She leans forward, stealing all my thoughts as she wraps her sweet mouth around my crown, the happy sounds in her throat almost more than I can take.

"You've never....done this with Ryan?" She said she's never given head before. I don't know why I'm asking. I guess I just need to hear her say it.

My cock falls from her mouth. "No," she says, and goes back to licking me.

"You just fucked, huh?" She inches back and strokes my cock as her other hand goes to my balls. I curl into her. "That's good, Maize."

"I'm not even sure what we did was fucking, Christian. I didn't know it could be so good."

"You haven't felt anything yet, babe," I boast, because I plan to fuck her so thoroughly she's not going to be able to walk for a month. Which means I get to keep her here with me longer. A wave of happiness goes through me at that thought.

"Get that condom on me now."

She works the condom over my girth and once I'm sheathed, I take her shoulders and set her back onto the pillow. A little whimper works its way out of her throat as I fall over her, taking one nipple into my mouth. I really haven't spent enough time here. Next time. Her legs go around my back as I slide up and capture her lush lips for a deep, hard kiss, born of need—weeks of need.

My crown instinctively finds her hot, wet opening, and I jerk my hips forward to give her an inch.

"Ooh," she says as I stretch her open. She wiggles beneath me, but I need to take it slow. I don't want her sore. I don't want her to feel anything but pleasure. "Christian," she murmurs, and I revel in the sound as I slide in a little deeper.

"You good?"

"So good," she purrs, and rakes her fingers through my hair. Her hips move and I bite the inside of my cheek to keep it together. "More, please."

I slide deeper, and deeper, until I'm buried inside her, every inch squeezed by her hot tight muscles. I don't move when I hit her cervix, I don't even breathe. I want to stay like this for an extra second and bask in the intense pleasure prowling through my veins, and try not to come as it tugs my balls.

"You are so goddamn tight, this is going to be hard for me," I admit.

She chuckles slightly. "Hard being the key word here, Christian."

Her teasing brings a laugh to my lips and it's funny, really. I've never laughed during sex before.

"It's okay if you don't last," she says, and cups my cheeks. I frown at her, because it's not okay at all. "I probably won't come again."

"What makes you say that?"

"I don't think I...can."

"Mind if I try?"

She smiles. "Not at all. Don't feel bad if I don't, though, because we can do it again later."

I smile and kiss her. "Yeah, we can, can't we?"

Her grin falls, and she orders in a commanding voice, "Now fuck me, Christian."

My head rears back and I stare at her for a long second, then I laugh. "Okay then. The woman gets what the woman wants." I take her hands, knowing how she likes when I restrain her, I put them above her head and hold them there. Her chest heaves with approval, her breathing growing a little rough. I pull almost all the way out and with one quick thrust, fill her again. Her mouth and eyes open wide, but no sound comes. Yeah, that's it. That's exactly what it's going to take to make her come again. She'd better hang on for the ride.

I move my hips, my pelvis stroking her clit with each thrust, and she lays there immobile, like she no longer remembers how to move, but that's okay. I'm happy to take over. I pound into her, hitting her cervix with each thrust and her eyes gloss over with pleasure. I take it she's never had a full-body orgasm before. That changes now.

"Christian..." she whimpers as my balls ache, needing release, but I hold on. Right now, this is all about her. She grows wetter, and my cock slides in and out, pushing her open, stretching her with each thrust. I let one hand go, and reposition to apply constant pressure to her clit.

She begins to chant my name, and her hand goes to my back. Her nails drag skin as she claws at me, like she's struggling for something to grasp on to, something to ground her, but I don't want her grounded, I want her to fly because I'll be here to catch her. She's safe with me and she needs to know that.

"I've got you, Maize." I slide one hand around her back, and hold her to me, our chests pressed together as I fuck her hard and stroke her clit. "Let go, I've got you."

A cry escapes her lips and her pussy clenches so hard around my cock, I swear to God, I nearly black out. I take a few fast breaths as her hot juices sear my dick, a sweet torturous heat that teases my own release. I push deep, and unable to hold back for one more second, I spill my seed into my condom, wishing for the first time in my entire life, there wasn't a barrier separating us.

"Sweet Jesus," I murmur as our bodies quake together, moisture sealing us as one, as I collapse on top of her. I find her mouth, kiss her deeply, and snuggle into her, unable to get close enough. We hold onto one another, and with my cock still buried inside her, her small chuckle reverberates through me. I lift my head, angle it, when I see the corners of her mouth turning up. "Something funny?" I ask, this strange lightness inside me, bringing on my own laugh.

She laughs harder, and unable to help myself I do to. My God, it's so good to let go. It's like the weight of the world is suddenly off my shoulders. After the laughter subsides, I shake my head.

"Why the hell were we laughing?"

"I don't know about you, but I don't think I've ever felt this good in my entire life. I get a ton of endorphins from running, but not like this." She laughs again and adds, "If I'd known sex was like this, I'd have been doing it every night since I first enrolled at Kingston."

"Every night?" I ask. "What about the chafing?"

That brings on another burst of laughter, and our bodies rock together as we let go and enjoy the moment. I pull out of her, and slide to the side, our laughter still filling the room. Quickly discarding the condom, I wipe up and grab a few tissues to clean her. She reaches for them, but I wave her hands away, and she watches me closely as I wipe between her legs.

Her cheeks are red, her eyes glossy, and so sated my chest swells with pride as I toss the tissues away and roll toward her. That's when a loud bang assaults our ears, and someone kicks in my door. What the fuck?

14

MAIZE

y heart jumps into my throat as Christian's door gets kicked in and in falls a very drunk baller. He hits the floor with a loud bang, and curses spill from his lips. Christian jumps up, quickly reaches for his jeans, and tugs them on. As the guy struggles to get up, Christian turns to me, pulls the blankets up to my neck and sits on the edge of the bed to shield me from anyone's view. I try to look around him to see what all the commotion is about, but he's too wide.

"What the fuck are you doing, Channing?"

The guy named Channing grumbles something, and while I can't see him, from the sounds he's making, I'm guessing he's trying to stand and is having a hard time doing it. Suddenly there is another set of footsteps in the room.

"Do you two mind?" Christian says, his voice a warning growl through clenched teeth. His back muscles are so tight, I fear if I touch him, something might snap.

"Oh, who are you with?" the second person asks, and Christian leans back to prevent him from seeing. "None of your fucking business. What the hell is going on, Evan?"

"We were just fucking around. Didn't mean to bust your lock. Since when do you lock your door anyway?"

"Since none of your fucking business. Now get out."

"What the hell has gotten into you?" Evan asks. "You used to be more fun."

"You have two seconds to leave before I show you how fun my fist is."

"Fine, fine, we're going." An oomph sound fills the room as Christian shifts on the bed, and scrubs his face. "Let's go, Channing," Evan grumbles. The two disappear and the door slams shut. Christian turns my way, his blue eyes hard, mean.

"I'm sorry, Maize." He gives a shake of his head. "Those assholes can get out of control after a win."

"It's okay," I say and put my hand on his chest, his heartbeat strong against my palm.

"I didn't want them to see you."

"I don't think they did," I say, part of me assuming it's because I'm naked while another part of me worries that he doesn't want anyone to know he's slept with the nerdy track star.

He worshipped you, Maize.

Wanting that thought to overrule all others, I pull him to me, take pleasure in his strength and warmth. "You're too far away."

He stiffens and inches back and worry once again creeps in, takes hold of my stomach and pushes back my post-orgasmic bliss.

"I can't believe they broke the fucking lock." He stands, glances over his shoulder and adjusts the blanket around me, until I'm mummified. Once I'm immobilized, he grabs a chair and puts it under the knob, testing it to make sure no one can get in. "I'll get this fixed first thing tomorrow."

"Okay," I say, and stare at his tight back as he leaves the room without a word, without looking at me. I watch him go into the bathroom, and can't help but think he's more upset than he should be. If he's never locked his door before, surely to God, one of the guys in the house must have walked in on him and one of his hookups in the past. Privacy doesn't seem to be a big deal around here, yet when it comes to me, he's very secretive. Old insecurities come back to haunt me, and I try really, really hard to push them down. Tonight was perfect, and I can't get into my head, can't start overthinking things, and let the past ruin what beautiful things I just experienced here.

The shower turns on and my heart sinks into my stomach. So this is what post-sex looks like with Christian Moore. We have mind-blowing orgasms, and he walks away afterward, discarding me without a word and leaving me in his bed, a hot mess, while he showers. I lay there and stare at the white ceiling, trying not to cry, and the next thing I know he's standing over me, his mood a bit more mellow.

"I thought you were sleeping, you were so still."

"You wrapped me pretty tight, Christian. I can't move."

He laughs lightly. "I just wanted to make sure you were covered in case one of those assholes came in here again." He tugs the blankets and frees me. "Come here," he says, and tugs me until I'm sitting. "How's your ankle?"

For a second, I have no idea what he's talking about, then my brain starts working again. "It's good."

"Okay," he says and scoops me up.

I yelp as he carries me into the bathroom and sets me on the edge of the tub. My stupid heart takes that moment to thump. He was in here running a bath for me, when I thought he was just discarding me. I reach down and touch warm, inviting water.

He crouches down beside me, and brushes my hair over my shoulder, and the fact that I'm naked and he's only in his jeans really sinks in. More importantly, I'm okay with it. It feels so natural to be with him like this.

"Need me to help you in?" he asks.

I take in his deep blue eyes, the softness in them as his gaze moves over my face. "Yes, please."

He carefully picks me up and sets me in the tub, but then I make a big splash, soaking his chest, his jeans, the floor.

"Oops," I say innocently.

He grins. "You're telling me you didn't do that on purpose?"

I bat my lashes at him. "I never said that."

He angles his head, a grin toying with the corners of his mouth. "You're saying you did do it on purpose."

"I never said that either."

"Then what—"

"If you'd stop talking for a second, I could tell you that I soaked you because this tub is big enough for two and I'd really like it if you got out of those wet pants and joined me."

He inches back a bit, his eyes wide. "Really?" he asks, like the thought of us bathing together is ludicrous. What, has he never gotten into the tub with a girl before? Maybe he hasn't. I sure as hell haven't bathed with a guy before and I kind of like the idea that I could be his first—for something.

He pushes to his feet, reaches for the button on his jeans and tugs. "Wait. If I get naked, you're not going to try to put your mouth on my cock again, are you?"

I chuckle at his playfulness. "No."

He snaps his fingers. "It was worth a try," he grumps, his mood light now, and it pulls an airy laugh from my throat. I lean forward to make room for him, and he climbs in behind me, his legs stretching out beside mine. We both go quiet for a long time, lost in our thoughts, and I lightly run my fingers along the top of the water.

"Christian," I finally say, breaking the comfortable quiet.

"Yeah."

"I really like...fucking you."

He pulls me back, until my head is against his hard chest, and he lifts his hands from the water and lets the droplets fall over my nipples. "I really like fucking you too."

"We're going to do more of that, right?" I roll my eyes. *Way not to sound eager, Maize.*

"Yeah, sweetness. We're going to do that again. A lot. You said yourself you should have been doing it since first year. We have a lot of fucking to make up for."

I settle against him, never having felt so comfortable with any guy, in any situation, sexual or otherwise. "Okay," I say quietly. He runs his hands over my arms and upper thighs, and I let my lids close. "How long do you think the party will go on tonight?"

"Too long," he says, and I angle my head at the tightness in his voice. "I should have moved out a long time ago."

"My place isn't noisy, it's just run down." I frown, realizing it won't be totally run down for long. Kaitlyn said the roofers had already started, which of course makes it noisy, and soon enough my ankle will be healed, and I'll be able to move back. Jeez, I wish that didn't give me a stupid lump in my throat. This situation is temporary, and I'd be wise to remember that.

He gives an easy laugh. "Maybe we should both move into a place together."

I laugh at that too, because he's kidding. At least I think he's kidding. Yeah, he's kidding. "Soon enough I'll be healed and out of your hair, Christian." I wait for a second, and what he says next is like a slap to the face.

"Yeah..."

What, did I think he was going to try to convince me he was serious and that we should really shack up in a place, where I'm not a prisoner in his bedroom? Not that I'm a prisoner, but I usually only come and go out the back door and when no one else is around.

Not wanting to ruin our mellow moods, but wanting to bring it up just the same, I start, "I need to talk to you about something."

"Sounds serious." He runs his hand along my neck, and smooths my hair from my face, his touch brings on goosebumps and I sink deeper into the water, his now flaccid cock against my back.

"You paid my medical bills, didn't you?"

He stiffens for the briefest of seconds, but it's enough for me to know I'm right. "What makes you think that?"

I sit up, turn in the tub and spread my sore leg out until it's across his lap. He lightly strokes it, his hand a gentle sweep that seeps into my bones, and warms me in a way I've never been warmed before. My heart thumps as I look at him, take in the curves of his face, the warmth in his eyes. My God, not only is he the handsomest man on the planet, he's the sweetest, too. I can't be reading this guy wrong. I just can't be.

"I'm going to pay you back," I state adamantly.

"Okay," he says.

That's it? Okay? That's all he has to say. He's not even going to ask me how? Does he not believe me?

"Christian, I mean it." I tug the hairs on one of his legs and he yelps and pulls back. I grin. "Don't mess with me. I can be mean." Not true. I really don't have a mean bone in my body, though at times, I wish I did.

"Okay," he says again. "I won't mess with you, killer. You're going to pay me back. I get it."

"Like you, I stand behind my word."

A warm, barely there smile touches the corner of his mouth. He likes that I have faith in him. It makes me wonder though, has no one ever trusted this guy, believed in him? Or is it just that he never lets anyone in. *Is he really letting you in, though, Maize?* You slept with him. That's all. Why the hell then does it feel like so much more. Oh, maybe because I'm a ridiculous, emotional girl and there is a part of me that's still back in that closet wanting to be liked by the boy who set out to ridicule me, and the mean girls waiting to laugh from the other side of the door. I thought I'd left her behind, but maybe she's always going to be a part of me.

"I just don't know how yet," I say and reach for his body wash.

"I believe you're a woman of your word too, Maize. I just didn't want you worrying about it right now. You have graduate applications, keeping your grades up, and summer internships to keep you up at night."

Feeling brave I say, "The only thing I want keeping me up at night is you."

He grins. "I like the way you think."

"And I like the way you feel." I pour a generous amount of bodywash on my hands, soap it up and rub it over his chest.

He moans. "We don't need to worry about anything right now, though. We just need to see about this mouth."

He wraps his hand around my neck, and brings my mouth to his. He kisses me so tenderly, my eyes open to take in his features. I have to say, for two people who are just fucking, he sure kisses like it's a whole lot more. Although really, what would I know what a whole lot more looked like? I'm so inexperienced. But this guy, for as long as I'm here, he's going to fix that.

I press my forehead to his and give a small sigh. "Seriously, Christian, that was very sneaky and very considerate of you."

"Shh, don't tell anyone."

I laugh. Hard to believe the guy who pulled his pants down and ruined my reputation in high school would turn out to be a nice guy. Sure, he sleeps around a lot, but so what? That doesn't mean he doesn't have kindness or integrity in him, and he only 'bought' me at the auction not to own me, control me, or finish what we started back in school—which we did and I'm so grateful—but because he's a man who stands up to his responsibilities.

He lathers his hands, and scrubs me down. "Let me help you up and we'll get rinsed off. He shifts, stands, and puts his hands under my arms to lift me to him. I touch his chest as he puts on the shower, and once we're all rinsed, he climbs from the tub, rubs us both with a big fluffy towel, and carries me to his bed. He slides in beside me and pulls me to him.

The party continues downstairs, and with my head on his chest, his rumbling stomach sounds loud. "You need food."

"Yeah, but I'm not going out there."

"Can we order in? Maybe pizza."

He laughs. "It wouldn't make it up the stairs."

"I think I might have a granola bar in my purse."

He tugs me in tighter and flicks on the TV. "How about we just hang out, and once they all go to bed, which shouldn't be too long, everyone is exhausted, we'll go downstairs, and we'll make something."

"Okay," I say. We've pretty much been eating cereal, sandwiches or takeout for the last couple of weeks, so something home-cooked would be nice. So much for me waiting on him and cooking and cleaning. He's not made me do any of those things.

I snuggle into him, while he flicks through the stations and stops when he comes to an MMA fight. "Oh, hell no," I say and snatch the remote from him.

He laughs. "Fine, what do you want to watch?"

"Not that."

He groans. "Please don't put on a chick flick."

I come across an old college movie about a girl going home for Thanksgiving. "I love this one."

"If you say so."

"Are you still planning to go to Aspen for Thanksgiving, after your big game on Friday?"

He nods. "That depends. Are you still planning on going home?"

"Yes." Once again, an invitation lingers on my tongue. My mom would lose her mind—in a good way—if I brought Christian home, but I can't let her think I'm involved with him. This is so not a relationship and she'd jump to conclusions.

"They call that the big turkey dump." he says and having no idea what he's talking about, I lift my head and frown. He grins. "You know when someone leaves home for college, leaving their boyfriend or girlfriend behind, and starts a new exciting life. Then they go back home at Thanksgiving and end up dumping the one they were with. It's the big turkey dump."

I burst out laughing. "How do you know that?"

"I don't know, and with the way you're looking at me, I'm kind of embarrassed that I do." He eyes me. "You don't have anyone at home waiting for you do you. Like Ryan?"

"No, what about you?"

"Nope. No former, present or future girlfriends," he says.

"Why is that, Christian?"

15

CHRISTIAN

I don't answer her. Instead, I stare at the television and pretend I didn't hear. Honestly, I don't mean to be a rude prick. This girl just opened up to me sexually and handed herself over, but I don't want to get into my past, or my demons. I'm not about to drag her into my fucked-up world, although there is some weird needy part of me that wants to open up to her, but what's the point? She's not going to be in my life much longer. She basically said so herself, and I should be okay with that.

Why the hell aren't I? Maybe I don't want to examine that too closely.

She falls quiet, and turns away, aware that I've gone silent, that it's a subject I'm not ready to delve into. We snuggle, and watch the movie until the end, until the house quiets down, and when the credits roll, I glance down at her, figuring she'd fallen asleep, but no, she smiles up at me and my heart wobbles in my too-tight chest as I gaze back. Jesus, she's so sweet, innocent and beautiful. I don't think she's been told enough how special she really is.

"Hey," I say quietly. "Want to go get something to eat?"

"Yes, I'm starving."

I slide from the bed and grab a pair of sweatpants and a big sweatshirt. "These are big, but should be okay."

As she dresses and puts her boot back on, I tug on my jeans, and grab a clean T-shirt. I move the chair from the door, still pissed that Channing broke the lock, and glance up and down the hall.

"Coast is clear," I say and hold my hand out. She slides her small palm into mine and I can't help but think the fit is perfect, that her hand might just be made for mine, and mine alone, but as that thought moves around my brain, I'm worried that I might have to cash in my man card. Laughing quietly to myself, we head downstairs and I'm seconds from scooping her up, when she shakes her head.

"It's okay. I can walk."

In the kitchen, I take two glasses from the cupboard, and find her heading to the fridge. She pulls out the water jug, and I swallow against a dry throat, not because I'm thirsty, but because seeing her in my clothes fucks me over just a tiny bit.

"So just you and your mom huh?" I ask, and while I'd love for her to stay here over the holidays or come to Aspen with me, family is important to her and I'd never want to come between their tight relationship.

I like the smile on her mouth when she says, "Yeah."

"Do you mind if I ask about your dad? Is he in the picture?"

She shakes her head, and fills our glasses with water. "No, he was a cheater, and left when I was young. Gone, never to be heard from again."

"He didn't take care of you guys?" I ask, wanting to know more, everything, about her, even though I ignored her personal question.

"No."

"What a prick."

She smiles. "Why don't you tell me what you really think?"

What I really think is she's had it rough, and probably has some deep-rooted trust issues with men that began very early on in life. Pulling my pants down in the closet, that really doesn't seem like something she'd do, but I guess people will go to extremes to fit in.

"Just did."

She comes from behind and wraps her arms around my waist, pressing her chest to my back and while I'm used to physical contact being about sex, this isn't. She's touching me with tender hands, this embrace is the furthest thing from sex, and probably the nicest hug I've ever felt. I take a deep breath, let it out slowly, and put my hands on hers as she links them over my stomach. Her skin is so soft to the touch, so warm, and like her, does the weirdest thing to me, makes me want to spill all my secrets, and open up to her in a way I never have to another. What the hell is going on with me?

"I'm sorry for not answering your question earlier," I say.

"I never should have asked it. It's not my business and I'm sorry."

I turn to her, lean against the kitchen counter, and widen my legs to position her in between. She puts her hands around my neck and smiles at me, asking nothing from me. She never has, actually, and I'm not really used to that. Everyone wants something from the quarterback.

"Sex should never be used to trap anyone."

Her eyes go saucer wide and she tries to inch back. "Christian...I...never..."

"No, no, no that didn't come out right," I say quickly. "You're the last person who'd ever use anyone for anything, Maize."

"No, I wouldn't."

I tug on my hair. "I just...I didn't mean to blurt that out. This isn't easy for me to say, and to be honest, it's not something I ever talk about."

She goes quiet, and just stands there and lets me work this out in my head without judgement or input. It's what I need right now and somehow, she knows that. I make a mental note never to underestimate this girl. She's fucking smart. I really love that about her.

Love?

Well, I like it, I mean.

"Mom met Dad in college. Like you, he wanted to go to law school. It was love at first sight. That's how Mom tells the story anyway." I give a humorless laugh. "Grandma, she tells it quite differently." She nods and I continue with. "Anyway, Dad got accepted into Harvard law, and they were having quite a bit of relationship troubles. Arguing all the time, because she wanted to go with him, wanted to set up house, but he wasn't ready for that. He had a long, hard four years ahead of him and he wanted to concentrate on his studies. He just wanted to get a quiet place where he could focus, but Mom wanted to move in with him."

"I can actually understand your father wanting a quiet place. That's my goal too, and I wouldn't want anything distracting me from that and Harvard is expensive."

"They broke up, and Dad was ready to move on when Mom announced she was pregnant with me."

Her head rears back. "Oh wow."

"She got pregnant to trap Dad, because she knew he came from money and was going to be successful himself, and would give her the life she wanted. She had plans to go to college too, now she didn't have to. She could just marry into the life she wanted. She was a social climber."

"Did you and your mother ever talk about it?" She puts her palm on my cheek and I lean into her warmth. "Did you ever question your grandmother?"

"I didn't want to believe it." I snort and shake my head. "Who wants to think they were only born as a pawn?"

"No one. At least I know I was the product of love. There was a time Dad was faithful and according to Mom, there was a time he loved me. I guess I just wasn't enough for the love to last."

I shake my head. "This isn't on you, Maize. You can't own that. Your father did what was best for him. You being enough had nothing to do with it, because you are enough." I push her hair from her face, and take in her eyes. She blinks and glances down, but not before I read what's written there —somewhere deep inside her, she doesn't think she's enough.

Fuck that.

"I guess I could put that on you too, Christian. Maybe you weren't born out of love, but that doesn't mean your parents don't love you."

"Yeah, that's why they don't come to my games," I say with a laugh, but I don't want her pity. No, I don't want anyone feeling sorry for me. "Look, it's okay. I know what I am and I know what I'm not."

"What does that mean?"

"I was a means to an end. Dad and I might not be close, but that doesn't mean he doesn't have good traits. Grandma raised him to be a guy who always does the right thing."

"I guess you get that from him."

"He loves law and I love sports. You know, if we didn't look alike, I'd even wonder if I was his." She angles her head, her eyes wide. "Oh, believe me if you saw him, you wouldn't question it."

"Handsome, is he?" she says with a teasing grin.

I shake my head. "Is that all I am to you? A pretty face?"

She touches my chin, runs her finger along my cheek. "Yeah, but keep talking," she says and even though she's kidding, it still stings.

"I have an amazing grandmother. She might not like Mom, but she loves me. She often came to D.C. to spend time with me while Dad was at work and Mom was off doing her thing. We did a lot together and it was hard leaving my friends when we moved to So Cal, but she was here, and that made it easier." I smile. "You would like her."

"It sounds like she is awesome, but I'm pretty sure we'll never meet."

I go quiet for a long time and consider that, remembering what this is and what it isn't. "Yeah, you're right," I say, noting the strange knot tightening in my gut, one that shouldn't be there in the first place.

"So all that?" she asks with a frown. "Your mother's betrayal, your parents, their neglect, that turned you off relationships?"

"I guess."

"You're not your father, Christian." She taps my nose. "You're better than that."

I give a humorless laugh as my stomach growls, a reminder that it's been far too long since I've eaten. "Thanks for the vote of confidence." I slap her backside and she yelps. "Now why don't you take a seat over there, and you can watch these hands work magic."

"I thought I already had."

I laugh at that, liking the way she makes me feel. She's about to move, but someone stumbles into the hall, and I reposition the two of us until she's the one pressed against the counter behind me. I do not need one of my drunken brethren coming in here and making crude remarks, or looking at her inappropriately. She deserves better than that, and I'd rather be inside the kitchen with her than outside Wolf House beating the crap out of someone. I'm not sure what it is, but when it comes to her, I can't help but be possessive...obsessive.

We stand there in silence for a moment, until whoever is in the other room collapses onto the sofa with a loud groan. I seriously need to get out of this place. I'm not even sure if I can tough it out until graduation.

"Wait a second." She nods and I head to the massive living room to find Barrett face down on the sofa. I turn his head to the side so he doesn't suffocate and head back to the kitchen to find Maize exactly where I left her, a worried look on her face.

"You okay?" I ask, and step up to her. She nods and unable to help myself I press a soft kiss to her mouth.

"What was that for?" she asks when I break it.

"You're irresistible."

She laughs like she's not sure if she believes me and takes a seat at the long oaken table, dented and bruised from one too many kitchen parties. She covers her mouth as she yawns.

"Keeping you up, am I?" I ask as I grab eggs, milk and vanilla from the fridge.

"I don't mind. I can sleep in for a bit tomorrow, and then I have study group."

I set the ingredients on the counter. "Are you sure I can't help?"

"Positive."

She falls quiet as I go about making us some French toast. Nothing fancy tonight, because we're both tired. "Want to go out to dinner tomorrow night?" I wait for her to answer and when none comes, I turn to her, and find her nibbling on her bottom lip. "What?"

"We usually just eat in."

"I thought it might be fun to do something else. You must be feeling a bit cooped up in my bedroom."

"Not really."

"Still, let's go out. I know this great little place over in Barrington."

She laughs. "Do you have something against the food around here?"

I stir the eggs and dip the bread in. "Nothing against the food. Just something against everyone knowing me wherever I go."

"You're a private guy, aren't you?"

I arch a brow and take in the astonishment in her eyes. "You say that like you're surprised."

"I am, actually." She rubs her arms like she might have a chill. "You're a football star, Christian. Everyone is always screaming your name, yet deep inside, you don't really like it." Her voice is soft, incredulous, like she just had a huge epiphany.

"You're right, I don't like it. I love football. I love the game, the plays, the comraderie and the competitiveness, but I don't need everyone chanting my name. I don't like everyone in my business. When I was young, I was always forced to go to Dad's functions, and behave like the perfect little boy. I was always on display, my every move scrutinized."

"It still is," she says.

"Yeah, you're right. I have to keep on the straight and narrow or it could be detrimental to my father's career. That's why I take my private time very seriously. I don't like anyone knowing my business. Football is one thing, but what I do behind closed doors—"

"Is pretty fantastic," she says with a smile. She stands, comes up behind me and puts her arms around me as I toss the bread into the hot pan. "But I get it. I really do. I'm private too, and yet I'm a track star with thousands of eyes on me at every race."

I touch her hand, rub it with my thumb, and she rests her cheek on the back of my shoulder. My heart thumps just a little harder, everything about the way she's touching me is doing the weirdest things to my insides.

"What do you want to do after football, Christian?"

"I'd like to teach, maybe become a high school gym teacher."

She makes a sound, like she's impressed. "I think you'd be a good teacher."

"Do you now?"

She chuckles. "I know things."

"Have you always wanted to be a lawyer?"

"For as long as I can remember." I tap her hands to move her, so she doesn't get burned as I plate the food. She steps back, and is about to sit when I place her food on the counter, in front of the stool next to me. I want her close. She folds her arms, and there is a small smile on her face as I divvy up the breakfast. "I have this thing for the underdog."

"Yeah, I kind of figured that, and you know what, you'll be a great lawyer because I know things too. You'll get into Harvard, Maize. I know it."

"Still working on my essay."

"I'm sure you'll blow them away." I wink at her. "Maybe I'll drop your name if I see Dean Saunders in Aspen."

"Don't you dare." She gives me a warning glare and I like that she's a girl who wants to make it on her own, but hell, we all need a little help once in a while. Right?

I grab silverware and syrup and we sit close at the counter. "You see this," I say as I hold up a piece of French toast. She arches her brow as she chews. "This, my friend, is simply a mechanism for transporting syrup."

She laughs, and we fall into an easy quiet as we eat. Once we're done, we tidy up, and we head back upstairs, and the second she falls into my bed, I know in an instant, the cot in my room is no longer needed.

"Can you take me again, Maize?" I ask as my cock thickens.

She crooks her finger, and widens her long, silky legs as she gestures me closer. "Let's find out."

16

MAIZE

I close my textbook and press my fingers to my eyeballs. My God, I've been studying so hard, for so long, my brain is a blur. Here it is the Thursday before Thanksgiving, and the break can't come quick enough. I'm about to lay my head on my books, and steal a nap right here in the library—Christian has been keeping me up late at night—when my best friend waves to me, and comes walking over.

"Hey, have you seen my former best friend around?" she asks and plunks down across from me. "Her name is Maize Malone."

I cringe. All my time has gone to my studies, or to Christian. I'm a terrible friend and it's no wonder she's mad at me. "I know, I know. I'm so sorry."

She grins. "It's okay, at least one of us is getting it." She leans across the table all conspiratorial like. "So tell me everything. I want all the details."

I laugh. For the last month now, she's been trying to get me to give her the nitty gritty on my bedroom time with Christian, but I don't kiss and tell. "Wait, why are you not getting any?" I ask. She shrugs and her gaze goes across the room to Barrett. I gasp. "Don't tell me you've gone and fallen for a footballer?"

"Not really. I don't know. You know we hooked up last month, right?"

"Yeah, and now you like him?"

"No, I hate him. We were supposed to meet up again last night, and he blew me off for some card game."

"Yeah?"

She leans in closer. "Apparently, there's more than secret auctions that go on at Wolf House. We're talking illegal card games with high stakes, and it's not just college boys partici- pating either. Sometimes their rich daddies and uncles join in, along with some millionaires looking for a little fun."

"How do you know all this?"

She shrugs. "Wait, this conversation isn't supposed to be about me, it's about you. How's the ankle?"

"Good, the boot is gone. My appointment this morning was fast. I didn't want Christian to take me, but he insisted."

She grins. "I'm sure he did."

"It's a huge relief to have it off. My God, I was so worried I'd still have it on for Thanksgiving. Christian and I are going to go out to dinner tonight to celebrate."

"I wonder..." she asks with a grin.

"What?"

"How many times you can say Christian's name in a minute."

I shrug and make light of it. "He took me to my appointment, and I have been staying with him."

"Dinner, huh? Where are you going?"

"To one of his favorite spots. Christian..." She grins and I catch myself and take a breath. "He's headed to Aspen after Friday night's game, and I'm headed home, so this is a last dinner or something." Maybe it's a goodbye dinner, one last hurrah, before I go back to my place. Maybe he's planning on breaking that to me tonight. I knew it was coming and I'm fine with that.

Are you really, Maize?

"I read your Harvard letter, made a couple of suggestions, and sent it back to you." She reaches across the table and takes my hand. "You've got this, Maize. But I'm going to miss you when you go to Massachusetts. Soon enough you're going to start talking funny, taking drives in your 'cah', and going to the 'bah'. But you'll be a wicked good student."

I laugh as she puts on a Boston accent. "Speaking of cah, what time are we leaving tomorrow?" Just thinking of Mom's turkey dressing has me salivating.

"One. Right after class." She glances around, her gaze falling over the footballers across the room. "I'm looking forward to getting out of this place."

Just then my phone pings and my heart jumps in my chest. It's crazy how happy I get every time Christian texts or calls me, but he knows I'm in the library, and he's still in class, so this is strange, and really I need to stop being so happy to hear from him. I'm sure after tonight, I'll be back in my house and he'll be back in the bed of some hot cheerleader. I grab my phone and it's not a text, it's a call coming in from my mother.

I frown. "That's odd." I glance at Kaitlyn, take in her worried look. "It's Mom. I'll be right back."

I hurry outside to take the call, my stomach tight. It's not like Mom to call in the middle of the day like this. I slide my finger across the screen. "Hey Mom, what's up?" I ask.

"Am I catching you at a bad time?"

"No," I say and sink onto the stairs when I hear the strain in her voice. "Are you okay?"

"I am, but I'm not," she says with a sigh. "I have to work all weekend. One of the girls went on maternity leave early, and we're short-staffed. I'm sorry, honey. You can still come home, I just won't be able to make us a big meal and I'll be at the hospital most of the time you're home."

Disappointment courses through me but I'm not going to complain. Mom is the only family I have, and things could have been a whole lot worse. "I understand. Maybe I'll just stay here and study."

"I feel awful."

"Don't. Life happens and before you know it, it'll be Christmas and we can gorge on turkey then."

She laughs. "That sounds wonderful, Maize. I've been so busy lately we haven't had much of a chance to talk." A bell chimes in the background, and she covers the phone for a second.

"It's okay, Mom. I know you're busy. I've been busy too. I miss you, though."

"Okay, hun. I have to run. We'll catch up at Christmas."

She hangs up and I stare at my phone for a second. I'm disappointed, but a really strange sense of relief goes through me because Mom would have asked about my races and I would have had to lie. This way, I won't have to and by rights, now that my ankle is healed, I should probably move back into my house. That thought sits heavy as I push to my feet and head back inside.

"Everything okay?" Kaitlyn asks.

"Mom has to work through Thanksgiving."

"That sucks. Why don't you come home with me?"

"As nice as that offer is, I think I'll just stay here and get some work done."

"Okay," she says and stands, looking a little unfocused when Barrett gets up and heads for the door. "I'll talk to you soon."

"Kaitlyn?"

"Yeah?" she asks and turns back to me, still looking a bit rattled.

"I'm going to move back home." I lift my leg. "There's no reason for me to stay with Christian any longer. I'm all healed now, and I can probably get a part time job and start paying him back."

She winks at me. "You have been paying him back, sugar baby."

"I am not..." I laugh. "Okay maybe I am, but once I pay him back, I won't be."

She nods. "Whatever you decide let me know, but if I were you..." She snaps her fingers. "I'd stay put and get it, gurl." I smile and she goes serious. "Hey, are you okay?"

"Fine," I fib and put on my best happy face. "Just bummed about Thanksgiving."

She eyes me for a moment and I try not to fidget. "You sure this doesn't happen to have anything to do with a football player and you falling for him?"

"I am not falling for Christian," I say as much to myself as to Kaitlyn. "We're very different people and neither of us is looking for any sort of a relationship."

"Sometimes things change, girlfriend," she says, hiking her backpack up and leaving me with that very real thought.

I sit there for a moment, that uneasy feeling in my stomach mushrooming, and when the library starts to empty, I pack my books and head back to Wolf House. I go in around the back, habit now, even though I don't have the boot on any longer, and thanks to the key Christian gave me, I let myself in. I make my way to Christian's room, moving through the quiet house. Many of the guys have already left for the long weekend.

In Christian's room, I glance around, and my heart is heavy as I look at my things all scattered about. I should just pack up and go, and forget about dinner tonight, before I get in any deeper with this guy, if that's even possible. But seriously, there's no sense in prolonging the inevitable. I grab my bag and start stuffing my things into it, when the door creaks open behind me. My heart jumps as I turn. Warm and wonderful sensations move through my body when I find Christian standing there smiling at me.

"Hey sweetness. Getting ready to go home?" he asks, his gaze going to my bag.

I take a breath. "Actually, no." I plop down onto the bed. "Mom has to work all weekend, so we postponed turkey until Christmas."

His face falls and he crosses the room, pulls me to my feet and puts his arms around me for a big bear hug, catching me by surprise. "I'm so sorry, Maize...I know how much you've been looking forward to it."

"Yeah, it's okay. I'm still limping a bit and this saves me from explaining what's really been going on in my life."

He inches back, and puts his hands on my shoulders. "Why are you packing, then?"

I shrug. "I figured since my ankle was better now, and the roof is fixed at my place."

"You're not going anywhere." His voice is so deep, so hard, and so adamant, my body stiffens.

"What are you talking about?"

He grins, a playful little gleam in his eyes. "You owe me."

I nod. "I know. I plan to pay you back every cent. I told you that."

"No, you owe me. I was cutting you some slack because you were in a boot, but now sweetness, you're mine, bought and paid for. I own you and it's time you started serving me the proper way."

I grin, the pulse at the base of my throat picking up pace at the teasing, yet hungry look in his eyes. "Oh, is that right?"

"That's exactly right," he says and grips the hem of my T-shirt. "I've been patient, but now that you're not going anywhere this weekend, I think I might just tie you to that bed, and do dirty things to you." He walks around me, his breath hot on my neck as he moves my hair from my shoulders and presses hot, open mouth kisses to my tingling flesh. "Now that your leg is better..." he says, grabbing my hips and moving my body. "You're going to be a good little servant, and do everything I tell you to do."

"What...what do you want me to do?" I ask, my voice hoarse and low, full of arousal.

"I think I'm going to need you to take these pants to your knees. I don't want them all the way off though. Just enough to show me your hot little pussy."

I gulp, heat coursing through my body, amping up my arousal.

"You see, I've not really been able to do everything I wanted with you, with that boot on." He gives a low, slow whistle. "Now I'm going to fuck you in all the ways I've been dreaming of."

"What have you been dreaming of?"

He laughs. "Such a dirty little girl, wanting to hear about all the ways I'm going to fuck her."

My body vibrates as he circles me again, dropping to his knees behind me to pull my yoga pants to my knees. He grabs my ass and squeezes my cheeks. My sex clenches, and I reach down to part my wet lips and touch myself. It pulls a growl from Christian.

"You can touch yourself, Maize...but your orgasm is mine." I stroke my clit as he rakes his teeth over my ass. I grow so much wetter. His teeth scraping skin feels so good, so naughty. Maybe I am his dirty girl, for wanting and enjoying this.

"I want you bent over the bed. I want to see your hot, tight pussy."

He moves me, until I'm facing the bed. I stand there as he removes my shirt, and bra, and circles my waist to grab my breasts. He squeezes, and pinches my nipples, and the sting travels all the way to my aching pussy. Yeah, I know. I was planning on leaving before I got in any deeper, but what is one more fuck between friends?

He toys with my breasts for another minute, and kisses my neck, his soft moans curling around me. His mouth goes to my ear. "On the floor, and bend over this bed. Keep your legs together."

Holy God.

I sink to my knees, able to do the move easily now with no boot, and press my breasts to the mattress.

He goes to his knees behind me. "So goddamn beautiful," he says and slides one thick finger into me. I let loose a loud moan, uncaring if anyone hears. If this is going to be our last time together, I'm going to enjoy the hell right out of it.

"You're so wet, Maize. Have you been thinking about fucking me?"

"Yes." I murmur into the bedding, and wiggle my ass, wanting him inside me.

"I'm back early. Were you going to lay on this bed and put your fingers inside yourself."

I groan, loving the way he talks to me. I squeeze my legs together, and his growl of approval burns through my blood.

"So hot and tight for me." He slides another finger inside for a snug fit, and I move, rubbing my clit against his bedding.

My brain cells stop firing as white-hot pleasure grips my entire body.

"Fuck, Maize," he growls, as small spasms start in my core and clamp around his finger. The sound of his zipper releasing fills the room and I moan.

"Yes," I cry out. "Put your cock in me, Christian."

He goes still for a second, clearly surprised by my demands and while I'm not usually so vocal, I really just don't care. Like I said if this is our last time, I'm leaving here with a bang —literally and figuratively.

"You need my cock, Maize..."

"Yes. I need it. I need you to fill me. I need you to fuck me."

He falls over me, presses kisses to my back. "You don't even have your pants all the way off yet."

"I don't care. Just put your cock in me," I cry as my spasms grow stronger. I have never in my life had such a full-body experience before. Foil crinkles and the next thing I know, he's driving into me so hard and deep it pushes me into the mattress and pulls all the air from my lungs.

"Ohmigod," I cry out and gasp as he rocks into me, hitting my cervix and every other pleasure zone in my body. I grasp the bedding, claw at it, as the world closes in on me.

"This what you need, sweetness?"

"It's what I need," I manage to say past a dry throat. I gasp, cry, buck back against him as he pulls almost all the way out. "More."

He grips my hips, his fingers biting into my flesh as he rams into me, hard blunt strokes that steal my last working brain cell. My body burns, aches, as he pounds, bringing on an orgasm that renders me senseless. He groans as I come around his thick, pistoning cock, and I love it. I love what he's doing to me, what I'm doing to him. I love the honesty in this, the raw, primal way we're fucking. Both of us are a hot mess as we give and take with unfettered need.

I soak his cock, and I quiver as my juices drip down my thighs. He changes the pace and rhythm, driving home as he chases his own release. I move with him, meet and welcome each hard thrust, as I encourage him to just take...take everything he needs from me, the same way I took from him.

His breathing grows harsh, each breath a hot blow against my back, and I close my eyes against the sensation. Stupid tears press against the back of my lids and I try to blink them away. I don't want my heart to hurt right now. I just want to enjoy the physical aspects of this, but dammit, I've been keeping my emotions at bay so long now, and the way he's taking me right now, it just feels more...more than just fucking.

It's not, Maize. Don't go confusing love and sex.

I swallow and push back all the girly feelings as he goes still high inside me, and a second later, his cock throbs. "I feel you," I murmur.

"So good, Maize," he whispers, as he comes and comes and comes some more, and I worry he's going to overfill the condom, and it's going to burst. He falls over me, his cock still buried deep, his mouth warm and wet on my back. As he presses me to the bed, I sink into the mattress, warm, sated, unable to move a single muscle. We stay like that for a long time, and when he finally pulls out, I miss the connection.

He disposes of the condom, and I stay exactly as I am as he disappears into the bathroom, coming back with a warm cloth for me. I get rid of my clothes and my heart misses a few beats as he cleans me, and a few minutes later, I find myself positioned in the middle of the bed, Christian beside me, running his big, warm fingers up and down my arm. I've been studying so hard, and staying up so late, that with his body wrapped around mine, sleep pulls at me, but I force my eyes open, and turn to find Christian watching me, his eyes narrowed, deep in thought.

"Hey," I say and put my hand on his cheek.

"Why were you leaving?" he asks, his voice serious, his eyes dark and intense.

"I can't stay here forever," I explain, my heart crashing hard against my ribs, I fear one could break. "My ankle is better, and I figured we didn't need this arrangement anymore. I can still help you with things if you want, as payment until I can actually pay you, but I don't have to be living here, right?"

Please tell me I'm wrong.

After a long moment, he nods in agreement. "I guess you're right," he says with a frown, and rolls to the side to look at the ceiling, and I can't help but wonder what is going through his brain. "But it will have to wait until we're back from Aspen."

"What do you mean...we?"

17

CHRISTIAN

It's Saturday, and night has fallen over the mountain town as I pull the rental car up to the massive lodge. After our winning game Friday night, which Maize came to watch, we went to bed early, and got up early to catch our flights, and plan to go back Monday. I'll miss my Sunday afternoons at the hospital visiting the kids, and we'll both miss a few classes, but most students travel Monday instead of Sunday to extend their time at home. While we don't have a lot of time here, I plan to make the best of it. I turn to take in the wide smile on Maize's face as she gazes around with childlike wonderment. My heart pinches in my chest, wanting to put that smile on her face every single day.

"You like it?"

Flabbergasted she looks at me, her eyes full of joy. "Like? Christian," she says, her voice high and excited, even though we're both tired from an early morning followed by our flight. But seeing the look on her face is worth it. "This place is gorgeous." I turn to the massive log cabin structure and try to see it through her innocent eyes. I've been here so many times, it's easy to forget the beauty of the place. I take an extra minute to glance around, and take pleasure in the snow-covered peaks. Maize might not be able to ski, but that doesn't mean we can't do other outdoor activities, and a few indoor ones too.

I give her hand a little squeeze. "Come on. Let's go check it out."

We exit the vehicle and I meet her at the front of the car, where I take her bare hand in mine. I'm pretty sure she didn't pack gloves, but we're going to need them, and hats too.

"I can't believe this place." She looks up to the dark, star studded sky and breathes in the fresh air. "You come here every year?"

"Yeah. The air is so fresh, much different from California, huh?" She nods, then glances at her feet, her thoughts elsewhere. "What?"

"I don't know." She swings my hand. "I guess..." She crinkles her nose. "Does it get lonely?"

I shrug. "There's a big difference between alone and lonely. I think you've realized that I'm a bit of an introvert by now. I don't mind being here alone, eating alone, skiing alone. Sleeping alone, however..." I tease.

We walk up to the massive carved door, and I tug it open for her, and the warmth from the fire inside bursts over us. But it's easy to tell from the way her brow is furrowed that she has something on her mind.

"What is it, Maize?" We enter the huge lobby and her steps slow.

"Do you...I mean...have you ever brought anyone here with you before?"

"No. Not here. Not ever. This place is my escape."

She freezes. "Maybe I shouldn't have come."

I reach for her, touch her shoulders, and give a squeeze to put her at ease. "No, Maize. I want you here with me." I lean toward her and lightly brush my lips over hers. "I'd rather be here with you than be here alone." She gives me a worried look, and I shake my head. "I mean it. Now go check out the lobby while I get our room key."

Her movements are hesitant as she turns and heads toward the huge stone fireplace, a few kids around it, roasting marshmallows. She walks around, looking at the brochures as I head to the check-in counter, my mind going through all the ways I can prove to her just how much I want her here with me. After a fast check-in, I step up behind her and put my hands around her stomach as she reads one of the glossy brochures.

"Find anything good?"

"They have an art museum." She scoops up a few more pamphlets. "Have you ever been?"

"Nope, but we'll go, if that's what you want to do." The scent of her shampooed hair fills my senses as I breathe her in. "We can do all the things you want to do."

"What about this ghost tour?"

I shrug. "If you want."

"No, I'm kind of a chicken," she says with a chuckle and I pick up the brochure for the snowmobile tours through the mountain.

"What about this?"

"You know how to ride a snowmobile?"

"Yeah, and it would be gorgeous going through the mountains. If your ankle is up for it."

"It is, but maybe I just want to stay in our room." She turns and my heart beats just a little bit faster when she goes up on her toes and presses a kiss to my nose. I love seeing her this excited. Up until now, I never knew that pleasing someone else would give me such pleasure. I guess I must be growing up.

"While I like that idea, I want you to enjoy this place. When we get back home, we can stay in our room all we like." I consider that, and my stomach tightens because yeah, we agreed that she'd go back to her off-campus house when we returned and when did I start thinking of *my* room as *our* room. She was packing and getting ready to leave Thursday and I had better get my shit together, because no matter how much I want to keep her with me, she's not mine. Not really. I grab our bags, and lead her to the elevator. We go to the top floor, and I usher her off and down the hall. The second I open the door to our room, she gasps and looks at me.

"Christian, this is too much," she blurts out and starts to back up.

I capture her arm and stop her. "This is the room the family always gets. We have a standing reservation for certain times of year, and Thanksgiving is one of those times, but if you don't like it..."

"Like it?" she says as I drag her inside and shut the door behind us. "I love it. I think it might be bigger than all of Wolf House."

I laugh. "Not exactly," I say and head toward the patio doors. I glance over my shoulder. "Come on in, Maize. Make yourself at home."

She takes a hesitant step inside and brushes her hand over one of the side tables. "Your family is okay if we just use it?"

"It would just go to waste if we didn't." I press a button and the blinds lift to showcase a hot tub with the ski hills lit up in the backdrop.

"So gorgeous," she murmurs, and her gaze drops to take in the hot tub. "No way." I laugh and she says, "I didn't bring a bathing suit."

"You don't need one." She grins at me. "Although there is a heated pool outside which you might want to use. There's a gift shop. We can get whatever we don't have."

"I can make do with what I have," she says and shakes her head. I grin, loving that about her. She's definitely not a girl to take, which makes me want to give her things all the more.

She spins and admires the massive living area, kitchenette, and big fireplace. "You know," she says, her voice a low playful whisper that teases my dick. "I've never made love in front of a fireplace before." As soon as the words leave her mouth, she pales slightly. "I didn't mean make love," she says quickly, trying to backtrack, but the thought of making love to her on that carpet holds more appeal to me than I wish it would. She laughs, but it holds a measure of unease. Her hands go out, palms up. "I think the romance of this place is getting to me."

Leaving that comment lingering, I flick on the propane fire. "If I get it really hot in here, it's going to force us both to get naked, and while I like the thought of that, let's go get something to eat first. That airplane food is just not cutting it."

We head back to the main lobby, and I put my hand on the small of her back, stepping close to her as I guide her into the elegant dining room with the floor-to-ceiling windows, giving a majestic view of the mountains.

"Christian, welcome back," Sandra says with a big wide smile as she grabs two menus, her gaze moving over Maize with deep curiosity. "How have you been?"

"Doing great." I glance around the near empty restaurant. I love being here this time of year. The slopes open on Thanksgiving weekend and it's usually fairly quiet. Christmas however, it's insane. Maybe I'll go back home at Christmas. Maybe Maize and I can hang out. "Happy to be back here for the weekend."

"We're happy to have you, and your...friend."

I laugh, because subtlety is not Sandra's forte. "Sandra, this is Maize. We both go to Kingston."

They exchange pleasantries, and then Sandra guides us to the best table in the place, asking me about my classes and football like we're long lost friends. I do consider her a friend. I ask her about her husband and her son Ben, who was accepted to Penn State this year. We sit, and when Sandra leaves, I find Maize grinning at me.

"What?"

She shakes her head and laughs. "What is it with you and all the middle-aged hostesses anyway?"

I laugh out loud. "I don't know. I guess they all think I need a mother figure since my own is so absent."

"Your mother never comes here?"

"She has, when I was younger, but we did our own thing, and I'm not really sure the staff liked her all that much."

She reaches out and takes my hand. "I think it's nice the way you treat everyone as equals. No matter who they are or what they do for a living."

It's clear to me that she had preconceived notions about those with money. I can understand it, considering how she was treated in high school. Our server comes and Maize orders a glass of wine, and I get a beer.

"I really wish I could hit the slopes with you," she says as she gazes longingly at the mountain, a few skiers dotting the hills.

"I don't have to ski. I can hang out with you."

"Nope." She shakes her head. "I'm not keeping you from the slopes. Besides, I brought my books, and reading by the fire sounds just about perfect. I like my alone time too, Christian."

Our drinks arrive and we clink glasses before taking a big sip. "Did you tell your mom you were coming here?" I ask.

She chuckles. "No, I didn't have time. You mentioned it Thursday and I didn't even have a chance to catch my breath before I was getting up at the crack of dawn to catch a plane."

"You had all of Friday to call her."

Her smile falls off, and worry moves in to take its place. "I don't really want to tell her about us—not that there is an us, but you know what I mean. She's always saying I work too hard and every Thanksgiving she asks if I'm bringing someone home."

Understanding she doesn't want me to meet her mother—and not sure how I feel about that—I lean toward her. "I like that she cares so much about you. I wish I had that kind of closeness with my family, to be honest."

"You have all the servers and hostesses mothering you wherever you go." She gives me a smile, but we both know it's not the same thing.

"I'd never want to be an absent parent." My humorless laugh curls around us. "Not that I'd know how to be a present one." She opens her mouth to say something, but before she can get a word out, someone speaks over her.

"Christian," a familiar female voice says as her steps come to an abrupt stop at our table. "I thought that was you."

I turn, not at all surprised to find Cynthia Saunders smiling at me. I stand and pull her into my arms. "Cynthia, it's so nice to see you."

"You too." I break the hug and she smiles at Maize.

"This is my friend, Maize," I say, waving my hand toward her. "We go to Kingston together. Next year though..." I give her a wink. "She'll be in Harvard Law, just like you."

"Really?" she asks. "That's fantastic. I look forward to getting to know you. Any friend of Christian's..." She gives a laugh. "Although I must warn you. The dean is kind of a tyrant. I'm not sure I'm going to do well at the interviews. We might not be classmates at all."

"He's a tyrant?" Maize's eyes go wide, a little frightened.

"Maize, this is Cynthia Saunders, Dean Saunders's daughter. She's kidding. Sort of."

"Oh," she says with a laugh, as she playfully taps her head. "I get it. A little slow. Sorry."

"Not slow at all. It's been a long day," I say to Cynthia. "We just got in, actually."

"I'm not going to keep you, then." Her brow arches hopefully. "You need to get all the nourishment you can for the slopes tomorrow. Can't wait to race you down, Christian—and win of course." She gives Maize a wink. "He's yet to beat me."

"That's because you cheat," I say as I lean in to give her another hug. "I don't know how you cheat, but you do."

"Such a frail male ego," she says with a laugh. She lowers her voice and whispers into my ear. "I like her, Christian." We break the hug, and she turns to Maize. "See you guys later. Enjoy dinner." She walks off and I smile as I sit back down, remembering all our fond times together.

"She's really pretty," Maize says.

"Yeah, I guess," I say. I think of Cynthia as a sister. We spent a lot of time here together as kids and teens.

"Did you two ever..." She holds out an index finger and circles it.

I mimic her actions. "Did we ever circle our finger at each other?" I ask, even though I know exactly what she's getting at.

She whacks my hand away. "You know what I mean."

"No. We're just friends." I take in the tightening of Maize's lips. "If I didn't know better, I'd think you were jealous."

She gives a fast shake of her head. "I'm not, not at all. I was just curious."

"She's a childhood friend," I explain again, and lift my beer to salute her before taking a long pull.

She looks at me thoughtfully. "So how does an NFL draft work?" she asks, changing the subject. We order our food, and I spend the next half hour talking about the draft and how it works, and that I'm a draft prospect, and chances of getting picked up are pretty good. She listens intently as our meal comes and we eat, and I know she's not faking interest because she nods and asks questions at all the right times. I finally set my fork down.

"I've been hogging the entire conversation," I say with a laugh.

"I like hearing about your future." She wipes her mouth and sets her napkin down on the table. "You said you wanted to be a teacher someday, after your NFL career. Do you think you'll settle in California?"

"You know, I'm close to my grandmother, but living in California isn't a must. I can live and teach anywhere. What about you? Where do you want to practice?"

She laughs. "I haven't thought that far ahead. All I can think about right now is getting into Harvard."

The server comes back with dessert menus, and we decide to get a big piece of chocolate cake to take back to our room, and I'm glad. I want to get behind closed doors and relax with Maize, no interruptions.

After our cake arrives, we make our way back to the room, and I shut and lock the world out behind us. The place is smoking hot, and I'm beginning to rethink my brilliant plan of leaving the fire on.

"Ohmigod, Christian, it's a million degrees in here," Maize says and swipes at her forehead.

I crack the patio door to let the heat out, and when I turn back, Maize is stripping her clothes off, and in that instant, I decide leaving the fire on was the absolute right decision.

She plays coy and glances at me over her shoulder. "Are you going to stand there and gawk, or are you going to help me check sex in front of the fire off my bucket list?"

"Like you even have to ask."

I rip my shirt off and make my way to her, my heart beating faster than it should, because no matter how hard I try, how much I know I have to, I'm not sure I can let her walk out of my life. She turns, drops to her knees, and pops the button on my pants. Her hands capture my cock, and I groan as her sweet lips wrap around me. That's when I realize just how fucked I really am.

In so many ways.

18

MAIZE

"This is only the best chocolate cake I've ever eaten," I moan before I shove another forkful into my mouth.

Christian laughs, and glances at the clock. "Cake always tastes great at eight in the morning."

"Hey don't judge me." I point my fork at him as I cross the room, and sit on the coffee table across from him as he sips his coffee. "We're on vacation, and what we eat, and when we eat, doesn't matter." I cut into the cake and hold it out for him. He takes the bite and moans. "Also," I add. "Calories don't count on vacation either."

"You might be right. That is the best thing I've ever put in my mouth. Or maybe the second." He grins and points between my legs. "Or third." He points to my right breast. "Or fourth." He points to my left breast. Laughing he adds, "I guess you get my drift. It's the best thing I've put in my mouth, after you."

I laugh and he hands me his coffee. I take a sip to wash down the cake. It's weird, sharing food and drinks like this. Deeply intimate. I almost laugh. We've been having crazy sex, and yet I find drinking from his mug more intimate. That ball to the head must have messed me up more than I realized.

A knock comes on the door. "That's breakfast," he says and pushes to his feet.

I set the cake plate down. "I didn't know you ordered."

"You were in the shower."

"Is that who you were talking to when I came into the room?" A short while ago after showering, I entered the room and found him on the phone, talking quietly, like he didn't want me to overhear him.

Instead of answering, he reaches for his wallet and walks to the door. Okay, so avoiding that question isn't strange at all. Unless it wasn't room service he was talking to.

A burst of old insecurities crash through me and I quickly push them down. I am spending this last weekend with him, and I damn well plan on enjoying every second. If he was on the phone making plans with some girl for when our time together is over, it's none of my business.

I glance at the full tray with silver domes covering the plates as he rolls it toward the table. "How much did you order?"

"I wasn't sure what you felt like."

My heart wobbles. He really is so sweet. "I think I might be too full from the cake." I didn't realize he was ordering in, and when I came from the shower and saw the cake from last night, I couldn't help myself. Usually, I'm much more disciplined. I think Christian is ruining me, and I'm not even mad about it...because of that decadent cake.

"If I had known, I wouldn't have eaten the cake." I stand and head to the table. "Why didn't you tell me?"

His smile is so soft and tender, it wraps around my stupid heart and squeezes. "Because if you want cake, you should have cake."

He begins to remove the silver domes and a silly laugh catches in my throat. "I have never had room service before, Christian." As I take in the abundance of food, it drives home the fact that Christian and I really are from different worlds.

"You're kidding. Not even when you traveled for competitions?"

"Nope, we all ate like cattle in the buffet line." I take the lid off one and find a plate of bacon. I snatch up a slice and bite into it.

"I thought you were too full."

I give him a look that suggests he's insane. "There's always room for bacon."

He laughs and gestures for me to sit. "So fancy," I say as he removes all the lids and puts the plates in the center of the table. "Want to hear something funny?"

"Always."

He sits and we each help ourselves to what we want. I go straight for the strawberries. "When I was young, do you know what represented wealth to me?"

He shakes his head and bites into a sausage. "No, what?"

"Those vertical venetian blinds," I say with a laugh, and when he narrows his eyes and cocks his head, I explain it to him. "You know those long blinds that you open and close with a cord."

He grins and nods. "We had those. I just called them curtains."

"I thought if you owned venetian blinds, you were rich. Remember when Chelsea Haverstock invited me to her party that night..." I pause, although he probably doesn't need a minute to remember the night he pulled his pants down.

"I remember."

"She had venetian blinds and wall-to-wall carpet. I was like, this is posh. I thought someday, when I grow up and become a success, I was going to have blinds and all that carpeting."

"That's funny. Wealth to me was a trip to Disney."

"You must have done that."

"Actually, no. I've never been there."

His eyes open at the shock on my face. I'm surprised for sure, but why would he lie about that? "You're kidding me?"

"No, why? Have you?" he asks.

"No, but why did that represent wealth to you?" I wave my hands around the place. "You had this resort, and I'm sure you've been all over the world."

"Most trips were business, and we'd tag along. Maybe Disney didn't represent wealth, maybe it represented family. Now that I think about it, that's it I guess." He cuts into his egg, takes a bite, and looks thoughtful. "My friends would go with their families. I was so envious. Even though I had everything

I could want, what I really wanted was just time with my parents. I wanted us to do things as a family, like I'd see all the other kids around me doing."

"I get it, Christian. I really do." I used to envy the rich people who could have whatever they wanted whenever they wanted. I was clearly looking through rose-colored glasses. Christian has given me a much clearer vision, and truth be told, I wouldn't trade what my mom and I had for all the money or trips in the world.

"Maybe someday you'll have that family, and you can all go to Disney."

He snorts. "Like I said last night, what do I know about being there for someone?"

"Christian, you've been there for me through my whole injury, and don't forget you had your grandmother. She taught you what family was all about." He takes a sip of coffee and glances at me over the rim, his eyes unfocused, like he's a million miles away.

Finally, instead of agreeing or disagreeing with my comment, he says, "I'm going to hit the slopes for a bit. Afterward, do you want to explore the town, and hit up the art museum?"

"I would love that. I'm going to sit in the lobby, and if it warms up enough, I'll grab one of the outdoor Adirondack chairs overlooking the hill so I can watch."

"You're sure you don't mind me leaving you here?"

"I like alone time, remember, and I want you to enjoy yourself, Christian." I give a wave of my hand. "Go, have fun. I'll be here waiting for you when you get back."

"I like the sound of that, Maize."

"Now finish eating, or you'll miss all that fresh snow."

He nods and once we finish eating, he jumps in the shower, and I head out to the patio to breathe in the clean morning air. A girl could really get used to vacationing in a place like this.

I stay there for a long time, enjoying the scenery and basking in the fresh air when a set of hands wrap around my waist and warm lips find my neck.

I lean back. "I love it here so much. I might never go back."

"We can come again, another time."

I nod, even though that will never happen and it's so sweet of Christian to make the offer. I tap his hands. "You better get out there. Show Cynthia what you've got."

He chuckles at that and the sound reverberates through me, wraps around my heart and gives a loving squeeze. "Okay, and then later, by the fire, I'll show you what I've got."

"I know what you've got." I turn in his arms. "And I like it."

We stand there and exchange a low slow kiss, like neither of us are in a hurry to go. I finally break it and give him a little shove. He groans, and I follow him inside, locking the door behind me. Twenty minutes later, I'm kissing him at the lobby door before he disappears and I stand there and watch, my arms wrapped around myself for warmth as he puts on his skis and heads to the lift. That might be fun, going up on a lift, seeing the town from way up high. Only problem is, I'd have to drop to my rear end and slide all the way down, because I am not risking another ankle injury. I didn't say anything to Christian, but it's sort of aching in this cold weather.

I hike my backpack up higher on my shoulder and find a comfy chair by the big window. I order a big mug of hot chocolate and marshmallows—calories don't count on vacation, remember—and settle in to do some studying. Minutes turn into hours and every now and then I peek at the hill. When I see two people coming down together, I stand to get a better look. I can make out Christian because I know what he's wearing, and I can only assume the girl with him is Cynthia. I drop back into my seat and try not to feel a measure of worry. It's silly, he said they were never together, and we're not really together, so I have no reason to be jealous. Was it her he called and whispered to earlier this morning?

Ugh, stop.

I push those thoughts from my brain and drop back into my chair. I turn my focus to my books and work to concentrate. Over the next half hour, the lobby fills up a little more, a tour bus drops off a few skiers, and the chatter and commotion make it a bit hard to concentrate. I stretch and check the time, and consider going back to the room for a quick nap, when someone moves my hair and presses their lips to my neck.

I gasp and jump from my chair, and nearly twist my damn ankle.

"Whoa, easy," Christian says, his lips twisted. "I didn't mean to frighten you. Sorry about that."

I laugh it off. "It's okay. I have no idea why I was so jumpy."

He pulls me to him, and I smell the fresh air on his clothes and skin as he presses his lips to mine for a soft kiss.

"Did you have fun?" I ask.

"Yeah, I love the slopes, but I kept thinking about you back here by yourself."

"I told you I'm a big girl. I can take care of myself."

He gives me a playful grin. "But isn't it more fun when I take care of you?"

I put my hands on his chest, and his coat is cold against my fingers. "Do you have something in mind?"

He checks his watch and I try not to give into the disappointment in my gut. Does he have somewhere else to be, something more important pressing at him?

"Yes, but it will have to wait."

"Okay," I say and go to sit down again when he stops me.

"What are you doing?"

"You have somewhere to be, so I'll get some more studying done."

"Where I'm going, you're coming," he says, and scoops up my backpack. He shoves my books inside and I stand there frowning at him, having no idea what he's talking about.

"Are we getting something to eat?" I ask, noting it's well past lunch time and he's probably starving from all the exercise.

"Eventually." He takes my hand and leads me to the lodge ski shop that carries every expensive brand of winter clothing known to mankind. "You need a better coat, hat, and mitts for what I have in mind."

I pull my hand from his, and back up an inch. "Christian, no. I don't need anything."

He puts his hands on my shoulders. "Right now, you're still mine, remember? So I'm taking care of you, whether you like it or not." I'm about to shake my head when he cups my face to stop me. "If it makes you feel better, you can pay me back."

"Like my medical bills, and all you put out for my tuition and lodging?"

"We can just add this to the list. Now say yes, so I can show you something spectacular, something you're not going to want to miss."

"As long as I can pay you back."

"Uh huh," he says, so noncommittal I almost argue, but there is a part of me that really just wants to escape with him, so I agree.

"Fine."

He grins, like he just won the battle of the century, but I think he already won that ages ago when he set money down to have me as his. The retail clerk steps up to us, and after ten minutes, I'm all decked out in new clothing, and ready to melt to the floor because we're still inside and I'm sweating to death.

After he pays, we drop my backpack at the front counter, and Christian takes my hand, leading me out. "Where are we going?" I ask as the brisk air washes over me and I feel nothing but heat. He leads me down a path, going slow because of my ankle, and we come upon a shop.

"Your chariot awaits, my lady."

I stop in my tracks when I see the long row of snowmobiles, all lined up and ready to be rented.

"Are you serious?"

"You said you wanted to see the top of the mountain." He pulls me close and kisses me.

"You didn't know that. I never said that to you." At least I don't think I did. I'd only thought it in my head, I'm sure.

"I saw the way you were looking at the ski hills when we first arrived. You wanted to go up, but had no way to get there. Now we have a way."

Wow, he doesn't miss a thing, and I really like that about him. "Why didn't you tell me?"

"I wanted it to be a surprise."

"This is...this morning...the phone."

"Yeah, sorry for not answering. I wanted it to be a surprise." I shake my head, astounded by his sweetness. "You want to go, don't you? It shouldn't hurt your ankle, and this is a great way to get to the top. Wait until you see what's up there."

I laugh, hard, like a load has been lifted off my shoulders, and he looks at me like I might have just escaped an asylum.

"I'll take that as a yes."

"Yes." I throw my arms around him and give him a kiss. "This is a great surprise."

"Remind me to surprise you more often," he says as I go back down on my feet. He puts his arm around my waist, and we head inside the warm building. Less than ten minutes later, Christian is latching my helmet and helping me onto the beast of a snowmobile. I slide my hands around him and hang on.

"You know what you're doing, right?"

"I'd never put you in danger, sweetness."

He pats my hand, and the next thing I know, we're on the snow-beaten trail, the wind in my face. I might have been frightened by this new adventure, going through the woods and up a mountain, but I feel completely secure as I hold on to the guy I'm really, really starting to like.

Starting?

That's possibly a lie. I might have hated him in the past, but so much has changed since I started sharing his room. He slows and points, and I catch a bunny hopping into the snowy underbrush. A wide smile splits my lips.

"A bunny," I squeal and steal a glance at the gorgeous, white-tipped trees. It's quite breathtaking out here, and I really wish I could walk without fear of injuring my ankle. I wrap my hands around him tighter, and press my body to his, needing the contact as my emotions rev faster than the beast we're on. I can't quite remember the last time I was this happy.

We go a little further up the hill and we wave to a couple coming down on another machine. Christian slows, and points again, but I don't see any wildlife.

"Deer tracks."

"Amazing. Wait, are there bears here?"

"Probably hibernating right now, so we're good."

I relax a little and he revs the gas, and we take off again. I watch the scenery, a sense of peace washing over me, all worries about school, my future with Christian, and life slipping away as I breathe in the refreshing mountain air and let it soothe my soul. We finally reach the top and a quaint little log building comes into view.

Christian kills the engine. "You must be starving?" he asks as he removes his helmet. I fuss with mine, unable to get the clip to snap open and he shoos my hands away and easily removes it, much the same skill with which he always removes my bra. It comes with experience, I guess, and I am not going to think about that for one more second.

The scent of fresh coffee reaches me and my stomach growls. "They have a coffee shop here?"

"Amazing food too."

We head inside, and customers and staff alike greet us like we're all a part of one big family. We take a seat by the window and order the soup and biscuits, and coffee. I peel my heavy clothes off, the fire in the hearth washing over me, creating a warm glow inside my body. I glance at Christian, and I can't seem to keep the ridiculous smile from my face.

"I really love it here."

"I'm so glad." The server comes with our coffee, and I pour a bit of milk into mine. "I'm not sure if you were watching or not, but I ran into Cynthia on the hill."

"Yeah, I thought I saw you with someone," I say casually. "Did you finally beat her?"

He laughs. "Hell no, she's too good, and like I said, I think she cheats." He reaches across the table. "I forgot to tell you, she invited us to have dinner with her and her family tonight."

"Oh, how nice," I say a bit disappointed because I really just wanted a quiet night with Christian. We don't have too many of those left. He angles his head and arches a brow like he's waiting for some light bulb to go off. "What?"

"Did you forget her father is the dean of the law department at Harvard?"

I gasp. "Ohmigod, I can't believe I forgot that." Then again, I'm so wrapped up in Christian, I can't seem to concentrate on much else.

Maize, you're having dinner with the dean of the law department!

My nerves jump as I think about sitting down with him and his family. While this might be a dream come true for most, I'm not one to schmooze, and don't even know what I'm supposed to say in a situation like that. God, I really am out of my realm here. "I can't...I'm not prepared."

He gives a small wave of his hand, like it's nothing, but it's not nothing. It's something big and he knows it too. "You don't have anything to prepare for, this is just dinner, and a networking opportunity."

"Christian, did you do this? Did you set this up for me?"

"I wanted you to meet him, but Cynthia is the one who put the invite on the table." He gives me an apologetic look and adds, "I might have mentioned something about eating at the restaurant tonight. But Cynthia liked you. She wants to get to know you."

"That's nice," I say absently as I swallow, hard. Opportunities like this don't normally present themselves to a girl like me. I'm so used to doing everything on my own, the hard way, but Christian here is changing all that, putting me in situations I wouldn't normally find myself in and making it easy for me to forget I come from the wrong side of the tracks. None of that seems to matter to him. I wouldn't be here and he wouldn't be introducing me to his friends if it did matter, right? Unless of course, somewhere deep inside him, he needs the girl he's been spending time with to be a Harvard student, because only then would she be good enough.

But Christian isn't like that. We only go to restaurants far outside of Kingston because they're his favorite, and taking the back door to Wolf House was all about my injured ankle.

Right?

19

CHRISTIAN

I glance at a very tired Maize as we take the late flight back to Kingston. She's trying so hard to stay awake, but she keeps drifting off, a cute, contented smile on her face. It makes me happy to see her like this. She damn well deserves to be worshipped, and treated to a relaxing weekend. I'd love to take her back here. I really wasn't kidding when I put that offer on the table and once again, she reminded me we were done this weekend.

I take her blanket and tuck it around her, and she moans something to me. I settle in myself, my mind going back to our dinner with the Saunders family. Maize was so nervous, but once she got talking about her love of law, she calmed down and we all had a terrific night—one that ended with Dean Saunders talking about some summer internships he thought she might be perfect for, giving her his card and asking her to call to set up a meeting.

It couldn't have gone better and we all had a laugh when Cynthia leaned in to remind Maize her father was an ogre, which of course he's not, but it's clearly a private joke between them. He's a great and fair man and I think he was very impressed with my girl here.

My girl.

I want to make her my girl. I want to keep her at my place longer—at least until Christmas. Maybe I'll go over to her place and break a pipe or something. That thought makes me laugh as I adjust my pillow and doze a bit.

The next thing I know, the plane is landing and Maize is waking me. I take in her tired eyes, her mess of hair and the smile still tugging at the corners of her mouth. Once we get our luggage and hop into my vehicle, I begin the drive home. My hand creeps across the seat, and I capture hers. Her head turns my way and she takes me in as I drive in silence, a little lost in my thoughts.

She perks up a bit as I take the turn to my place, and not hers. "I should...probably head back to my place."

"Tomorrow," I say. "It's too late now, and I don't want you to wake anyone." She falls silent and I'm about to open my mouth, determined to convince her, when she nods. Her phone pings, and she takes it from her purse and smiles.

"It's Kaitlyn," she tells me. "She just got back from being with her family and is asking how my weekend is going." She sends her a text back and relaxes against the seat. "I told her I'd be moving back home tomorrow."

"Okay," is all I say. The house is dark, very quiet as I pull up and park in my spot. The guys are all probably tired from travel or not even back yet.

"The place is pretty dark," she says.

"Yeah, let's go in the front, and be really quiet. I don't want to wake anyone."

She nods, and for a second I think she has something on her mind, but whatever it is, she pushed it away and smiles at me. "I really had a great time."

"Me too."

We step outside, and the air is so much warmer here. I snatch the bags from the back and we quietly head inside. I usher her up the stairs and follow her to my room.

"Home sweet home," she says and collapses on my bed, her arms and legs moving as if she's making snow angels. I take in her curves, the way she looks so perfect, so right on my bed.

I open my small fridge and grab a bottle of water. I screw off the cap and give it to her for a drink.

"Thanks, I'm parched."

She drinks, and hands it back. I take a big swig and set it on the nightstand, and go straight to undressing. She rolls to her side, a smile on her face as she watches me. "I'm going to jump in the shower." I hold my hand out. "If you're not too tired, want to join me?"

She gives a slow nod. "I'm tired, but I think we should end this vacation with a bang, don't you?"

I hate hearing the word end on her lips, and I want to ask her to stay—at least until Christmas vacation—and then we can reevaluate afterward. I'm not normally a fucking coward, but I can't bring myself to ask. What if she rejects my proposition?

What if she doesn't?

I walk to the bathroom naked, and she strips, so comfortable in her skin around me as I adjust the spray and guide her in. We just stand there, letting the hot water fall over us. Her mood matches mine, mellow, lazy as exhaustion seeps into our bones. We sure as hell packed a lot into the weekend, both of us clinging to every minute and not wanting to sleep. Maybe it's possible that she's feeling more too. But in the end, where could this possibly go? We have different lives, different futures ahead of us.

We wash each other with unhurried hands, taking our time touching, like it could very well be our last. She lets loose a small sigh as I remove the nozzle and spray the soap from her flesh.

"I am so sleepy," she says, her eyes half-lidded.

"Me too."

I shut off the water, wrap her in a big towel, and dry myself off quickly. She dries off, drops the towel and climbs into bed, and I slide in beside her, our bodies slightly damp and so warm. I've been inside her numerous times, yet suddenly I need the connection more than I need air.

I run my hand down her stomach and she sighs with delight. I touch her legs and no matter how exhausted she is, she widens them for me. Her inner thighs are hot as I lightly caress them, and her whimper fills the quiet in the room as I go higher and higher until I find her damp lips. But this dampness isn't from the shower. No, she's wet and slick from my touch. This is what I do to her and I damn well love it.

I touch her clit, brush it lightly with my thumb, and her sleepy moans stroke my cock. I'm so goddamn tired I could barely think straight to begin with, but now, with all the blood racing to my cock, I have zero intellect left.

I stroke her a little more, and put my finger inside her. Her hips lift, and her head falls to the side. Such a needy girl. Grinning, and wanting her to come tonight with me inside her, I climb over her, and push her legs open wider.

"I need to be inside you, sweetness."

She wiggles, and the second my crown penetrates her hot pussy, something niggles in the back of my lust-rattled brain. Fuck, what is it I'm supposed to remember? Her muscles squeeze me as I enter, and that's when it hits me, and I quickly pull out.

"Shit, we need a condom," I say. Her eyes go wide at first, then they soften as she places a hand on my cheek.

"It's okay, Christian. After our first time, I went to the doctor and went on the pill. I wanted the added protection, because neither of us want kids."

"Right," I say, an odd tightness in my chest, not because I want kids, but because Maize deserves to have a family of her own, and the thoughts of her having a family that doesn't include me in the picture simply adds to the pressure in my body.

"So you see, we can have sex without protection."

"Why didn't you tell me before this?"

She frowns. "It takes a full cycle before I'm protected."

I nod, although I sense that's not the entire truth. Maybe she was frightened by the idea of skin on skin. I've never had sex without a condom, either. Never wanted to. Right now, there isn't anything I want more in the world, although I'm afraid it could fuck me over, and that taking her with no barriers, her hot flesh on mine as I orgasm, leaving a part of me in her body, might be something I can't quite come back from.

"You sure about this, Maize?"

She wraps her arms around my neck, and presses her lips to mine, answering without words, and I press my crown to her opening and jerk my hips forward, entering her deeply. We both moan as intense pleasure moves through us, and I brush her hair from her face, pressing kisses to her eyes, nose, mouth, and cheeks as my heart pounds erratically against my ribcage. We move in synch and she hugs me tighter, our chests crushed together.

I glide in and out of her slickness, and she grows hotter, wetter with each thrust. Her body moves in rhythm to mine, our moves those of long-time lovers who know how to give and how to take. Never in my life have I had anyone like Maize in my bed, and lovemaking had never ever been this good with anyone.

Lovemaking.

She was right when she said that's what we're doing. Pretty crazy for a man who fucks and doesn't do relationships, right? What can I say? I'm falling for this woman and there isn't a damn thing I can do to stop it, even though it can only end with loss. She's not looking for a future with me and I'm not looking for one with her. It could never work. Right?

"Christian," she murmurs and presses her lips to my neck as her muscles tighten around me, her keening cry filling the room as she lets go, and tumbles into an orgasm. I breathe deep, revel in each hard clench as she milks my own release.

"Maize..." I murmur and pound into her. She scrapes her nails along my back and the sensations reach my balls. They tighten, and the world goes dark around me as I press my mouth to her shoulder and fill her with my seed. I groan as I spurt inside her, the lack of barrier bringing on the hardest orgasm of my life. Who knew it would be so good without a condom? Then again, would it be this good with anyone, or is every nerve ending tingling because it's Maize in my arms?

I deplete myself and fall over her, our mouths seeking one another. I kiss her long and deep, contentment prowling through our bodies, dragging us under. "Now we sleep," I say as her eyes fall shut and she gives a slow nod. I roll off her and her soft sleeping sounds fill the room as I chuckle quietly to myself. She stays asleep as I grab a cloth to clean her, and I can't help but think about her transition. When she first came here, she was jumpy, awake more than she wasn't, and now I'm sure she could sleep through an earthquake.

I snuggle in beside her, tug the blankets up and the next thing I know, my alarm is going off. Groaning, I reach for my phone, turn it off and make sure it hasn't woken Maize. I find her sound asleep and the thought of leaving her in bed and going to practice make my stomach cramp.

But I don't want to disappoint the coach or my teammates, so I crawl out from the covers and steal one last glance at Maize. The need to wake her and beg her to stay until Christmas pulls at me, but maybe I should let her cut loose now, before I'm in too deep. A sound catches in my throat and I put my hand over my mouth to silence myself. Honestly, is there any part of me that thinks I could actually get in deeper with her?

I quietly grab my gear and scribble a note, letting her know I had to go to practice. I don't want her to think I just took off. I stand there, debating on asking her if we can talk later. What the hell do I do? I quickly ask if she wants to grab lunch later, and to send me a text.

Leaving the ball in her court, I head outside, and the early morning sun shines down on me. I make my way to the field, and meet up with my buddy Linc. He throws his arm around me.

"Where have you been, anyway? You don't come out anymore. You don't text."

"Aww, what's the matter, is Linc missing his girlfriend?" Kyle teases.

"Fuck you," Linc says and I know he's right. I've been so caught up in Maize.

"Just been busy."

"How were the slopes?" he asks and gives me a push to back me up so we can toss the ball.

I can't keep the stupid smile from my face as my thoughts go to Maize. "That good, huh?" he says. "Did you get some pussy?"

"Don't do that," I blurt out, and he looks at me like I might have sprouted a second head. The guys can be crude, but the thoughts of him talking about Maize like that doesn't sit well with me. Although he has no idea she came with me. I've been keeping things pretty low key, wanting her just for myself.

"Shit, man, I'm sorry. You know I didn't mean anything." He eyes me. "Dude, is it Maize?"

I swallow and reach for my helmet. "Yeah." No point in lying.

"You really like her, huh?"

I nod. "She's not like everyone said she was, Linc." I toss the ball back to him, the need to defend her strong.

"I never thought she was corn on the cob." He grins at me, producing the dimple that drives girls crazy. "She seems more like a ball buster."

I laugh, as I think about the way she glared at me, like she wanted to neuter me after I took her down with my ball. "She's not. Well, she is, but once you get to know her, she's really sweet." I frown. "We're not really a couple."

"What is that supposed to mean?"

I step toward him and lower my voice. "I just bought her."

"And now you like her, right? I've seen it happen."

"I'm just not sure how she feels."

"Then find out. How about a double date? Let me get to know her better, see you two together. You've been hiding out in that room of yours so much, I didn't think you lived at Wolf House anymore."

"Yeah, I know."

"Double date then?"

I don't want to hurt his feelings, but Steph has never been one of my favorite people. Linc likes her and as long as he's happy, that's enough for me. I'd never say anything bad about her, but she walks around with a sense of entitlement, and easily fits in with the mean girls. I really didn't like the look she gave Kaitlyn the day Maize hurt her ankle.

"What do you think?" he presses.

"Actually, I think Maize is moving back to her place today."

"Fuck, man, what the hell?"

"It's just messed up."

He eyes me and is about to ask more questions when the coach calls out to us. For the next couple of hours, we practice, and after we hit the showers, I catch Linc looking at me like he wants to talk, but I have to get to class. I check my phone, disappointed that there's no message from Maize.

My stomach drops. By now, she's back at her own place. Am I seriously going to let that happen? Am I not a guy who fights for what he wants? Maybe I should go over there caveman-style and take her back. But I'm not going to do that if it's not what she wants, and a few more months of fucking isn't going to help me get over her.

Head down, I hurry outside and walk home, wanting to drop my stuff off before class, but come to an abrupt halt when I crash into Kaitlyn outside Wolf House.

"Whoa," she says and falters. I quickly grab her.

"Shit, I'm sorry."

"In a hurry much?"

"Yeah, I... sorry." I glance up at my window and the curtains are still drawn. It brings a smile to my face when I think about Maize's venetian blind story.

"Something funny?"

"No, sorry, just some things on my mind. Are you here for Maize?"

"Yeah, I've been texting, and she hasn't been answering."

Maybe she's still here. My heart leaps at that possibility.

"She might still be sleeping. It was a busy weekend."

She grins like she knows all the details and it's possible she does. They say guys brag, but I think girls are worse. I kind of like the thought of Maize bragging, and yes that makes me an egotistical dick, but I want her happy, and want to do nice things for her.

I gesture toward the front door. "Do you want to come up with me?"

She shifts from one foot to another, her eyes narrow in worry. "No, but can you give her a message for me."

"Yeah, sure. What is it?"

She frowns and looks past my shoulders. "It's bad news." My heart thumps. Maize has been through enough already; more bad news is something she doesn't need to hear. "And maybe it's better coming from you than me." She snorts. "Shoot the messenger and all."

"What is it?" I ask, my heart still thumping. Did something bad happen back home? Christ, her mother is all she has, if anything happened... I take a breath and try not to get too ahead of myself, and the truth is, her mother might be her only family, but she has others she can count on, like Kaitlyn and me.

"First, let me thank you for getting our deadbeat landlord off his fat ass. He's been getting things done around the place," she says, and I nod, wanting her to get to the point. "The bad news is, they were banging around, and a pipe broke. The place is a mess, and we won't have any hot water for a while." A stupid ridiculous smile tugs up the corners of my mouth and I scrub my face to hide it. "I know it's an imposition, but is there any chance she can stay with you a little longer. I know it's a lot, and you've put out—"

" I like to put out," I blurt out like an idiot, and she bites her lips to hide her smile. "I mean, sure, if that's what she needs.

She's more than welcome to stay for as long as she wants. She'll be going home for Christmas, but until then..." Why am I babbling and why do I have this ridiculous need to keep her until the next holiday?

She shakes her head and kicks a pebble. "Bad luck seems to follow her."

"Yeah, that's too bad."

Too bad for her, but great for me. Best I keep that to myself.

20

MAIZE

"Freedom!" Christian blurts out as he comes racing into his room, excited like a child on Christmas morning, and with the holidays just around the corner, why shouldn't he be?

I spin, his loud voice and high energy surprising me. I love his enthusiasm and I am excited to go home for a couple of weeks, but maybe I'm a little less excited than he is, which sounds awful and selfish. After spending all my time at Christian's—thank you, broken pipe—I'm not quite ready to go home. He'll be going his way, and I'll be going mine, and honestly since the accident, I've not gone more than a day without seeing him. He still disappears on Sundays for a few hours, and whatever he's doing he's keeping it secret. I have to respect that—and try not to read too much into it—because I know he's a very private person. But even when he was on the road for a game, we always texted or video messaged. I've gotten entirely too used to it.

"I take it you did well on your exam," I say, as I fold our laundry. Crazy that we've been doing our laundry together since

Thanksgiving, our clothes and underwear mingling in the washer and dryer. It's odd how that makes me giggle just a little bit.

"Fantastic. How did yours go?"

I crinkle my nose. "It went."

"Come on, you've been studying for weeks. You must have nailed it. Or maybe you weren't studying like you said you were. I could never find you when I went to the library. You always just seemed to have..." he pauses to do quotes around the words, 'Just finished.' He arches his brow playfully, but I don't miss the questions lingering in his eyes—was I really at the library, and if not, why would I lie about it? He's going to find out soon.

I gaze at the man who has worked his way into my heart. Honestly, I don't want our time to be over and I'm damn tired of being afraid that he doesn't care for me the way I care for him. He's kind, sincere, always there for me. I can't help but think he wouldn't be if he didn't want something deeper. This goes beyond responsibility for hitting me with the ball. This morning when I woke, I came to the conclusion that right after Christmas, when we agreed this arrangement would end, I'd have a talk with him on the way home in the car, and get to the bottom of where we stand once and for all.

"Yeah, your timing really sucks, and speaking of nailed it," I tease, wanting to change the subject, because he's right. Most times I fibbed, saying I was at the library, even though I wasn't. I don't like to lie, but those little ones were quite necessary. Living here with him, and being together all the time, prevented me from having too much alone time, and alone time was needed for what I've been planning.

"Oh, something on your mind?" He pulls me into his arms and plants a kiss onto my mouth like it's the most natural thing in the world...like I'm his and he's mine.

"We both rushed out of here so fast, with nothing but a granola bar in our stomachs, I'm thinking of food."

"You want to grab a late breakfast before we hit the road home?"

I give him a mischievous smile. "Something like that."

"Drive to Juleps Café?"

"Actually, I was thinking more along the lines of having breakfast here." I run my hands through his mess of hair, and smooth it back to showcase his handsome face. Unable to help myself, I lean into him and press a soft kiss to his lips. I linger there for a moment, and expel a contented sigh.

"I can make us something," he says.

"Nope, I'm cooking," I whisper back. "I am your servant, right?"

He laughs. "You know I was kidding. I just wanted into your panties."

I grin. "Still, I want to cook."

He slaps my ass. "Okay, let me wash up and we'll cook." He goes into the bathroom and he speaks over the running tap. "You must be excited to see your Mom tonight."

"I can't wait. How about you? What's Christmas like for you?" I once again almost ask him if he'd like to spend time at my place. But I don't want to put the cart before the horse. We need to have an honest and open conversation before I even let Mom know he exists, because there's a chance this is all in my head.

He peeks his head out as he wipes his wet hands on a towel. "My family will be there. Grandmother, and cousins and some aunts and uncles. Pretty much the one and only time we're all together."

"You must be looking forward to that, and having all the family around the dining room table for Christmas dinner." I used to dream about such things. Living in a fancy house, with a big family, all laughing around the table as we exchange stories. I guess it's not really like it's portrayed in the movies, and while it's only Mom and me, we have the nicest time.

He gives a humorless laugh. "Oh yeah, watching Mom and Dad pretend to like each other. It's like dinner and a movie."

I laugh at that as he comes from the room and put my hands on his chest to stop him. "Sit," I tell him and point to his favorite comfy chair.

"I thought we were cooking."

I hand him the remote. "I'm sure there's some game on some where. You sit, and I'm bringing breakfast to you."

He grabs my hand and tugs until my mouth is inches from his. "What are you up to, Maize Malone?"

I give him a quick peck. "You'll find out."

As he continues to eye me, I grin at him, and give a little finger wave as I exit his room and tug the door shut behind me. I might not have the money to get him a proper Christmas gift, but that doesn't mean I can't give him some-thing I know he likes. Besides, Christmas isn't about the amount you spend, it's about spending time and doing nice things for those you care about. That's my look on it, anyway.

I hurry to the kitchen and get straight to work. I might not have been studying those times at the library, but that doesn't mean I haven't been learning new things. I put all my focus into what I'm doing and less than thirty minutes later, I find a serving tray beside the fridge, and place our plates, and mugs of coffee on it, putting only sugar in Christian's. I head back up to his room, and the sound of a football game on the TV reaches my ears.

Unable to open the door, I give it a couple taps with my foot and the next thing I know, Christian is standing on the other side of the door, his jaw slack when his gaze drops to the tray.

"What the hell?"

I laugh a little, giddy inside that I can surprise him like this.

"Can I come in?"

"What did you do?" he asks as I move past him and set the food down onto his small table, and put one plate where he sits, and one where I sit. Then I set our coffees down.

"I made us a late breakfast."

He scratches his head, perplexed. "You made eggs benny?"

"I did." I wave to his chair. "Sit down and dig in."

He's still a little shocked as he drops into the chair, picks up his fork, and takes his first bite. "Jesus," he says around a mouthful of egg and hollandaise sauce. "This tastes just like the eggs benny at Juleps."

"I know."

"What did you do?" he asks again as he takes a sip of coffee and moans.

I push to my feet, lean across the table and plant a kiss on his mouth. "Merry Christmas, Christian."

"This is the best Christmas present ever. Even the coffee is perfect."

I laugh at that. "I thought you might like it, and I have a confession." His brow raises. "I borrowed a friend's car and drove to Juleps. I had a nice conversation with your favorite server, and she got me this recipe. I've been practicing. That's why you could never find me at the library. I was taking my mistakes to my Kaitlyn and my roommates. They're kind of sick of eggs and hollandaise."

"You've got to be kidding me." His smile is so sweet, and sincere it wraps around my heart and tugs tight. I am so damn crazy about this guy.

"You're the best, Maize Malone."

"Yeah, I know."

We both laugh and talk about our exams as we eat, and once the plates are cleared, Christian insists on doing up the dishes while I finish packing. I walk around the room, and note how many things I actually have here now. I flick through the TV stations and turn on a talk show as I gather a few of my clothes and toss them into my bag. I don't need many, since I still have things at Mom's. I grab my toiletries from the bathroom, and before I shove my laptop into my backpack, I open it and check my messages. A gasp catches in my throat when I see one from Dean Saunders. I sink down onto the bed, my heart jumping into my throat. I read the message once, and then again. The door opens and I can't stop grinning when Christian walks in.

He comes toward me, his gaze going from my face to my laptop back to my face. "What?"

"You're not going to believe this," I squeal.

"Try me."

I set my laptop down, and throw my arms around him. "Dean Saunders received my application, and wants to have a conversation over the holidays. He asked me to set up a time."

Christian picks me up and spins me around. "I knew he'd been impressed, Maize."

"I can't believe this."

He kisses my forehead and sets me on my feet. "I can. You worked hard for this."

I tap his nose and grin. "Our dinner in Aspen didn't hurt, either. You're a big part of this, Christian. Thank you."

"No thanks needed." He slaps my ass. "Now message him back, and then let's get going. I'm sure you're going to want to tell your mom this news in person."

"Do you think tomorrow is too soon to set up a call?"

"The sooner the better," he says.

I open my laptop and respond and not expecting an answer so fast, I'm about to close it when his email pops up, giving me a time. "It's a go. We're on for tomorrow."

"Nice. Your mom is going to be so proud of you." He makes a fist and nudges my chin playfully. "I know I am."

I honestly love how he thinks of my mother, and really seems to cherish the relationship we have. I hate that his mother and father are so absent. He deserves so much better than that. I finish getting my things together and less than an hour later, we head to his car.

"I really appreciate you driving me home." Kaitlyn had finished up yesterday and had no problem waiting an extra day to drive me home, but Christian jumped at the chance.

"Oh, did you think I was driving you home?" he says his lips twitching. "I'm just driving you to the closest bus stop."

"After that meal I just made, I'd think a rolled out red carpet from Wolf House to the car was in order."

He tosses our bags into the trunk and something moves over his face, something I can't quite identify. Reaching past me, he opens my door and I slide in. I take his dark, contemplative expression as he circles the Jeep and slides in beside me.

"You okay?" I ask.

He puts on a smile. "I'm good."

I study his profile as he backs out of his spot, and I don't get the sense that he's good at all. His quick change of mood is enough to give me whiplash, but I go silent and chalk it up to going home. We both have very different things waiting for us.

When one of my favorite songs comes on the radio, I jack it up and sing along, and I don't care that I can't carry a tune or that Christian is grinning at me. I shake my head and laugh. It's crazy how far Christian and I have come since high school. Never in a million years would the old me believe that I'd be in his car singing, or in his bed fucking. Although lately, his touch has felt far more emotional than physical.

"You have to guide me," he says when we get close to home, and I nod, having forgotten that he doesn't know where I live. I was the poor girl who took three buses to get to his school. I guide him through town, and point to the house two doors down from mine—Ryan's house.

He leans toward me and glances out the window. "This is where you grew up?" I turn and take in the small white bungalow with the broken shutter to the left of the main window. Ryan and I broke that when we were playing in the yard one day and it's been like that for years.

"No, actually, I live in the gray house back there."

He turns to look, a frown pulling at his face. "Then why are we here?"

I crinkle my nose almost apologetically. "If Mom sees me being dropped off by a guy, I'll never hear the end of it." He turns the radio down, like he needs quiet to tell me something, but a bang has both our heads lifting. I turn and see Ryan come rushing from his front door. He pulls open my door, and practically drags me out.

"Wait, I'm belted in," I say laughing, and once I get it unlatched, he drags me to him and gives me a big hug. For a second, I think I hear a growl rumbling in Christian's throat. I turn to him, and he's glaring at us, his fingers tapping the steering wheel.

"Hey, little Maize Daisy," Ryan says, and I whack him.

"Don't call me that."

"Who's your friend?" Christian asks, his voice a measure deeper.

"Christian, this is Ryan. You remember me mentioning him." He nods, slowly, and sizes up Ryan. "Ryan this is Christian, uh, my friend."

Ryan leans forward to see Christian, and I can almost hear his brain spinning. "Nice to meet you, Christian."

"Yeah, same."

Suddenly, like a lightbulb just went off in his head, Ryan says, "Christian...wait..." he glances at me. "Is this the same Christian who—"

"Thanks for the drive, Christian," I blurt out, not wanting to talk about that closet incident right now. "Can you pop the back so I can get my things?"

"I'll get them," Ryan says.

Christian kills the ignition and climbs from the car. Without a word, he goes to the back of the Jeep, opens the door and pulls out my bag. He hands it to me, and there is almost a frightening intensity about him when he glances over my shoulder at Ryan—no wonder he's so intimidating on the football field—and says, "You good, Maize?"

"I'm...good."

His head dips and his knuckles brush mine. He opens his mouth like he wants to say something, then scrubs his face, and turns from me. He taps his hands on the roof of the Jeep before he gets in, and says, "Knock Saunders dead, okay?"

"I will. Merry Christmas, Christian."

He stares at me long and hard before he says, "Merry Christmas," and I'm not sure why, but it sounded a whole lot more like goodbye.

21

CHRISTIAN

I'm in a pretty bad fucking mood by the time I cross town and pull into my parents' driveway. My phone pings and it's Linc checking to see if I want to go out for a beer. I give a humorless laugh. He seems to be about as happy as I am at being back home. I text back to let him know I'll be up for it later, and that I have to go say hello to the family.

I kill the ignition and climb from my Jeep, trying to shake off the uneasy feeling eating at me. Ryan is Maize's friend. Sure, he wrapped her up in a big hug and looked at her with pure adoration in his eyes, and she did the same. But they're just friends, right? Maybe they're still friends with benefits. Damned if that doesn't burn a hole in my gut and make me want to go back there and beat the shit out of him. Oh, but I can't do that.

Why the fuck didn't you lay claim already, dude?

Isn't that the question of the century. If I was being honest with myself, I'm a bit of a chicken shit. My whole life, I was adamant that I wasn't going to get involved in a serious relationship. I didn't want to fall into the pattern my parents did. The love, or infatuation, or whatever it is, fades, and you end up resenting one another, yet you have a kid, so you stick it out and live un-happily ever after. Real fucking fairy tale that is.

I open the front door, and step into the spacious front entry. Dropping my bag, I call out to my mother.

"Christian," Mom says and comes to greet me, looking completely put together with her perfect clothes, hair and makeup. After a hug, she tucks a blond strand behind her ear and stands back. "Let me look at you." She takes me in, and probably doesn't like that I'm dressed in jeans and my football jacket, but instead of saying anything, she smiles and leans in for another hug. It's been four months since I've last been home, and I haven't changed physically. In other ways, maybe, but I'm still fit from football and exercise. "So good to see you, but you do need a haircut."

I run my fingers through my hair, and nod in agreement. "It's good to be home," I say as her familiar expensive perfume fills the air around us. "Dad back yet?"

"He doesn't get in until tomorrow afternoon." She plasters on a smile. "Why don't you put your things into your room, and come back down for coffee." There's a strain in her voice when she adds, "Your grandmother is on her way over. She's bringing your favorite cookies. We thought you'd be home by now."

"Sorry, got a little tied up and couldn't get away until later." Even though I'm not a kid anymore, Grandma still likes to bake for me, and I like it, too. "Give me a sec to drop my bag in my room." I dart up the stairs and set my bag onto my bed and instantly go on a trip down memory lane as I glance around the spacious room. My bedroom is exactly as I left it four years ago. But I definitely feel different than I did when I left for college. In so many ways, ways that actually scare me a bit. The front door opens and I hear Grandma's voice, so I head to the stairs, taking them two at a time, and throw my arms around her.

"Grandma, I missed you."

She laughs and whacks me as she shoves a container of cookies at me. "Oh, phooey, you missed my peanut butter chocolate chip cookies."

"That's true, too." I laugh as I take the container, and for a brief second I think of tucking a few away for Maize. Although by the time I pick her up to go back to Kingston, they'd be stale. Unless, of course, I made a special trip across town.

She doesn't want her mom to know about you, dude.

"Now, let me have a look at you." I laugh, despite the storm going on inside me, and spread my arms. I spin to let her examine me, see that nothing is broken. She never was a lover of football and is always worried I'm going to get hurt. I love her for that, but football is my calling, and down the road, maybe teaching or coaching. A ridiculous image of Maize and me living in the city together, any city, while she practices law, and I teach, coming home to our own place afterward, careens through my brain. I shake it off, but don't miss the way Grandma is studying me with those perceptive eyes of hers.

"Still in one piece, Grandma." She narrows her blue eyes and gives me a once over.

"There's something different."

"Maybe it's that I'm not a teenager anymore." I laugh and brush off her concerns, not wanting her to delve any deeper.

"Nope, that's not it. You keeping your grades up?"

"Always."

Mom stands there quietly, her brow furrowed. She clearly can't quite figure out what Grandma is seeing. Why would she? She's never taken the time to really look below the surface where I was concerned. No, I was a means to an end, a pawn in her marriage plot.

I hold my arms out for Mom and Grandma. "Come on, let's go have a cup of coffee and some cookies."

I guide them into the kitchen and Grandma sits as Mom pours three cups of coffee, and I dig into the container of cookies like a five-year-old.

"Thanks, Mom," I say when she sets my coffee in front of me.

She pats my arm. "Let me grab the cream."

"I don't take cream, remember? Just sugar, lots of sugar."

"Oh right." She hands the cream to Grandma and I smile to myself. Maize remembered I like my coffee with just sugar. She also went to extreme measures to make me the perfect breakfast. I still can't believe she did that. Then again, maybe I can. My stomach tightens. Jesus, how the hell am I going to go through the entire Christmas break without seeing her? I'm not, and she's just going to have to deal with that.

No, dude, she doesn't want you at her place.

To fucking bad.

"What's her name?" Grandma asks, pulling my thoughts back as she drops two sugar cubes into her mug and stirs it.

My head lifts, the ridiculous smile on my face dissolving faster than her sugar. "What?"

Grandma takes a sip of coffee and looks at me over the rim. I grab a cookie and practically shove the whole thing into my mouth so I don't have to talk, but she's a patient woman. She'll wait until I eat the whole container and then resume her questioning.

"Are you seeing someone, Christian?" Mom asks, a hopeful look in her eyes as I hold the container of cookies to her. She's always pushing for me to get serious. I guess my single, play the field status doesn't look good to her.

"Uh, no." I give a fast shake of my head and set the container down when she holds her hand up, palm out. "Too busy with football and studying."

Mom adjusts the silk scarf around her neck. "It's not right, Christian. You should be thinking about your future wife and children at this point in your life."

I almost choke on my cookie. Why the hell would she care? She trapped my father, for Christ's sake. Does she think she's going to be a better grandparent than she was a parent? Grandma makes a scoffing sound, and Mom casts her a quick glance. Like I said, Grandma never really was a fan of my mother, but she's always been good to me.

"I am thinking about my future, Mom." I should have joined Linc for that beer. But this conversation would have happened sooner or later, so I might as well get it out of the way now.

I exhale and go for another cookie, and brace myself. "Many of your friends are engaged now, Christian. Just last week Wanda told me that Megan was planning her spring wedding."

"Oh yeah, good for Megan. Not everyone has to get engaged straight out of college. It's not a crime to stay single."

Ignoring me she continues. "Megan plans to bring her fiancé to the Christmas party. Perhaps she has a few single friends. I'll ask her mother."

"Please don't." Jesus, I hate the annual Christmas party. Hate Mom trying to set me up with one of her friends' daughters. AKA the mean girls from my high school years, and I'm not interested in getting fixed up or hooking up with any of them.

"I ran into Chelsea the other day," Mom continues. "She's at Princeton, doing a literature degree. She's a lovely girl, Christian."

"Leave the boy alone," Grandma says, and Mom stiffens. "He'll get married when he's ready and not a day before." There's a warning in Grandma's voice and my mother's face pales in response.

"More coffee?" Mom asks and stands.

I take a huge sip of mine. "I'm good." My phone pings and my heart leaps, hoping it's Maize. I leave it for now, because both Mom and Grandma hate phones at the table and I'd probably start smiling like the village idiot again. Grandma already suspects something as it is.

"Maybe you should get that," Grandma says, taking me by surprise. My gaze flies to hers, but her face is expressionless, and I grin at her. She's far too wise for any of us.

I tug my phone from my pocket, and it's a message from Linc letting me know he gathered up some of the guys and they were all headed out to shoot some pool. I'm not sure why, but I have a feeling something is up with him. I've been so caught up in myself, I've been a shitty friend. "It's Linc."

"How is he?" Mom asks. "I do hope he's coming to the party this year. He always has an open invitation, but never comes."

"He's busy with his own family." I reach for another cookie, and turn the conversation around, asking Mom about her Thanksgiving weekend, and Grandma about all her clubs. Soon enough, it's time for Grandma to head back home, and even though she's in her late sixties, she's still driving and still going strong.

I walk her to her car and give her a big hug, promising I'll visit. She drives off and I check the time. My guess is the guys are still at the pub, and dammit I could use a drink or two right about now. I hurry back in the house, and Mom is sitting at the table, her day planner out.

"I'm going to head out and meet the guys." I put my hands in my pockets. "Shoot some pool."

She smiles up at me. "You aren't staying for dinner?"

"No, I'll grab something when I'm out." When she looks like she's going to protest, I add, "You're right. I should catch up with the old crew." Her smile widens, because she thinks the old crew means some of the girls she's interested in setting me up with. It's all for show with her, though. It doesn't look good at the country club that her son is still playing the field, so to speak. I head to the cupboard, and take out a small plastic bag.

Mom's eyes narrow, confusion all over her face, as I pack up a few cookies. "What on earth are you doing, Christian?"

"You know how much Linc loves Grandma's cookies," I fib, and honestly I don't even know what I'm doing. My thoughts are so consumed with Maize it has me fucked up and acting out of character. My mother, who knows so little about me, is even picking up on my strange behavior. "I'll catch up with you later. We'll play some games, or maybe a puzzle."

She smiles, happy with that. "Keep tomorrow evening free. We have dinner plans at La Fresca when your dad gets back."

"Okay." I drop a kiss onto her cheek, and her perfume gets on my skin. "Don't wait up for me."

I head back outside, jump into my Jeep and my insides are a twisted mess as I drive to our favorite pub. I try to get Maize out of my mind, and brush off the unease in my gut as I walk inside to find Linc and two of our buddies at the pool table. I gesture the server for a round of beer for us all, and make my way over.

"Hey bud, you made it," Linc says and puts his hand on my shoulder, but there's a new sadness about him. "How's the fam?"

I laugh, not wanting to ask him right out what's wrong in front of everyone. "Same old, same old. You're invited to the Christmas party this year," I tell him. "Please come and take some of the attention off me."

He cringes and I don't blame him. Mom's parties are so goddamn pretentious and boring, the only thing I can do is drink copious amounts of tequila to get through them. For a moment, I picture Maize at the party. She'd hate everything about it, and while everyone on the guest list walks around with their noses in the air, Maize is the one who is too good for them all.

"I think I have surgery that day," Linc says, with a grin that seems forced. Yeah, something is definitely off. "I have to have my spleen removed."

I laugh and reach for a pool cue as Curtis and Finn come over and greet me. They were both on our high school football team and both now play for Georgia. They're tight, like Linc and I are. "Dude, it's been too long," they both say and take turns shaking my hand and embracing me at the same time, the weird way guys do.

"What have you two been up to?" I ask, and lean against the wall as the server comes with our beers. She gives me a big smile, and while I would normally flirt back, I'm not much in the mood for it today.

She walks away and Finn whistles. "Now that's some tight pussy."

I shake my head, offended at his crude comment. "Come on, dude. That's just wrong. Respect."

Curtis takes a shot and glances at me. "What's up your ass, Christian? Last year you said the same thing about our server." I nod. He's right, and I hate myself for it. Fuck, things have certainly changed a lot since our last pool game.

"You pussy-whipped or something? Like our man Linc?"

"Don't be jealous that I'm getting it on a regular basis and you're not," Linc says with a grin that doesn't reach his eyes. Shit, there must be something going on with him and Steph. I can feel it in my bones.

We all laugh, and I take another drink of my beer. "How's the fam?" I ask him.

"Oh you know, putting their favorite son on a pedestal."

"Did you hear Chelsea is having a party at the country club?" Finn says. "A reunion of sorts before we all graduate and move on."

"No, never heard," I say. "Can't imagine I'll be going."

"One last blowout. Why not?" Curtis asks.

"I have plans," I say and grin at Linc as Curtis sinks the last ball and wins. "Gallbladder removal." I push off the wall and look at Linc. "Partners?"

For the next few hours we play, and shoot the shit and a few more of our buddies join us, and so do some of the girls I used to hang with. Linc orders some finger food for us all, and when Chelsea comes in, she gives me a big hug.

"Hey," I say, as she lingers in front of me, and runs her finger down my chest. "I was talking to Fiona. She said she ran into you at the hospital."

"Yeah, a friend got hurt." I inch back, as she pushes against me.

"You're friends with corn on the cob now, are you?"

Anger sears my blood and I work to keep my cool. "Don't talk about her like that."

She stares at me for a moment, and then laughs. "You can't be serious, Christian."

"Leave it," I say and wonder why I ever went out with her, considering that stunt in the closet. She never paid any attention to me until I became a baller. I knew who she was and what she was about, and I guess my behavior says more about me and who I was. I'm not that guy anymore.

She runs her tongue over her bottom lip. "I thought we'd hang out, get to know each other again this Christmas."

"I'm kind of busy," I say and move to the other side of the table to take a shot. I don't need to lift my head to know she's pissed off and glaring at me. I don't want to hurt her feelings or anything, I'm not about that, but I can't be with her. I'm not a cheater, even though Maize isn't mine. Yet.

I glance at my watch, and put my cue back on the rack. "I have to run," I say to Linc.

He nods. "Yeah, I do too."

We say goodbye and walk outside together. "You okay?" I ask when we're alone. "Did something happen with Steph?"

"Yeah, I gave her a diamond necklace for Christmas, and she gave me my walking papers."

My heart lurches. "Fuck, man, I'm sorry."

"I was totally fucking blindsided. Never saw it coming." He gives a humorless laugh. "I guess you never do."

My stomach clenches, because he's right. No one ever sees a break-up coming. Shit, for all I know, this is the end for Maize and me. Christmas was our deadline, and I don't want to stick to it. What does she want?

"How about you? You okay?" he asks.

I shrug. "I don't know."

He puts his hand on my back. "Why don't you go see her?"

I stare at him. "You think?"

"I know."

It's late when I turn off my lamp and check my phone one last time before I crawl into bed. No calls or texts. Disappointment hits harder than that wayward football. Maybe I should just text him first. It's the twenty-first century, for God's sake. A girl can make the first move. I giggle at that thought, because I've been sleeping with Christian for months, living with him, and I'm debating on whether to send him a text or not.

I flop onto my pillow, deciding to do just that, when his message pops up.

Hey.

My heart races, and my fingers are a bit shaky as I text him back.

Hey yourself.

Busy?

Just getting ready for bed.

What are you wearing?

I laugh out loud and cover my mouth. Mom is still up and I don't want her coming in here to check on me.

Oh, just a little something called lingerie.

It's a lie, I'm in my pajama shorts and T-shirt.

You have any of those little white panties with you?

I chuckle. I have no idea why he's so obsessed with my white cotton panties, but he is.

Maybe.

Go to your window.

My pulse jumps. Is Christian outside? I turn my lamp on, jump from my bed, and pull open my curtain, and a giddy sound catches in my throat when I find him standing beneath the streetlamp. I quietly open my window and in hushed words I say, "What are you doing here?" He waves and starts walking toward me, and I do love the way the man walks with such a sexy swagger.

"Hurry," I say and glance over my shoulder to make sure Mom isn't standing in my doorway, an admonishing look on her face. Up until this second, I've never had a hookup in this bedroom, never worried about my mother walking in on us. My freaking door doesn't even have a lock on it. This is a bad idea. Such a bad idea.

Then why aren't you stopping it, Maize?

He casually steps up to my window, and leans against the frame, looking so damn hot my ovaries clench. "I'm not catching you at a bad time, am I?"

I look past his shoulders, and down the street. "No, now get in here before someone sees you."

"Embarrassed to be caught with me, Maize?"

I just don't want the neighbors talking, or for my mother to get the wrong idea. He grabs the ledge and effortlessly hoists himself up. Two seconds later, he's in my small, childhood bedroom, his presence overwhelming the space and me. He grins as he pushes his hair back and glances around.

He walks over to my dresser and drops something on it. I'm about to ask what he's doing, but he turns and says, "So this is your room, huh?"

"This is it."

"Looks like a high school girl still lives here."

I laugh. "Mom hasn't changed a thing."

"Neither has mine. I still have a shelf above my bed displaying all my trophies."

"I'd love to see that."

He nods. "I'll send you pictures tonight, after I get home."

My heart sinks a little and it shouldn't. I didn't want him to meet my family, either.

"That would be fun to see, and it sounds like they are proud of you, Christian. If they keep all your trophies displayed."

"There displayed in my room where no one goes. But my successes make *them* look good, Maize. That's all. It's all about image with them, associating with the right people, and putting a proper appearance out to the world. Honestly, I've always walked the straight and narrow, always followed the rules."

My heart sinks. "Until me...until..."

Before I can say anything more, he steps up to me, wraps his arm around my waist and drags me to him. The smell of beer, mingling with perfume, hits me hard. I put my hand on his chest.

"Where were you?" Unease worms its way through my body. Was he out with the right people?

"Met the guys for a drink."

"That's why you smell like beer, but why do you smell like perfume?"

"If you're wondering if I was with another girl, the answer is no. You're the only girl I can think about. That's why I'm here, Maize..." My insides flutter, and there is nothing on his face to suggest he's been in someone else's bed. "Tell me I can stay. I really need to put my cock in you."

My legs quiver. "God, when you put it like that."

He glances the length of me, takes in my shorts and T-shirt. "New pajamas?"

"No, I just didn't take them to Kingston with me."

"I'd ask you to put on your little white panties, but I'm going to have you out of these in a second anyway." My body heats as he turns, and his face falls slightly as he glances at my unmade bed. "Did you sleep with Ryan in that bed?"

"No, we were in his..." He focuses back in on me. "I've...never slept with any guy in that bed."

Catching me by surprise, he picks me up, and sets me on my bed. "How about we rectify that."

"My door, it doesn't lock," I whisper.

"Then you'd better not scream too much, Maize." He shrugs out of his coat, and reaches over his back to take off his T-shirt, and my gaze goes to his body. Even though I want to look at him, admire him, I reach over and turn out the light.

"You want me to feel my way around, do you?" he asks in the dark.

I chuckle. "Just in case Mom walks in."

The bed creaks as he climbs in beside me, and I tug the blankets up to cover us up. A weird little giggle crawls out of my throat. "My God, this feels so..."

"Good."

"Yeah, but risky...my mom."

"Worried about getting caught can be half the fun." I want to protest, but goddammit, I can't, and when he presses his lips to mine, and spreads my legs as he positions himself in between them, my brain stops working.

"Yes," I murmur, and run my hands through his hair as his lips leave mine to go to my neck. His mouth is hot, like fire on my skin and I writhe beneath him as I tug the blankets over us. He pushes his pelvis against mine, his rock-hard cock straining against his jeans. He slides to my side and puts his hand into my shorts. "Christian," I moan, moving against his fingers as he circles my clit. I lift my hips, wanting him inside me.

"Need something, sweetness?" he asks.

"I need you." He rewards me with a finger, and slides it deep inside me. He fucks me with it, and it's insane how close I already am. He fills me with a second finger, and rubs the heel of his hand against my clit. My breathing changes, becomes labored, and under the covers, it's hard to get air, but air is overrated anyway. Pleasure grips every nerve in my body and I put my hand over my mouth and bite down to stop from crying out. My body clenches, and my sex squeezes his probing fingers as my climax peaks. A keening sound rises in my throat as I ride out each powerful wave. My God, sex with Christian is amazing. I'm pretty certain by this point he's ruined me for any other man.

He keeps his fingers inside me until I stop spasming, and then he takes my hand away from my mouth. Warm lips press against mine.

"You missed me, huh?" he teases.

"Apparently."

He chuckles, and I give him a hard shove. He lets out a little oomph when I put my hand on his chest and pin him to my bed. I can't see his face, but I'm sure he's wondering what I'm up to. Grabbing the blankets, I pull them up until we're both underneath and I kiss his bare chest. His moan curls around me and I go lower, until I reach his jeans. I pop the button, unzip them and tug them down to free his cock.

"Fuck yeah," he groans as I take his hardness into my mouth, wanting to devour every inch, even though he's too big for that. My lips stretch around his cock and I cup his balls for a soft massage and his hips lift, driving his cock a little deeper into my throat. I love how aroused he is, that it's my bed he's in—that it's me he wants to be with.

Pre-cum drips from his crown, and I taste it with my tongue, savor his tangy flavor. His hands fist my hair and he tugs, but I'm not quite done with him yet. Yes, this is risky, and inappropriate with my mother in the other room, but it's also kind of fun and exciting. I was never a teenager who snuck boys into her room, and I have to say, it's something everyone should experience, sooner or later.

He swells even more in my mouth, and tugs on my hair, and while I'd like for him to come in my throat, I desperately need him inside me. I lift my head and in one quick movement, he has me on my back, pinned beneath him, my shorts at my ankles. He tosses them away and growls at me. God, I love when he does that.

"My cock, in you, now."

The wild urgency in his voice sends heat charging through me. "Yes." I open my legs, and he centers his cock and powers into me, going so deep it sends my head spinning and tilts my world on its axis.

"Christian," I murmur, and bite his shoulder as he fills me, physically and emotionally. With my heart full, bursting with all the things I feel for this man, I rake my nails over his muscular back and move with him, meeting each blunt stroke, as he pounds into me. I'm not even sure I've ever seen this kind of intensity in him, this kind of hunger in his body.

"Maize, you feel so good," he says, his voice a low soft whisper as he puts his lips to the hollow in my throat and presses soft kisses, a contrast to the fierce way he's pounding into my body.

"You do too." I close my eyes, lose myself in the sensation, while I concentrate on the pleasure building between my legs. I struggle to breathe as I roll my head from side to side, and when he grinds against my clit, another wave builds inside me. "God," I whisper.

"Come all over my cock, babe," he whispers, and as soon as the words leave his mouth, they taunt my sex, and I let go. I bite down to suppress a cry as I clench around him. He groans in my ear, a tortured sound as he holds on.

"Let me feel you," I whisper. "Fill me, Christian." Under the covers, we can barely see each other, but I know he's staring, just like I'm staring at him, taking in his silhouette as he pushes deep and lets go. A quiver goes through my body as he spurts into me and I squeeze his cock, wanting every last drop. "So good."

He nods, and his lips find mine for a deep, sensual kiss. Our tongues tangle, taste, leisurely explore, neither of us in a hurry to break the connection.

"I'm so glad you came," I say, pushing the blankets off us so I can see him, and the corners of his mouth turn up.

"Was I taking too long or something?"

I laugh and whack him. "I'm glad you came by tonight, and I'm glad you came too." A giggle catches in my throat.

He slowly pulls out of me. "Do you have tissue?"

"Yeah." With my body and limbs so lethargic, I slowly reach over and grab the box. He pulls out a few tissues and wipes us both up and drops them into my trashcan.

I hear a creak in the hall and put my finger to my lips. We wait, and when the sound passes by my door, I exhale the breath I was holding.

"I should get out of here, huh?"

A knock sounds on my door. "Maize, are you up?"

I push Christian so hard he falls off the side of the bed with a thump, and I grab my book and toss it to the floor. My door creaks open and I pull my blankets up to my chin.

"Everything okay? I thought I heard voices and then a bang."

"I, uh, fell asleep with my book, it must have fallen off the bed."

Oh, Maize how easily the lies are coming now.

"Did you need something?"

"I didn't mean to wake you. I thought you were up, and I wanted to let you know my shift got changed. I have to go in early tomorrow, but that means we can have dinner tomorrow night. Why don't you see if Ryan wants to come over, then we can all watch a movie or something?"

"That sounds like a great plan." I stretch to give her the hint.

"Okay, you get back to sleep. I'm off to bed in a few minutes too."

"Night, Mom."

"Night, love."

My door clicks shut and I lay there for a second until her footsteps are down the hall. I lean over the bed and find a stark-naked Christian on his back, his hands covering his manly parts. "Sorry," I whisper and cover my mouth to stifle a chuckle.

"You don't look sorry. You look like you're laughing and I nearly flashed your mother."

I grab my shorts and shirt and tug them on. "Here, get dressed." I toss his clothes to him.

He dresses quickly and I sit on the bed crossed legged to watch him. "I feel like I'm back in high school," he grumbles.

"Got caught in a lot of girls' beds, did you?"

He gives me a playful wink. "Who says I got caught?"

"Then the part about being in a lot of girls' beds is true?" Damn, I hate the jealousy racing through me. The floor creaks again, and I walk quietly to my window. I turn and he tugs me to him, planting a very possessive kiss on my mouth. He kisses me hard, long and deep. It steals my breath and sets fire to my last working brain cell.

"What was that for?" I ask.

"When you're hanging with Ryan tomorrow, that kiss is what I want you thinking about."

There's something in his eyes, something soft and sincere, and it hits me in the chest, a little to the left. I am so completely in love with Christian.

"We're just friends."

"Yeah, with a guy that looks like Ryan-freaking-Reynolds."

He's jealous. I'm sure of it, and I love it. I tap my chin. "Do you think?"

He gestures with a nod to my bed and cracks his knuckles. "Yeah, I think. Keep him out of that bed."

"Sometimes we sit on it, Christian."

He angles his head, his blue eyes a deeper shade. "Are you trying to provoke me?"

A door closes in the hall. "You have to go."

He grumbles, and throws one leg out the window. "Text me after the dinner and movie."

"Why, are you planning to sneak into my room again?"

He frowns and glances down. "I won't be able to. Dad is getting home tomorrow and I'm expected to go to a family dinner."

"That sounds nice, Christian."

"Yeah, we'll see. Then Saturday there's this..." He blinks and lifts his head. "Doesn't matter. Are you going to miss me?"

"Terribly."

"Good," he says and slides out the window. He curses and I laugh, assuming he landed on one of the prickly bushes. I watch him hurry to his Jeep and climb in, and my body tingles all over, his touch still burning through my body.

My phone pings, and I jump on my bed and reach for it and read the text from Christian.

Still thinking about me, aren't you?

Maybe.

Why are you so obsessed with me?

Must be that first-born quality we both have.

Ah, yes, the reason we could never work out.

I stare at his message for a long time, not really knowing what to make of it. Is he reminding me this is just sex? Or is he waiting for me to jump in and tell him it's not true? As I sit and overthink it, wondering what it was he started to tell me about Saturday night, and then changed his mind, another message comes in.

I had a really nice time tonight, Maize.

Yeah, me too.

Check your dresser.

Having no idea what he's talking about, I jump up and go to my dresser to find a little baggie with cookies.

Grandma's famous cookies. Now go get some sleep. See you soon.

My heart beats wildly at the sweet gesture as I set my phone down, knowing sleep is the last thing I'll be getting tonight, even though I need to be bright and sharp tomorrow for my interview. No, I'm going to lay here and go over the events of tonight a million times, especially the jealousy I heard in his voice and his reminder that 'only children' aren't compatible. I know we both started out in different places, but we've grown and changed, and tonight, I really sensed he wanted the same things I do. Then again, I can't forget Ryan's reaction when Christian first dropped me off. He was floored when he realized it was Christian, and after he drove off, he gave me a good hard lecture about the rich kids from the right side of the tracks and how I should never trust them because I'd only end up hurt.

Can I trust Christian?

My stomach tightens. I was going to wait to talk to him on the drive home—figure out if we had a future together—but maybe I'd better do it sooner rather than later.

23

CHRISTIAN

With voices rising up from downstairs, I sit on the edge of my bed and quickly send Maize a text, and the pictures of my room I promised her. It was late last night when I got home and I didn't want to send them and wake her.

I really want to see her, desperately, but Mom's party is in full swing, and I'm expected to be here to mingle and find myself a fiancée. That thought makes me laugh. None of the girls here tonight can even compete with Maize. And while I want to be with her, she's busy with her mom and I don't want to interrupt their limited time together. That doesn't mean I'm not going to sulk about it, though.

I can understand her not wanting her mother to meet me and get the wrong idea, but once I give her the present Linc and I spent all day shopping for, I'm hoping she'll see that I'm serious and rethink what we have. Maybe then I can meet her mother. I of course want her to meet my family too, especially Grandma, but I'd never bring her to this pretentious bull shit party.

I stare at my phone, but no reply comes. I haven't heard much from her since she told me how well her phone interview went with Dean Saunders. She's going to get a full ride, and he's setting her up with some firms for their internship programs. She's spent many hard years working for this and now it's all in the palms of her hands. I'm happy that I could help the girl who never asks for help.

A rap comes on my door and before I can get to it, the knob turns and in walks Chelsea. She smiles and glances at the white-knuckled grip I have on my phone. "Are you coming down or are you going to play on your phone all night?" I stand, shove my phone into the front pocket of my dress pants, and she puts her hands on my chest to straighten my tie. "You clean up nice, Christian."

I laugh, and take in her tight black dress. It's low in the front, showcasing a hell of a lot of cleavage. "Like what you see?" she teases.

I was simply observing, not ogling. Christ, after Maize, all other girls pale in comparison, but I'm not rude, so I say, "You look nice, Chelsea."

"Nice," she says as her eyes narrow in on me. She spins to show me her body. "I think you could do better than that."

"Christian...oh..." Mom goes still when she sees Chelsea in the room with me. "Oh, sorry. I didn't realize you were up here, Chelsea." She smiles at the girl she believes would make me a suitable wife. "I was just checking to see if you were coming to the party."

"I was just on my way."

I wave my hand for Chelsea to exit first and we follow Mom down the stairs and into the living room. I grin when I see

Linc, and step up to him. "Surgery canceled? Spleen still intact?"

He laughs and hands me his beer. I take a big drink as he says. "You owe me one, bud."

He's dressed in a nice suit and tie, and he hates suits and ties. I can't help but think something is up. "Seriously, what are you doing here?"

"Heard a rumor." He frowns and shakes his head.

I eye him. "Do I want to know?"

"It involves you, so probably."

"I'm going to need a drink for this." I head to the bar and the man attending it pours two shots of tequila. We both knock them back.

"Chelsea wants you back," he tells me. "She made it perfectly clear at the pub the other night after you left. Gave hands-off warnings to her girlfriends."

"I had a feeling something was going on with her. It doesn't make sense, though. Why now?"

"Apparently, her boyfriend broke it off, and she's devastated. Graduating from college, no ring on her finger when many of her friends are engaged."

"She's barking up the wrong tree, dude."

"I know, but I thought you'd need a wingman tonight to help out. Chelsea has a way of always getting what she wants."

The bartender pours us another shot and we toss them back. He then hands us a couple beers from the fridge. My phone pings, and I snatch it from my pocket, hoping it's from Maize, but it's not. It's from our coach, sending out a group message reminding us to make good choices and stay fit over the holiday. I laugh just as Linc's phone pings with the same message.

I'm about to shove my phone in my pocket when someone bumps me, and it falls to the floor. I reach for it, but Mrs. Jackson puts her hand on my chest and gives me an apology, although I have a feeling she banged into me on purpose.

"I've got it," Linc tells me as he reaches for my phone while Mrs. Jackson keeps hold of me and drags me across the floor to say hello to her granddaughter. I cast a pleading glance over my shoulder, a cry for help, but Linc just shrugs and takes another drink of his beer. Some wingman he's turning out to be, but he's here to run interference with Chelsea and there's no rescuing anyone from Mrs. Jackson. She pretends to be a little old lady, but she's a shark with pointy teeth and right now she is trying to matchmake. Why does everyone think I need to be set up? I can get girls perfectly fine on my own. Sure, I let them know it can't go anywhere, but who I see, who I take to my bed, is my decision, not anyone else's.

"Katherine is all grown up," Mrs. Jackson says to me. "You'd hardly recognize her, but trust me, you two would make the cutest couple." She taps a blonde on the shoulder and she turns. Katherine smiles at her grandmother, until she realizes her grandmother has her arm latched around mine in a death grip, in case I try to run, I assume. "Katherine, you remember Christian?"

She nods. "I do. Nice to see you again."

"You too." I haven't seen her since I went off to Kingston and she was a junior in high school. She was pretty then, still pretty now. Her shyness hasn't changed either.

Mrs. Jackson releases me, and claps her hands together. "Isn't she lovely, Christian?" I turn to her and over her head I catch the way Chelsea is glaring at us.

"She is. Very lovely."

"I'll leave you two to get to know one another. Katherine, make sure you tell him all about Princeton."

Mrs. Jackson leaves, and Katherine rolls her eyes. "I'm so sorry."

I laugh, instantly at ease with her. "What is with the matchmaking? If I'm not mistaken, it's the twenty-first century." I see that her glass is almost empty. "Come on, let's get a fresh drink."

"Or ten."

I laugh at that. "It's not so bad," I say, and then check myself. "What am I saying? It's bad, it's really bad." She laughs with me and hands me her glass.

The bartender fills it with wine, and she gives me a grateful smile. "If we could just pretend we're falling for each other tonight, that would really help a girl out."

"My mother is at it too, so you could help me out. We can hang out, but you should know I'm with someone."

She glances around. "Oh, is she here?"

I give a fast shake of my head. "No, this isn't her kind of thing." I glance around the room, and frown. "She'd actually hate it."

"I like her already, and if you're worried about me trying to get a ring, don't. I'm more into Christinas than Christians."

I laugh at that, really liking her. "I wasn't worried, but I guess your grandmother doesn't know, huh?"

She exhales. "No, I haven't been able to break it to her."

"Sorry about that. I know it can't be easy." I put my arm around her shoulder like we're long lost friends, and guide her to a quiet spot in the room. We both take a seat, and for the next half hour, fall into easy conversation. I catch Linc's eye a few times as Chelsea and a few of the other girls in the room chat with him. He's got my back, keeping Chelsea occupied.

"I thought it might have been Chelsea you were with," Katherine says.

"Why's that?"

She takes a small sip of wine and crinkles her nose. "She looks like she wants to put me through a woodchipper."

I chuckle. "I guess it's a good thing we don't have one then." I stand and hold a hand out to her. "How about a breath of fresh air?"

We head out onto the back patio, and the cooler night air falls over us. We lean over the rail and take in the dark night. "Tell me more about Princeton," I say, and for the next half hour we talk about school, and football, and before I realize it, I'm talking about Maize, like nonstop, I need to shut up already. I'm sure I'm boring Katherine to death. I shake my head.

"I'm sorry, I don't know why I went off like that."

Katherine grins, like she knows something I don't. "I do. You really like her."

I laugh and shake my head. "I do like her."

She angles her head, her dark eyes moving over my face. "Does she know it?"

I rake my hand through my hair. "I...I've never actually told her, I guess."

"Maybe you should."

"When did you get so smart?" I ask and when she shivers, I put my arm around her and lead her back inside. Her grandmother gives us a big smile.

"She's going to be heartbroken," Katherine says with a sigh.

"You have to live your life, Katherine. You have to do what makes you happy."

"Great advice coming from a guy who's at a party when there's somewhere else he'd rather be."

I laugh. "You got me there."

She checks the time. "I think it's time for Grandmother to head home. It was so nice seeing you again, and I look forward to meeting Maize."

"You're going to love her."

She smiles at me and puts her palm on my face. "If you love her, everyone will love her."

I do. I do fucking love her.

I reach for my phone, to see if she returned any of my messages, and that's when I remember Linc has it.

"Take care, Katherine," I say and go in search of Linc. The party has died down quite a bit, many of the elderly guests long gone. Linc has had far too much to drink by the time I find him and I guess he's drowning his sorrows. He really seemed to like Steph, and this breakup has been hard on him. I want to help, but I don't know what the answer is. A hook up? Spending time alone? All I know is whatever he decides to do, I've got his back.

"You're sleeping here tonight, bud," I say and put my hand on his shoulder.

"Yeah, thinking that would probably be a good idea."

"Thanks for running interference."

He nods. "Was that Katherine?" His head bobs a little. "Chelsea wasn't very happy about you ignoring her."

"Yeah, it was Katherine, and I wasn't ignoring her. Besides, you kept her busy."

"I should go say hi to Katherine."

I stop him. "She's really sweet, too sweet for you dude, so forget it."

He laughs, and finishes his drink. "You're right. You know I'm going to have to beat the shit out of Kyle."

My head rears back. "Kyle, why?"

"I think Steph is with him."

"Fucker."

"Yeah."

"We can talk about Kyle tomorrow. Go upstairs, climb into one of the spare beds, and sleep it off."

"Okay, dude."

His shoulders are slightly slumped as he walks off, and my mother steps up to me. "Is Linc okay?"

I catch him stumbling a bit on the stairs. "He's going through a rough time."

She nods and smiles. "He seemed to be hitting it off with Chelsea."

"They're just friends," I say as he disappears up the stairs.

"What about you and Chelsea?" She waves a finger at me. "I caught you two in your room, remember."

"Friends."

"Yes, of course." Her diamond earrings glisten in the overhead light as she tucks a strand of hair behind her ear. "You seemed to be interested in Katherine. She's a lovely girl, Christian."

"I'm interested in someone else."

Her face lights with curiosity as she glances at the thinning crowd. "Is she still here?"

"No, she was never here, and you'll meet her when the time is right." I feign a yawn, and check my watch. "It's been a long day. I'm going to crawl into bed."

Her eyes are lit with excitement. "Okay, but tomorrow I want to hear all about this girl."

I nod, and head upstairs. I'm about to enter my room when I find the door shut. I know I left it open when I moved Chelsea out and headed down to the party. I check the two spare bedrooms and they're empty. I guess Linc stumbled into my room. I drop down onto the bed in one of the spare rooms and reach for my phone.

"Shit."

I go back to my bedroom door. My buddy is probably fast asleep. I'll just hurry in, grab my phone and get out. I don't want to wake him, he's clearly having a bad night, and needs to sleep it off. I try the door, only to find it locked. Fuck, he probably doesn't even realize he's locked it. I consider pounding on the door, I really want to see if Maize messaged me back, and after talking to Katherine, I really want to tell Maize how I feel—although doing it in person is a much better idea. Waiting until morning to talk to her might be torturous, but I can't go around pounding or breaking down doors. I'm about to walk away, when I hear a noise in my room—something that sounds a lot like giggling. What the fuck?

24

MAIZE

I t's the day before Christmas, my mom has the nightshift off, and we're both up early baking up a storm for tomorrow's feast. I should be happy. I should be smiling with joy and dancing around the kitchen. But I'm not. In fact, I'm completely confused. I sent Christian a dozen texts last night, and he's yet to answer any of them. He mentioned that he had something to do, somewhere to be on Saturday night, and while I wanted to ask—it's not like him to be vague—I didn't want to pry. Although he still has never told me where he goes every Sundays.

I guess if he wanted me to know he would have told me. Really though, it's Christmas and he's most likely busy with family. It's not like him to blow me off and I'm probably worried about nothing. Then again what if something happened and he couldn't text. What if he was hurt? With that thought rattling around inside my brain, I reach for the cookie sheet with shaky fingers, and it falls. The loud clanging sound pulls me from my reverie.

Mom touches my arm. "Are you okay?"

I nod. "I'm fine. I just didn't sleep well last night."

"Why don't you go lay down?" She waves her hand to shoo me away. "I've got this."

I shake my head. "No, I like baking with you. I just need more coffee." I head to the pot and pour a big mugful. As I drink my gaze goes to my phone, but again...nothing.

"Are you waiting for a call?" Mom asks, as she turns her rolling pin to hit the crust from a different angle.

"I plan to go shopping with Kaitlyn and Ryan later, so I was just checking to see if they left me a message." At least it's not an entire lie. We do have plans to shop. I take another big drink of coffee, and start dropping the shortbreads onto the tray. A smile creeps across my face as I think about the cookies Christian brought me. They were delicious and I must ask for the recipe. Maybe I can make them for him back at Kingston. He sure loved the eggs benny I perfected.

A knock sounds at the door and I nearly jump out of my socks. "I'll get it," I say quickly, and Mom gives me a strange look as I wipe my hands on my apron. I'm ninety-nine percent sure it's not Christian, but there is a small part of me that wants it to be him. I'm not ready for Mom to meet him, but I just want to see him, to know he's okay after not hearing from him last night.

I pull open the door and my face falls when I see it's Ryan. "Nice to see you too," he says with a smirk.

"Sorry, I just thought you were someone else."

"Thought I was the big football star you're sleeping with, did you?"

"Shh," I say and whack him. "Mom is in the kitchen." I frown and take in his just crawled out of bed look, messy hair, sleepy eyes, unshaven face. He does have a Ryan Reynolds vibe about him. "Wait, why are you here so early? I thought we weren't going shopping until this afternoon."

"We're not, but isn't today your baking day?"

"Yeah."

"Then it's my eating day." I laugh and shake my head. "I could smell the apple pie from my house," he says and inhales deeply. "Woke me up."

"You're crazy. Come on."

"Wait, what's wrong?" he asks, capturing my hand to pull me back.

God, I wish he couldn't read me so well, but we've been buddies since kindergarten, so I'm not surprised. "I just... haven't heard a word from Christian." I take a deep breath. "Don't," I say. It's too early for one of his lectures. He doesn't trust Christian or any of the kids from Sweetwater High, and with good reason after what they did to me. Christian has changed, though. I'm sure of it.

"All I'm going to say is it's Christmas, and he's probably busy with his country club or something. I heard something about Chelsea having a party."

I stiffen. "Was it last night?" Did he go to a party at the country club, with Chelsea, and not tell me? *Purposely* not tell me? I work to push down the unease.

"I really don't know. I was shooting pool at the pub. Dylan knows Chelsea from Princeton, and he ran into her and she mentioned something about a party, but I don't think the country club is his scene."

I try to play it off. "I'm sure he wants to catch up with all his friends." Ryan eyes me for a moment longer, and I try not to fidget.

"I'm sure it's nothing," he says, and I relax a bit.

"Hey Mrs. Malone," Ryan says, and moves past me into the kitchen, like he knows I might just need a minute alone.

"Oh, Ryan, stop calling me that. You're not a boy anymore, and you can call me Barb." As the two talk in the kitchen, I take a couple deep breaths to pull myself together. I walk back into the kitchen, and while it's pretty early, and he's likely still sleeping, I shoot off another text.

Hey Christian. Hitting up The Daily Grind, and going to do some shopping with Kaitlyn and Ryan. Catch up later?

I stand there for a second, and feel the burn of Ryan's eyes as I wait for a response. Three dots appear and my heart picks up tempo.

Busy, can't.

I stare at the two words, the air leaving my lungs like I'd just been sucker punched, and wait to see if he's going to come back with a reason, or something...anything. This response doesn't seem like something Christian would send. My mind goes back to the night he made love to me in my childhood bed. Yes, made love. No matter what he says or calls it, that's exactly what we did, and now this. Two simple words blowing me off.

"If you'll excuse me, I have to run to the bathroom."

I dart down the hall with my phone and even though Kaitlyn is likely still asleep, I call her anyway. She picks up on the third ring, sounding groggy.

"Did I wake you?" I ask.

"No, actually. I'm in the bathroom on the floor."

"Did you drink too much last night?" Kaitlyn isn't much of a drinker. It interferes with her sleep and training.

"I had one drink with my brother. I should not be this sick. Ugh."

"Sorry. We can cancel plans for shopping."

"No, I want to go. I'm sure this will pass. Wait, why are you calling so early?"

I take a deep breath and let it out slowly. "Christian."

"What did he do?" she says, her voice a bit stronger.

"I don't know...I just got this strange response from him." I tell her what happened and she goes quiet for a second. "It's weird right. That doesn't sound like him."

"I don't know, Maize. You know him better than I do, and maybe now that he's home, he's back to the guy he used to be. I don't know if that's true. I just don't know what to say." She goes quiet for a second, and I blink the stupid tears pressing against my eyes. "Why don't you text back?"

I shake my head, even though she can't see me. "No, I don't want to do that. Maybe I'll just give it some time. He might be crazy busy or something." My mind goes to the party at the country club, and unease rakes across my skin.

"Okay if that's what you think is best." I hear the toilet flush. "I'm going to go lay down for a bit."

"We don't have to go if you're not up to it."

"I'll text you later."

We hang up and I splash some cold water onto my face, and try to pull off casual as I walk back into the kitchen to find Ryan taking a tray of cookies from the oven. "These smell amazing," he says and I'm glad he's acting like his normal self in front of Mom.

"Were you talking to someone in there?" Mom asks.

"Yeah, Kaitlyn. She's not feeling great so she might not be joining us for shopping."

"What's wrong with her?" Ryan asks. "I was texting with her last night and she seemed fine."

"Sounds like the flu. It must have come on quickly." I glance around as Ryan takes a hot cookie from the tray and yelps because it burns him. "Do you not have any patience?" I ask and turn the cold water on for him. He puts his hand under the tap as he shoves the cookie into his mouth and then dances around because the burn stings, and he has a hot cookie in his mouth.

"It's hard to have sympathy," I say, and he laughs around a mouthful of cookie. Mom just shakes her head, and it's clear to see that she's so happy her kitchen is full of fun and laughter today. We spend the next few hours baking and chat-ting about Harvard and Stanford, where Ryan is attending, also on a full ride. He's a whiz on computers, and has a lead on a startup that wants him. Headhunters from some of the other big tech companies want him, but he's all about the startups.

The morning passes quickly and I honestly don't even want to know how many times I checked my phone. If I had to ballpark it, I'd say around a hundred. When it finally pings, I jump a little higher than I did when Ryan came to the door. I snatch it up quickly.

"It's Kaitlyn," I say injecting a measure of enthusiasm into my voice. While I'm happy to hear from her, I was really hoping it was Christian. "She's feeling much better and said she's good to meet for coffee and shopping."

"Where are you going for coffee?" Mom asks.

"The Daily Grind. It's her favorite."

"I hate that place," Ryan says. "Who charges one hundred dollars for a latte anyway?"

I laugh. "It's not a hundred dollars." He's right though, it's a coffee shop for the rich and famous, but Kaitlyn swears they make the best lattes on the planet and she treats herself to one every Christmas. With the meager amount of money in my account, I'm just going to get a regular drip.

"I'll take the last of the cookies out," Mom says. "You two go have some fun, you look like you could use it."

I give Mom a kiss on the cheek, run to my room to change my clothes, and tie my hair back. I'm not planning on seeing anyone other than Ryan and Kaitlyn, so no need to do hair or makeup. With my purse over my shoulder, I meet Ryan back in the kitchen, and we start down the sidewalk to his car.

"Are you changing?" I ask.

He grins. "No, the girls dig the just crawled out of bed look."

"Getting lots of play, are you?"

He laughs. "Getting enough." We reach his house, and jump into his car. It's an old beater he's had since high school. He's worked numerous jobs to keep it going, and I think he doesn't have the heart to part with it now.

We drive through the busy streets, everyone's out doing their last-minute shopping, and we circle the block forever before we can get a parking spot. The coffee shop is packed, but I spot Kaitlyn sitting at a table. She waves us over. I take her in and frown. Something's not right.

"You feeling okay?"

"Much better. I must have eaten something that didn't agree with me. I ordered for us all. On me. Merry Christmas."

I laugh as I sit across from her, and Ryan drops down beside her. We agreed a long time ago not to exchange gifts, but I let this one go. I still have to get Mom something. She had her eye on a pair of earrings, and I plan to get them for her. I'll put them on my credit card, and plan to get a part time job when I return to Kingston.

Kaitlyn's name is called, and she stands and comes back with three lattes. I take a sip and moan. "My God, that is good."

"Merry Christmas to me," Kaitlyn says, and takes a big drink. We laugh, but mine dies an abrupt death when someone calls out my name.

"Maize, I thought that was you."

I lift my head to see none other than Chelsea Haverstock coming our way. She turns to Kaitlyn, who snarls at her.

"Kaitlyn, so good to see you," Chelsea purrs. She blinks and glances at Ryan, who's changed so much over the years. Not that she knew him back in high school. He didn't go to Sweetwater. "You, I don't know," she says, her big fancy purse falling on her arm as she touches his shoulder.

"Ryan, meet Chelsea. Chelsea, meet Ryan."

"So nice to meet you," she says in a disgustingly flirty way as she sizes Ryan up. "Ooh, if I didn't have a boyfriend." She laughs as her friends join her. We all exchange pleasantries and I go back to my latte, hoping she'll get the hint and leave. "How funny running into you all here. I didn't think you came to this coffee shop." She stifles a yawn. "They better hurry up with my espresso. I need the caffeine after last night."

Don't ask.

Don't take the bait.

"What happened last night?" I ask and Ryan just shakes his head at me, but there's a part of me that wants to know if she had a party, and if Christian was there.

"Oh, it was Christian's annual Christmas party." She blinks at me. "You remember Christian Moore, don't you?"

I gulp and can physically feel the blood draining from my face. Before I can say anything, Ryan's hand goes to my knee and he gives it a squeeze. Chelsea continues with, "Let me tell you that boy does have *more*." She winks. "If you know what I mean." The two girls she's with are on their phones, completely ignoring us.

"You...you were at a party at Christian's?" I ask, shocked that my voice even works.

"Maize," Kaitlyn says, and I hold up my hand to stop her. I want...no need...to hear what Chelsea has to say. Her phone pings in her designer purse.

"That's probably him now." She chuckles. "I'm surprised he's up, though. We had a very late night." She fumbles with her phone, and then it slips from her hands and lands on our table. "I'm such a klutz when I'm tired."

My gaze goes to the phone, to the picture she has as her screensaver. What the hell. I lean forward, narrow my eyes, glance at the two people in bed. The picture is dark, a bit hard to make out, but behind the bed, I spot a shelf full of trophies. This is definitely Christian's room. I've looked at the pictures he sent a million times, so I'd know his room in an instant. I lean forward to get a better look at her phone, and study the couple entwined in the bed...My heart stops beating. "Is that..."

"Oops, that's private." She snatches her phone up.

I slowly lift my head and blink at her, as Ryan stands. "I'm going to kill him."

"Ryan, please don't." I grab his arm and tug until he's sitting. The last thing I want is for him and Christian to fight. This is my battle, not his.

Chelsea blinks dark lashes over big eyes as she gazes at Ryan like she has no idea what he's talking about. I must be wrong. I have to be wrong. I mean, lots of guys have shelves with trophies behind their beds, right?

You're not wrong, Maize...

"Is that..." God, I can't even bring myself to ask if it's her and Christian.

"Yeah, Christian and I hooked up last night at his Christmas party. We're an item now."

"Christian had a Christmas party," I mumble to myself.

Christian had a party at his house, and didn't invite me.

As that thought bounces around my brain, Chelsea's fingers fly over her phone as she shoots off a text—to who, I don't know. Maybe it's Christian. Her eyes move back to mine, and she laughs lightly. "Why do you seem so surprised? I don't think he ever got over me when I broke it off before college." She hugs her phone to her chest. "It was only a matter of time before we found each other again, and with my degree in literature, I won't be tied to a desk or one place. I can write anywhere, which means I'll be able to go on the road with him. God, we are so perfect for one another, don't you think?"

With the world closing in on me, my mind goes over everything, from our time in the closet in high school, to when he came to my bedroom the other night telling me he needed to be seen with the right kind of people. Blood drains to my toes as I consider the two word answer he gave me this morning, and I can't forget how we always went out of town for meals, and he hid me behind his big body every time we ran into someone at Wolf House. Is he embarrassed by me? My God, he must be. How could I have been so wrong about him? Was I nothing more than an easy lay, a girl from the wrong side of the tracks to have a little fun with, finish what he started back in that closet?

Was I nothing to him? Was he simply slumming?

As all sets of eyes stare at me, a couple with worry, a few with venom, I turn to Chelsea and spit out, "Yeah, you're perfect for each other."

25

CHRISTIAN

"Are you fucking serious?" With my nerves on edge, I pace back and forth in my bedroom, my phone in my hand. I keep glancing at it, but have yet to receive a response from Maize, which is making me a little—or a lot—insane. This isn't like her, and that has my brain running in a million different directions, none of them good.

"Yeah, okay, I get it." Linc leans forward and braces his elbows on his knees. "I'm a dick."

"Dude."

His head lifts, and I take in the dark circles around his eyes. My heart pinches, because I know he's hurting. Steph did a number on him and I don't want to beat him up over this, not when he's so down.

"I know...I slept with Chelsea, and I'm one hundred percent sure she thought I was you." He groans and I shake my head. I can't believe the giggling I heard last night was Chelsea, in bed with my best friend. I went with the theory that Linc had some girl on speakerphone, or that he was watching porn on his phone. I had no idea there was an actual girl in my room. What the hell was she thinking? Oh, probably that by sleeping with her again, I'd remember how good we were together, and ask her to marry me? But we weren't good together. Ever. Not like Maize and I are. Fuck, why isn't she answering me?

"I went with it anyway." He rubs at his sleepy eyes. "Hey, I did say I'd run interference, didn't I?" He grins, but it looks more like a cringe. "That's really taking one for the team."

"She must have known it was you come morning, right?" I ask and pace to my window to look out, check to make sure her car isn't on the street and she's still lurking somewhere in this house. My search comes up empty. "I can't have her thinking it was me."

"Yeah, she left quickly. Probably got one look at this hand-some face," he says and scrubs his chin. "And bolted after she realized she wasn't in bed with you."

"You sure?" Nervousness swells inside me.

"Yeah, I'm sure." He reaches for his phone. "Christ, I can ask her if you want."

I give a hard shake of my head as Linc looks at me through one eye, like it's too painful to open both with a hangover. "Let's just let it be. If she comes around, we'll talk about it." I check my phone again. Why the hell isn't Maize responding? She better not be out with that Ryan Reynolds lookalike. I take a couple fast breaths to calm myself down. I really didn't like the way he touched her the day I dropped her off. It makes me wonder if he's been in love with the girl next door all this time. "I thought she went home last night."

He pokes the mattress. "Nope, she was in this bed waiting to play hide the sausage." He shrugs. "There's a chance she knew it was me from the beginning, though. Maybe she heard you tell me to grab a room, and snuck up here first."

"Yeah, maybe."

He pinches the bridge of his nose. "I need coffee. Lots of it."

"Okay, come on." Since we're the same size, and I doubt he wants to climb back into his formal wear, I go to my closet and grab him a pair of jeans and a T-shirt.

He dresses and we head down to the kitchen and I find Dad sitting there reading the paper. He sets it down as we enter. "Good morning, son, Linc. Did you boys have a nice time last night?"

"Yeah, great night," I say. "How about you?"

"I always enjoy our annual Christmas party." He eyes Linc, and chuckles. "I think perhaps someone enjoyed it a bit too much."

"It's the tequila, it'll get you every time," Linc says with a laugh.

Dad takes a drink of coffee, and I notice the half empty cup in front of Mom's chair. I'm about to ask where she is, when she comes back into the room, her cell phone in her hand.

"Christian, I think it's a good time we had a talk, don't you?"

I stare at my mother and try to figure out what she's getting at but I'm so preoccupied, my mind on Maize's radio silence, on Linc sleeping in my bed with Chelsea, I can't comprehend her words. I arch a brow, and pour two mugs of coffee handing one to Linc, who looks like death as he drops down into one of the spare seats.

I toss a cube of sugar into my cup, and look at Mom. "What are you talking about?"

"This girl you mentioned last night." She gives me a big smile. "Tell me, who are her parents, and what do they do for a living."

"You don't know them, and why does it matter what they do for a living?" It's a stupid question, one I already know the answer to. Mom has always been a social climber, and I'm expected to be with someone from our circle.

She arches a curious brow, and lifts the basket of muffins from the middle of the table and holds it out to Linc. Linc takes one and casts me a glance. Worry dances in his eyes. Yeah, he knows what my mother is like and that she won't be happy when she finds out I'm with someone like Maize, someone without the right pedigree. Although, am I really with her? She's not even answering my text. Another wave of anxiety races through my blood.

A horrible thought hits me like a sucker punch. Now that she's had her interview with Dean Saunders, and has his stamp of approval, and that he's even going to see about internships for her, maybe she doesn't need to hang out with me anymore. I quickly strike that thought. She is not that girl. I might have run across plenty of them in life, but she's not like that. She's honest and caring, and...and why isn't she answering me?

"You don't know her, Mom. She goes to Kingston."

"Oh, a Kingston college girl." She claps her hands. "Where is she from?"

Dad ruffles his papers, obviously annoyed with my mother's prying. "What we should be asking is if he's qualified for a job if he gets injured in the NFL."

And just like that, I'm pissed off. Nothing will ever be good enough for him, not even football. If I had followed in his footsteps, maybe I'd be worthy of his attention. Getting into the NFL is hard fucking work, but I'm not going to rehash that old argument with them again. Sometimes I wonder if the fact that I chose sports over law is why he dislikes me and my choices. Maybe he simply never wanted me.

"Yes, I'm qualified for work," I say through clenched teeth.

My mother pinches her lips tight, and I grab her mug and refill it with coffee—she looks like she needs it. She drops sugar into it, and Linc blinks in agony as the spoon clinks against the side of the mug.

"I'd just like to know more about the girl my son is interested in," Mom says, clearly annoyed. "By the way, Christian. Evelyn Jackson called this morning and she said Katherine was quite smitten with you."

"Katherine and I are friends." I take a sip of coffee. "Nothing more."

Mom takes a bite of muffin and goes quiet as she chews. She finishes and says, "Yes, well, maybe you shouldn't have led her on, then. You were spending an awful lot of time with her."

Jesus, I can't catch a break here.

"I wasn't leading her on. We were talking."

Linc checks his watch. "Christian, we have to bounce. We have that thing."

"You have a thing?" Mom asks and wipes the corners of her mouth with her cloth napkin.

"At the country club," Linc says, and Mom's eyes widen.

"I didn't hear of any event at the country club."

"It's like a reunion thing, for Sweetwater kids. Nothing big." As Linc struggles, I just shake my head. He's trying to save me, but like me, he's not very good at lying.

"Oh, have fun then." We both stand and Mom frowns at our clothes. "Wait, you're not going dressed like that, are you?"

I glance at my jeans and T-shirt, a complete contrast to what I was wearing last night. I'm much more comfortable this way.

"It's just casual," I say with a shrug and before she can ask any more questions, Linc and I hurry out of the room. When we reach the front door, I fish my keys from my pocket and grin at him.

"A thing?" I slap him on the back. "Good one, bud."

"Give me a break. My fucking head is throbbing, and my brain isn't firing properly." His gaze drops as I check my phone again.

"Still nothing, huh?"

I shove my phone into my pocket. "Nothing."

"Want to pay her a visit? Make sure she's okay?"

I shrug. "I don't know. I don't want to just show up. She didn't want me to meet her mother, and what if I show up at her door and she's done with me?"

"Why would she be done with you, Christian? Did she do or say anything to make you think it was over?" I stare at him for a second, and his shoulders fall, no doubt thinking what I'm thinking, but don't want to put into words. Steph gave Linc no indication there was trouble in their relationship. He gives a heavy sigh. "Never mind."

I shade the sun from my eyes and glance around. "Maybe we can do a drive-by. Just to make sure nothing is out of the ordinary. Maybe there was an accident or something."

"Good plan."

We head to my Jeep and both jump in. I drive through the streets, go past the mall and the quaint coffee shops, and keep my eye out for her. Maybe she's doing some last-minute shopping. My search comes up empty and I head to the other side of town, and slow when we reach Maize's place. The curtains are all drawn, preventing me from seeing inside. I don't know if that's their normal or not, since she wouldn't let me drop her off at her place, and I've only ever been here at night, to sneak into her room.

I stop the car, and stare, and that's when I see her friend Ryan exiting his house. He turns my way, glares, and starts coming toward me, his pace fast, determined. As he gets closer, I note the tightness in his jaw, the way his hands are clenched and I instantly know something isn't right.

"What the fuck is his problem?" Linc asks.

"I don't know." I unbuckle and get out of the car, and Ryan keeps on coming until he's right up in my face.

His eyes are hard, unwavering when he asks, "What the fuck are you doing here, douchebag?"

Alrighty then. This guy clearly doesn't like me, and that's okay, I don't like him much either.

"It's none of your fucking business."

Linc gets out of the car, but Ryan doesn't take his eyes off me.

"You good, Christian?"

"I'm good."

Ryan laughs. "Like fuck you're good, and it is my business. Maize is one of my best friends, and she deserves better than you. I knew you were a dick back in high school, and once a dick, always a dick. Why don't you get back in your fancy Jeep and drive back to wherever the fuck you came from."

I have no idea what's up his ass, and at the moment I don't care. I just want to talk to Maize. I take a deep breath to keep my shit together, turn toward the house in time to see a curtain flutter.

"Is she inside?"

"She doesn't want to see you."

I glare at him. "You don't fucking know that."

He snorts. "Ask her."

I push past him and head toward the house, but the second I reach her steps, my phone pings, and I read the message from Maize.

Please go.

. . .

I stand there for a long time, just staring at my phone. It's crazy how two simple words have the ability to wrap around my heart and tear it clear from my chest. But this can't be right. It just can't be. We had a good thing. A great thing.

The best thing.

I have no idea how many minutes pass as I stand there on rubbery legs, my brain racing, but the next thing I know, a hand lands on my shoulder. I flinch, ready to turn and punch Ryan square in the face, when I find Linc standing there, the solemn look on his face hitting me over the head with a reality stick.

"Christian we need to go."

I turn, and the world blurs around me as Linc hops into the driver's seat. Walking on numb legs while Ryan continues to curse me out, I slide into the passenger seat, my lungs so tight, it's hard to breathe.

Ryan walks toward Maize's front door, and I reach for the handle, the sight filling me with blind rage. Linc grabs my arm to stop me.

"Don't make this worse," he says, and a good five seconds pass before I let the handle go, and nod.

"Get me out of here."

Linc backs out of the driveway, and heads toward home. "Where to?"

"Fuck," I swear and rake my hands through my hair. I grab my phone again and stare at her message. "I have no idea what's going on."

"Believe me, I know exactly how you feel."

I rub at the back of my neck, a headache brewing. "Yeah, I know, and I'm sorry you do."

He scoffs. "What a team we make. Want to hit up the bar, get shit-faced?"

"I can't think of anything else I'd rather do."

"Maybe a hot girl will help you get your mind off Maize."

"Did it work for you?"

He casts me a fast glance. "Only temporarily, but maybe that's what you need."

"Yeah…maybe."

26

MAIZE

With the late morning sun shining down on me, I wave goodbye to Mom as she stands at the door, with the promise that I'll be back right after spring finals. It's hard to leave, considering I haven't been home for long, but it's necessary. I slide into the passenger seat and glance at Kaitlyn. Her eyes are a bit heavy, dark smudges beneath them, and she's still rather pale.

"You don't have to come back with me."

She holds a finger up. "One, you're my best friend and I'm not letting you take a bus, so yeah, I do." A second finger joins the first. "Two, if he's there, I don't want you fucking facing him alone." A third finger joins the mix. "And three, I am done with all the food and family, and a million questions about my life. I just want to crawl into my own bed and sleep for two days."

I buckle up as she tightens her ponytail. "Are you sure you shouldn't go to the doctor?"

"I will, when we get back to campus. If I go here, Mom will freak out and make me take six million vitamins."

I laugh at that, even though inside I'm dead. My mind drifts to Christian, to the way he took care of me when I was down and out. He didn't fill me with vitamins, but he did make sure I had plenty to eat, took me to my appointments and paid my bills and expenses, which I plan to pay back, every last cent. With everything he's done for me, I honestly wouldn't have believed a word Chelsea said if I hadn't seen the two of them in his bed with my own eyes.

Stop. Stop. Stop.

I've cried enough, and I refuse to shed one more tear for a guy who could do that to me. I'm not sure why he bothered to come to my house Christmas eve. Maybe it was for one last 'other side of the tracks hook-up' before he announced he was with Chelsea. Anyway, none of that matters anymore, and there was no salvaging Christmas at that point.

I tried. I really did. But it was a struggle to put on a happy face Christmas morning in front of my Mom, and when I broke the news I was leaving today, she accepted it without question. She's smart enough to realize something is going on with me, and I appreciate her not pressing for information. But I wanted to get back early, before Christian, so I can clear the last of my things from his place and leave the key behind. I sit back and listen to the radio, and Kaitlyn casts me a glance.

"I'm here if you want to talk." Her voice is low, soft, concerned.

"I know. I think I would just rather forget." I pucker my lips. "I want to concentrate on school, and Harvard, and I'll need to find a part-time job when we get back."

"Okay, think about those things then." She turns the radio up, and we hit the highway. I let my eyes fall shut, but every time I do, all I can see are images of Christian.

Christian coming to the rescue after he injured me.

Christian carrying me up and down the stairs.

Christian touching me in the most amazing ways.

Christian sleeping with Chelsea.

A groan crawls out of my throat, and when I sense Kaitlyn checking in on me, I open my eyes, and turn my head to stare out the passenger side window. I focus on the trees and signs, anything to keep my thoughts from returning to him.

Kaitlyn makes a retching sound and I turn to her as she puts her mouth to the crook of her elbow. I sit up a little straighter, take in her paleness.

"Maybe I should drive," I say. I'm sad, but I'm not physically ill like her.

She takes a couple of breaths and shakes her head. "It'll pass. It always does. My God, I don't know what kind of bug I picked up. If I ate something bad, you'd think it would have been out of my system by now."

"Sometimes people get sick on vacation. The body needs to shut down and reboot. You've been working really hard, and competing non-stop. Maybe that's what's going on."

"Maybe, and it is true. I have been pushing myself."

"Either that or you're pregnant," I joke, but as soon as the words leave my mouth, her eyes pop open, and my pulse jumps.

"Ohmigod." She swallows hard. "You don't think I'm pregnant, do you?"

"I...I don't know. I was only joking. Is there a chance?"

Her eyes narrow, like she's doing mental math on the last date of her period and the longer she stares at the road without speaking, the more worried I become.

Her eyes are full of worry as she glances at me. "I might be a little late, but I always use a condom. I could be late because I'm sick, right?"

"Condoms aren't one hundred percent," I tell her. That's the reason I went on the pill. I was using two forms of contraception in the beginning with Christian, but once I got to know him better, came to trust him, we only used the pill. My heart stalls. God, I hope he didn't give me any STD's. I don't think he was with anyone when we were together, but now I'm questioning everything. Where did he sneak off to every Sunday?

"I'm on the pill, too, Maize." She frowns. "But last month...I was studying and running, and missed taking a couple on time." She grips the steering wheel tighter. "We'd better pick up a pregnancy test," she says.

I put my hand on her arm. "It'll be okay. No matter what, it'll be okay."

She nods, but she doesn't look like she agrees with me. She drives a little faster, passing vehicles in her hurry to get back to Kingston.

When we finally reach town limits, she pulls into the nearest pharmacy and I wait in the car until she comes back out with a little white bag. I notice her hands are a bit shaky as she sets it beside her on the seat. We drive by Wolf House, which we have to pass on the way to our place. We both stare out the window and check the parking lot.

She slows the car and glances at me. "It doesn't look like he's here. Let's get your stuff and get out."

"We don't have to go there first." I glance at the bag. "I know you want to..."

"I want to get this done, and not take a chance on him returning." She eases into the big parking lot, only one other vehicle in it and snatches up the bag. "Besides, while you pack up, I can use his bathroom and pee on this stick. Two birds and all."

"Okay," I say, and we go up the front steps. My stupid mind takes a fast trip down memory lane. Recalling all the times we went in the back way, and now I'm questioning everything. Was it because there were fewer steps, or was he just embarrassed to be seen with me? He's a private guy and doesn't like his business broadcasted, but still... If he loved me, really wanted to be with me, he'd want to tell the world, wouldn't he?

We step inside and the place is empty. "Come on, let's get this over with." We go straight to his room, and his scent washes over me as we enter. A little gasp catches in my throat.

"You okay?" Kaitlyn asks. I squeeze my eyes shut to keep the tears restrained. "Maybe I should have done this for you."

I breathe deep through my nose. "No, I'm okay." I point. "The bathroom is right there, and I'll be right here waiting for you. No matter what, I'll be here for you, Kaitlyn."

"Okay." She walks to the bathroom and the door clicks shut. I glance at the clock as I hurry around and gather up the last of my things. All the while trying not to think about the lump in my throat, or the way my insides feel like they've been raked raw.

I count the minutes as I stuff everything into a bag, and sit on the bed, to stare at the closed bathroom door. She's been in there at least four minutes, and the longer that door remains closed, the more I'm convinced she's pregnant.

A little shriek reaches my ears and I jump from the bed. "Kaitlyn," I say and walk to the door. It opens and relief washes through me when I see the smile on her face.

She holds the stick out. "Not pregnant."

My body goes weak after the big adrenaline dump, and I pull her into my arms. "No more taking your pills late and if you want, you can have mine. I won't be needing them anymore."

She pulls back and brushes my hair from my face. "Don't let Christian ruin anything for you. You deserve someone nice."

I nod. She's right. I do, but how can I give my heart to another when it's in so many fragmented pieces.

I hear a bang down the hall and my pulse jumps. "Let's get out of here."

"Let me just clean up my stuff." I follow her into the bathroom to pick up my toiletries, as she stuffs the stick and packaging material into the box. Once done, we leave his room, and as I shut his door, emotions crash over me like a turbulent wave, until I feel like I'm drowning. This is it. The very last I'll ever see Christian's room.

Why on earth did I let myself fall in love?

27

CHRISTIAN

The rain falls heavy as I drive across campus, and the dark and dreary day is a fitting match for my mood. It's the thirtieth of December, and I'm back early because we have practice tonight to prepare for next week's game. I couldn't wait to escape home. Watching Mom and Dad put on a show while they constantly bickered when they thought I wasn't within hearing vicinity—I always was—was enough to send me packing, and if I heard one more word about me finding myself a nice girl...

I don't get it. Why don't they just get a damn divorce? If they're staying together for my sake, if they've been doing that for years, they should probably know that staying in an unhealthy relationship does far more damage to the kid. Not that I'm a kid anymore, but my views on love and relationships were heavily influenced by what I heard and saw.

Were?

I guess those views changed after Maize, but what does that matter now? I need to put her out of my mind and focus on tonight's practice. I'm not in the mood for football. No, I haven't been in the mood for anything since Maize kicked me out of her life, with no explanation. The least she could have done was to let me know why. Steph had the decency to tell Linc she was interested in someone else and while it hurt him, he wasn't left hanging. I glance at the empty passenger seat and my fucking heart pinches tight as I hit the steering wheel. She should be beside me.

I park at Wolf House and sit there for a few seconds. I stare at my window, the curtains shut. To think I was going to have venetian blinds put on for Maize after she told me that funny story about her idea of wealth. I wanted her to have everything she's ever wanted. I guess in the end, I wasn't what she always wanted.

My phone pings and my heart jumps. I snatch it from the seat, and disappointment grips me when a text from Chelsea pops up. Fuck, I'm not sure why she won't take no for an answer. She was pretty adamant that we were going to be a couple before we both went off to our respective colleges. What she did to Maize and me in high school is unforgivable, but I guess a part of me feels sorry for her, knows the pressure she's under. I'm getting it from my folks too, but latching onto me out of fear... that's not good for either one of us.

I force myself to get out of the car, grab my bag from the back and trek slowly through the lot and up the stairs. I don't care if I get wet. I don't care about much these days, apparently. I reach my room, push open the door, and the first thing I'm hit with is Maize's lack of presence. The place looks the same as it did before she moved in, but it now feels a little colder, and a whole lot lonelier. Maybe I should go find her, demand answers. Linc heard through gossip that Maize and Kaitlyn had left home on the 26th, and came back here. No doubt she wanted to clear her things out without the risk of running into me.

I drop my bag, grab a bottle of water from my small fridge and take a big drink. If I didn't have practice tonight, I'd go for something stronger. A knock sounds on my door and I turn to find Thor standing there.

"How was your holidays?" he says, and stretches his hands over his head like he just crawled out of bed. His religion doesn't celebrate Christmas, so he stayed here over the break. His brother was flying in to spend time with him.

I put on my best face. "Good. Did you have a good visit with your brother?" He nods and steps into the room. From the tightness in his muscles to the clenching of his jaw, I can tell he has something on his mind. I turn to him, face him square on. "What's up?"

"I was here when she came back," he says and drops down into the small kitchen chair, the same one Maize sat in when she surprised me with eggs benny. Another day that cemented my love for her.

"Yeah." I try to show disinterest but really, I want to know all the details. "When was that?" Did that come out like I'm just making conversation and don't really care?

"The 26th, actually." I nod and take another sip of my water. "She packed all her things and bolted." A long pause. "Are you okay?"

"Yeah, I'm good, Thor." I stretch my arm out and fake a throw. "Looking forward to getting on the field."

"Afterward the beer is on me, okay?"

I smile, because I have a good tribe of guys who have my back. "Thanks, man." I eye my bed, hoping to get a bit of rest before practice tonight. I haven't been sleeping so well.

"Catch up with you later," he says and disappears, understanding I need some time alone, where I'll be lonely. I close the door behind him and set the lock. With zero energy, I walk over to my bed and flop down on it, but the enticing scent of her skin is all over my sheets. I pull her pillow over my face and breathe her sweet aroma into my lungs.

Fuck me.

With a bevy of emotions coursing through me, anger, sadness, love and need, I stand and tear the sheets off the mattress, dropping them on the floor before making a quick trip to the bathroom. The sight of the big tub instantly brings back happy memories of Maize, and I grip the edge of the sink, and hang my head to stare at the floor as I will those memories to go away.

Get it together, dude.

I have a fucking career to think about and grades to keep up. I can't be wallowing in self-pity like this. Something on the floor catches my attention, and I pick it up. It's a small square pamphlet. I open it up, and see that it's in Spanish. Good thing I remember some of it from high school classes. I drop down on the edge of the tub, and read through it, but I stumble over many of the words, so I head to the other room, grab my laptop and start a translation. Five minutes later I'm sitting at the table with my heart in my throat, and my stomach in one hell of a tight knot.

I grip my hair and tug, my eyes practically bulging out of my head as the tumblers fall into place. "Holy fuck," I say much too loudly.

Someone raps on my door, and my head lifts. I stare at it, unable to think, or speak. The rap comes again. A fast rhythm that matches my heart. The knob turns, whoever is out there impatient to get in.

"Are you okay?" Linc asks through the closed door.

I stand on shaky legs, unlock it with trembling fingers, and he takes one look at me and curses. "Jesus Christ, what's wrong?" I back up, stumble a bit, and drop back into the chair. "Talk to me, brother." Unable to find the words, I slide the small sheet of paper across the table. "What is this?"

"Read it," I push those two words past a dry throat, and jump to my feet, needing to move, do something to keep up with my racing thoughts.

He reads it once, then twice. His Spanish always was better than mine. His head slowly lifts, and I go still, meet eyes that are filled with worry, and confusion.

"Yeah, pregnant," I say.

He holds the paper up, and questions me. "How do you know this is hers?" I walk over to the counter, and show him her key. "She left this. She was here. I'm pretty sure no other girl would be in my bathroom taking a pregnancy test."

He frowns and goes quiet. I give him time to think. Hell, I need time too. He finally breaks the quiet with, "Didn't you guys use protection?"

"Of course, we did," I shoot back, and when he stiffens, I shake my head. "Sorry, man. I just...I'm fucked."

"You're not fucked. You don't know what the results were. We can't jump to conclusions just yet."

I throw myself onto my bed, and put my arm over my eyes as I think things through. "We stopped using a condom because she said she was on the pill."

"Okay, the pill is pretty safe. So maybe this is nothing."

"Not safe enough if she had to take a test." My mind screeches to a halt, and bile punches into my throat. "Fuck, you don't think..." I don't need to finish the sentence for Linc to know where my thoughts have gone. He knows everything about me, just like I know everything about him.

"I don't know what to think, but why would she tell you she was on the pill if she wasn't?"

I give a humorless laugh, and stare at the ceiling, shock preventing me from moving. "To trap me." Everything my grandmother told me about my parents' relationship seeps into my thoughts, and brings on my worst nightmare. I swore I never wanted a family, children. Never wanted to find myself in a situation like my parents.

I can hear Linc's throat work as he swallows. "Just because your mom..."

"Then why would she lie about being on the pill?"

"Maybe she's not lying. Not every girl is like your mother. Maybe she really is on the pill, and was late or something."

I think about the kind of girl Maize is. Sweet, innocent, a hard worker, always open and honest with me. She didn't even want me to introduce her to Dean Saunders. She wanted to get into Harvard on her own merits and I was the one who pushed for the meeting. Does that really sound like a girl out to trap a guy, for his money and influence?

"I told her I didn't want kids, that I didn't want to end up in a relationship like my parents."

"Maybe that's why she ran."

I rub the back of my tight neck. "What do you mean?"

He shrugs. "Maybe she's scared and running because you don't want kids, and she was afraid you'd think she was trying to trap you."

"That would mean she is pregnant." I consider that for a moment. She told me she never wanted to bring a child into the world either. I believed her. But things changed, we've changed, and I want different things now. Is Maize Malone the type of girl to trap me? She's ambitious, has her mind set on a law degree. Would she really get pregnant on purpose and blow that all off? I think about that long and hard, and come to one logical conclusion.

No, she wouldn't.

"But why did she break up with me before Christmas, before she took this test and knew the results?"

"That I can't answer."

I take a breath to slow my racing mind, and the second I do, the second I realize there could be more at play here, I stare at Linc, the world going a little fuzzy around the edges.

"What?" he asks.

"You had my phone. In my bedroom. Chelsea..."

"Fuck, Chelsea. Do you think she could have texted something to Maize?"

I shake my head. "She's always had it out for her. Fuck wait, maybe she sent her pictures of you guys in my bed."

"I wouldn't put anything past her, and I was drunk, Christian. She could have been taking pictures of the two of us, and I wouldn't remember."

The thoughts of Maize seeing pictures of Chelsea and Linc in bed—in my room—thinking it was Chelsea and me, turns the cup of coffee I drank earlier around and around in my stomach. "It's the only thing that makes sense." Maize isn't the kind of girl to use me for anything. Even though insecurities from past experiences crept into my brain, my heart always knew she'd never do anything hurtful, which is why this was so confusing and painful.

"Oh, this is bad." I tug on my hair. "So fucking bad." I glance at Linc, who is staring at me, like he's waiting for me to figure out how to fix this. "I need to talk to her."

"Yeah, I know, but..." He shakes his head, worry all over his face. "She made it pretty clear she didn't want to talk to you."

I can't let that stop me. Not now. Not with what I know. A plan forms and expands in my brain, and as my insides settle slightly. "I have an idea."

28

MAIZE

"Okay, get up. I'm sick of you moping around here like a sloth."

"A sloth? Sloths mope?"

"Well I don't know what mopes. I'll do a search and come up with a better simile later. Right now, I want you to put on some damn pants, brush your hair and maybe a little lipstick wouldn't kill you. Maybe some blush too. You look like death."

"Why thank you. I love you too, but I'm not going anywhere. I'm reading." I flip the page of my book. I've stared at the last page for so long, and I've yet to digest its words.

"Oh no you don't." She grabs the book and shoves it down the back of her pants.

"Give me that...wait, never mind. That is just nasty."

"Get dressed, or I'll do this with all your books, your computer and your e-reader."

"Wow, I remember when you were my nice best friend."

"I'm still your best friend, which is why you're going to do everything I tell you to do." I push up and adjust my pillow.

"What's going on, Kaitlyn?"

"Well," she says, "This is kind of about me. I'm sorry. I know you're going through a hard time, and I haven't wanted to make anything about me, but I need you."

My stomach drops. "I've been such a terrible friend. I'm so sorry."

"No, that's not true at all." She leans in and gives me a hug.

"Tell me what you need."

"There's a new band at the Growler tonight. The lead singer is soooo hot. I really want to go."

I bite my lip, and consider Christian's schedule. There's no game today, so the team won't be there to celebrate a win or loss, and truthfully, Kaitlyn has been there for me, through the highs and the lows, and I really want to be there for her when she needs me too.

"Give me a few minutes to get dressed, and we'll head out."

"Wear something sexy."

I chuckle. "I am not wearing anything sexy."

"Dress nice. No yoga pants."

"Why the hell not? Why would it matter in a dark pub?"

She folds her hands and presses them to her heart. "Because I want you to remember every detail of tonight. What everyone was wearing, what everyone was doing, when I first speak with my future husband."

I stare at her for a second, and then burst out laughing. "You're crazy, you know that?"

She grins. "No, I'm not, my mother had me tested."

I poke her nose. "And you watch too many TV sitcoms."

I make my way to the bathroom, and turn on the shower, so happy that we now have running water, all thanks to the guy who is dead to me. Well, he isn't. He's alive and breathing, and living rent-free in my stupid brain.

I brush my teeth, fix my hair, and since I look a little like I hadn't seen sun in a while, I put on a bit of blush and some lipstick. I change into a pair of jeans, and a light sweater. My hair, though, I clip it up, and let a few tendrils frame my cheeks.

I head downstairs, and find Kaitlyn talking to one of our roommates who came back early. I smile at Mia, and she gives me a hug. "Have fun tonight." She disappears and I arch a brow at Kaitlyn.

"Why is everyone acting so weird tonight?"

"You just haven't been out of your room enough and forget weird is our normal." She gives me a once over, twice. "You look good."

"I'm glad you approve." I frown, and glance at the clock. "I don't want to be out too late."

"Jesus girl, it's nine o'clock. When did you turn eighty?"

"Yesterday, and thanks for missing my birthday," I say and hike my purse up high over my shoulder.

She laughs. "It's good to see you still have your sense of humor."

I need to have my humor, otherwise I'd spend day and night crying. Kaitlyn loops her arm through mine. "Let's walk, in case we have too many drinks."

"I'm not having too many drinks."

The night is dark, the clouds heavy as we walk toward the Growler, and when we reach the pub and enter, I glance at the stage, but there's no band playing. Come to think of it, it's still officially holiday break, why would they schedule a band when half the students aren't back yet.

I turn to Kaitlyn, about to question her when a commotion catches my eye. More than half the football team is here, all eyes on Christian as he stands, his chair scraping the floor.

I fumble backward and grab Kaitlyn's arm. "What's going on?"

"Don't be mad at me."

My gaze goes from her to Christian, back to her again. "What have you done, Kaitlyn?"

"I need you to trust me on this."

"I'm leaving."

"Please, Maize. If you can't do this for you, do it for me."

My brain is a fuzzy mess, trying to figure out what she's talking about when Christian takes long strides and closes the distance between us. My God, he has dark patches under his eyes that match mine. Has he not slept in a week either?

There's a pleading look in his eyes when he says, "I need to talk to you."

"I don't have anything to say to you, Christian."

"That's okay. I don't need you to talk. I need you to listen."

I open my mouth to argue, but he cuts me off.

"The first thing I want to say is I know you're not like my mother. I know you'd never do it on purpose, Maize…and you don't have to do it alone. I'll always be there for you. I want to be there for you, if you'll let me. I didn't know that this was what I wanted until I met you."

I stand there staring at him, the mixture of sadness and hope mingling in his eyes, but I have no idea what he's talking about. *You're not like my mother.* What the hell? I open my mouth to ask, but he presses a finger to my lips to hush me.

"The second thing I have to say is I think you were given wrong information. I'm certain of it. Linc and I talked, and we put it together."

I glance around the room, and all eyes turn away, all except Kaitlyn's. She's keeping a close eye on me to make sure I'm okay, and I appreciate that. I realize she brought me here for a reason, and I trust her. There's something she needs me to hear, so I'll hear it, despite the fact that I'm is shaking so hard, it's near impossible to stand. I glance back at Christian, and my legs nearly give way. The mere sight of him is messing with my brain and my body. I slide onto the bar stool.

"Wrong information?" I'm seriously lost here. If he's talking about him in bed with Chelsea, I saw the pictures with my own damn eyes. At least, I think I did. I can for sure say it was his room, but the couple was dark. Why would anyone else be in his room, and in his bed, right? Something in the way that he looks at me tells me I'm about to find out, so I close my mouth and let him finish, hoping that everything he's saying will eventually make sense.

"Let me back up," he says and takes a deep breath.

"Every year my parents have a Christmas party. I hate it."

"Wait, it wasn't your party?"

"No, it's a big family party and I'm expected to be there, and Mom invites her friends, and everyone from her social circle..."

"Including Chelsea."

"Yes."

"Chelsea told me it was your party. I felt..." I glance down. "I ran into her at the coffee shop. I thought it was a weird coincidence."

"Jesus," he mutters, and takes another breath. "You thought I had a party and didn't invite you."

"Something like that."

"I'm sorry, Maize. You can't believe anything Chelsea tells you. And I know how that made you feel, actually. To think you weren't invited...wanted."

I blink up at him. "You do?"

"You asked me to drop you off two doors down, terrified your mother would see me."

I'm about to protest, but it's the truth. I did do that, not thinking how it would make him feel. We weren't officially a couple, but I was in love with him, and I never stopped to think how much that would hurt him.

"I'm sorry," I say, accepting responsibility. "I never stopped to think."

"It's okay, I understand. You didn't know where we stood, or how I felt and that's my fault. I should have told you how I felt, but there's a small chance I'm a bit of a chicken shit." My lips wobble, but he goes completely serious and adds, "The truth is, Maize, I didn't invite you because you would have hated it. I hate it. I only go because...well, because I always have to play the role of the good son. You know me, always having to do the right thing. I fucking hate it, but it's been ingrained into me since I was a boy. I wanted you at that party more than anything in the world. Not at the party because you'd hate it, but I wanted you with me. I thought about you the whole time, and sent you tons of texts before-hand, you just never responded."

"I did respond. I was busy with Mom when your messages came in and when I finally had a moment, I crawled into bed, and sent a dozen messages back, but I only got one message from you."

"What?" he asks, his eyes wide, filled with worry.

I take my phone from my back pocket, and show him the text that says I'd be at the coffee shop and his response of, *Busy, can't.*

"Fuck, I didn't write that. I would never be too busy for you."

I run my finger along the phone and show him all the texts I sent him.

He exhales and his shoulders sag. "I never got any of them." He hands me his phone. "Look."

I take a look, note the texts from me are gone. I shake my head. "I don't understand."

"I dropped my phone, and Linc had it. Chelsea must have gotten hold of it when she was in my room, answered you, then deleted them. That's how she knew you were at the coffee shop. It wasn't a coincidence and it's the only logical explanation."

"And the only logical explanation of the pictures I saw of your bedroom, with her in your bed was that she was there with Linc, not you."

"Yes. It's the honest to God's truth." I take in the intensity of his eyes, and there is nothing to suggest he's lying to me. In fact, there's a sense of panic about him. "You need to believe me. I did not send that text. I didn't even have my phone. Linc stumbled into my bed, where Chelsea was waiting for me, and I slept in the spare bedroom. If you don't believe me, you can ask Linc."

I take a huge breath, my brain once again going over every-thing this man has done for me since his wayward ball first hit me in the head. Honest to God, I actually hate myself that I thought badly of him. Old insecurities were too close to the surface. "That's not necessary."

He sucks in a breath, panic all over his face. "Please, Maize. Just ask him."

"No."

"If I found her there, Maize. I would have left. How could I ever sleep with another girl when I'm in love with you? You're the only one I want."

"You're...in love with me?"

"Yeah, I have been for a long time."

I put my hand on his arm. "Now I need for you to stop talking and start listening."

His lashes fall slowly over blue eyes, and my hand slides to his. "I thought you were just slumming, finally finishing what you started in that closet. I didn't want to believe it, though. It didn't make sense, but that stupid pants situation in the closet made me think on some level you were capable of being that mean. A mean boy." I crinkle my nose. "I know you're not that boy anymore, but old insecurities."

A humorless laugh rumbles out of his throat. "You should know I never pulled my pants down. I always thought you pulled them down, until I found out there was a third person in the closet with us, and he was supposed to pants us both. The closet was open before he could. We were both pranked, Maize. I never would have dated Chelsea had I known she was behind it."

My jaw drops open. Holy God, all this time I had it wrong. "I can't believe it."

"It's the truth. Chelsea was definitely one of the mean girls."

"I don't think that's ever going to change."

"I've never cheated on you. Even though we weren't a couple, I never cheated. I wanted to spend every waking second with you. Leaving every Sunday afternoon was hard, when all I wanted to do was stay in bed, or study with you. You trusted me then, didn't even ask where I was going, and I honestly hope you can trust me again."

"I don't need to know where you were going."

He smiles and leans in, not wanting anyone to hear, and that's just like Christian. Fiercely private. "I volunteer at the children's hospital. It's just something I do. I didn't need praise or glory, or have people thinking I was doing it to better my resume. That's why I never told anyone, but I probably should have told you." He swallows, and catches me off guard when he puts his hand on my stomach. "There's something else we need to talk about." A pause and then, "I know. I know everything."

The warmth of his hand seeps under my skin, brings on a quiver. "Know what?"

"When I said you were nothing like my mother..." He pinches the bridge of his nose, and takes a breath like he's trying to form his thoughts. "I want to be completely honest with you. At first, I thought you weren't really on the pill, that you were trying to trap me. Then I thought maybe you didn't need me anymore because you got into Harvard and the scholarship and internship, and then I thought maybe you ran away—"

I cut him off, unable to follow his ramblings. "Christian, what are you talking about?"

"The baby. I found a pamphlet for a pregnancy test in my bathroom."

The world tilts on its axis and I nearly fall off my stool as the pieces fall into place. "I'm not pregnant, Christian. It wasn't me who took the pregnancy test in your apartment. It was...a friend."

He lets loose a breath and for a moment I can't tell if it's relief or sadness, but there is one thing I do know. I lean away from him, and he stiffens. "You're a guy who does the right thing. You just said so yourself. But I don't want to be with you, or have you telling me you love me, because you think I'm pregnant and being devoted is the right thing." I slide off the stool, and stand with it between us. "I want to be with you because you want me."

He stares at me so long and hard, the room so quiet you could hear a pin drop, and I start to fidget self-consciously.

He turns from me, and tears pound behind my eyes as he offers me his back. I grip the bar counter, wait for Kaitlyn to come collect the mess that is me, but she's not moving. No one is moving. Everyone is watching Christian walk to the empty stage where no band is playing.

He takes a microphone, taps it twice. "Maize Malone, I love you. I've loved you for a long time now, and I hope in time you'll love me too, and come to see that I'm not such a bad guy."

My heart stops beating and time seems to stand still as I take him in, standing on the stage for all to see and hear his inner, most personal thoughts. What the ever-loving fuck! The guy who's private about everything is standing on a stage in front of his football buddies, professing his love for me. Have I died and gone to heaven? Has hell frozen over? Have I fallen again, and lost all consciousness?

"I want to be with you, because I want you. Now and forever. I want to have kids with you, and start a family with you. I want to be there when you become a lawyer and make the world a better place." He holds his hand out and I stare at it. "Can you come up here? I never got the chance to give you your Christmas present."

I'm not sure I can move, or even walk, but the next thing I know, I'm headed toward him, the tears in my eyes making it a little difficult. I reach him and he cups my face, and brushes the tears away with his thumbs.

"I know this is fast, but..." He drops to one knee and pulls out a ring. I gasp and there's a hush over those watching and now I'm glad I'm not in yoga pants. It's better that I'm nicely dressed for retelling this story to our kids. I turn and catch Kaitlyn's eye, knowing she was behind some of this. She smiles at me and gives me her nod of approval.

"We don't have to call it an engagement ring if you don't want to, if you're not ready for that. We can call it a promise ring. I want you to know that I don't want to be with anyone else but you. I want you to know I am committed to you."

"Christian," I whisper quietly as the tears fall harder.

"These last few months together have been the best of my life."

"I don't know if I'd say that," I tease.

He blinks, hurt registering in his eyes. "Aw, come on Maize. It wasn't so bad, was it?"

I laugh, and throw my arms around him, my insides soaring with the love I feel for him. "Not so bad, Christian. Not so bad at all."

I back up an inch and hold my hand out to him. Cheers erupt as he slides the ring on. He stands and I cup his cheeks, and go up on my toes to brush my lips over his. "These last few months weren't the best of your life, Christian." His brow furrows, and I laugh with all the joy inside me. "The best is yet to come."

AFTERWORD

Thank You!

Thank you so much for reading **Enemy Down**, book two in my End Zone series. I hope you enjoyed the story as much as I loved writing it. Please read on for an excerpt of **Keeping Score, available July 2021**.

Interested in leaving a review? Please do! Reviews help readers connect with books that work for them. I appreciate all reviews, whether positive or negative.

Happy Reading,

Cathryn

Hate is a pretty strong word.

It's not one I use frequently, or even flippantly. No, I use it when I mean it. When it's justly deserved, and when no other expression fits. Like that time when I was sixteen, and one of my foster parents dragged the new kid into the bathroom and flushed his head in the toilet because he didn't eat the broccoli on his plate—like getting a serving of fresh greens once a week was a privilege not a right.

Hate.

That's the only word to describe what I felt for that cruel bastard. He deserved the ass kicking I gave him for hurting a fellow foster kid, but I didn't take joy in hurting him, or in all the hating—and there was a lot of hating. That stunt landed me in a new foster home, with a whole new set of problems.

But that's not what I'm thinking about at the moment. Nope, I'm thinking about the only other person I can truly say I hate, and I'm currently sitting across the table from him, my legs relaxed, my feet kicked out in front of me, as beads of sweat trickle down Cochrane Montgomery's too perfect face as he stares at the cards in his hands.

I don't hate rich folks as a rule. Hey, whatever hand we're dealt is the hand we have to play right? I learned to deal with poverty and violence early on but Cochrane here, he's had it good up until now, which is why he's having a hell of a time dealing—or rather laying his cards down.

Am I taking enjoyment in his misery? Would it be awful if I said yes? Horrible if there's this satisfying pleasure washing over me as he squirms. I might have grown up on the mean streets of Chicago, and learned to use my fists for survival, but I like to think I'm a civilized human being—thanks to my grade ten gym coach. He saw potential in me, and taught me to use my hands for something other than crime. He even gave me his 1969 old Honda CB 750 motorcycle. No one has ever given me anything before, other than an ass kicking that I probably deserved. That bike has been with me since I graduated high school, when Coach handed her down to me —a ride for college, he'd said with pride, knowing he was a big part in shaping my future. I didn't want to take her, but he insisted. In return I promised I'd take good care of her and now she's my pride and joy and I wouldn't trade her for the world. Sometimes I think it's the bike—coach's belief in me— that gave me the motivation to make something more of myself and make him proud of me. That's why I'm here at Kingston College on a football scholarship, staring at the rich fuck who made my junior year miserable.

He licks his lips, and his head lifts. I almost laugh as he tries to play it off, play it cool, like I can't see right through him. Christ, I'm a hood rat, and can read a room, a situation, an opponent with my eyes closed, and if he thinks I'm not aware of his stress, of every muscle twitch in his body as he tries to beat me at poker, he's out of his fucking mind. I guess he figures a baller like me, a kid from the streets, must suck at math. He'd be wrong. Cards come naturally to me. Joining in the month's underground secret game at Wolf House however, not my thing...until tonight.

"Are you going to play or look at them all night," I taunt, shifting a little deeper into my seat, not at all worried he's going to win. I have a straight flush, and he's shit out of luck, in more ways than one. Rumor has it Daddy cut him off, put him on an allowance, because he'd been draining his account. The truth is Cochrane—I prefer to call him Dick, a play on his name, but mostly because he hates it—has a gambling problem.

But it's not Douche Bag's money I'm after. Rich boy just needs to be taken down a notch or two for treating me like trash when we roomed together first year. Guess he's not the cock-of-the-walk tonight. Back in our Freshman year, he's lucky I didn't give him a Burnside beatdown—that's what we called it back in our Burnside neighborhood—but my scholarship to bigger and better was far more important to me. Plus, revenge really is a dish best served cold, and while I'm quoting proverbial phrases...Karma is a bitch.

"Yeah, yeah," he says and swipes at his face. He might be rich, and tall and good looking, and might know how to charm the girls, but everything about him rubs me the wrong way. There's more to him, something insidious lurks beneath his perfect exterior. Maybe the girls are too dazzled by his perfect white teeth to see it.

"Come on Dick. We don't have all night."

He glares at me through beady blue eyes and I grin. My confidence is shaking him to his core and I almost—almost—give a shit.

"The name is Cochrane," he seethes through clenched teeth.

I glance around the basement of Wolf House, at the other intense, and illegal, games going on around me. I turn to our dealer, Andrew, as he waits for Cochrane to make a move. Andrew was the one who told me Cochrane was broke, and looking to win back some money. He's really one of the good guys. Rich, but treats everyone equally. We bonded my first year at Wolf house, when I was roommates with Cochrane. I have no idea who made that mix-up. Putting a scholarship baller in with the captain of the college's elite rowing team? Obviously, someone mixed the papers up or had a brain tumor. I suffered through Freshman year at Wolf House—I never belonged there to begin with—then switched houses during sophomore year, going off campus with a few of the guys I met on the football team. It was a much better fit, and I never looked back, until Andrew sent me a message about tonight's game.

"So, where's that sweet girl of your tonight?" I ask, knowing it will just rattle him. "Such a sweet thing." Reagan might be sweet to look at, the perfect California blonde and a killer body, but I don't like her much either. I don't hate her, no she doesn't deserve that harsh label, but she is one of the snotty rich girls, following in her folk's footsteps. Truthfully, I don't begrudge her that. Good for her for having the grades and ambition to aim for the senate like her parents. I don't know why I know that about her, only that I do. Really, she means nothing to me.

Then stop thinking about her, Rocco.

"Where she is and what she's doing is none of your business." He turns his attention back to his shit hand, and the table begins to vibrate with the nervous shaking of his foot.

I go silent, and just smirk at him. He takes a fast breath, and I'm pretty sure he's throwing up a silent prayer to the gods, which makes me laugh. Where the fuck was the mighty being when I was getting the living shit kicked out of me when I was barely a teen? Never mind that, where was my mother? Oh yeah, I remember. She fucked off when I was a toddler, leaving me with a mean bastard of a father, who resented everything about me, blamed me for her departure. When I got older, he used to like to show me how much he hated me, either with his fists, or his belt. He said it was to toughen me up, make a man out of me. He used to say that's what his father did to him, and he turned out just fine. Wrong. He did not turn out just fine. I have no idea where he is today, and I don't care.

He plays his hand, and I stare at the pair of kings. I exaggerate my movements, slowing everything down to drag out the moment as I lean forward, and lay my hand out, showcasing a gorgeous flush tens and Cochrane goes so silent, I think he might be having an out of body experience, and not a good one. His head lifts slowly, and his nostrils flare. He stares at me for a long moment.

"Pay up, buddy." I say breaking the silence between us as other games go on in the basement.

He glares at me his blue eyes hard, and almost...pleading. Man, it really shouldn't give me pleasure to see the guy who taunted me, called me gutter trash, and every other derogatory name under the sun, because I wasn't born into a prominent family, squirm. He got away with it, because I couldn't fight back and risk losing my scholarship. Guys like him with powerful fathers, would get me kicked out of college. I had a future to focus on. Still do, which is why showing up at this illegal game is out of character for me.

"Again?" He glances down, reaches for the cards, but I put my hand over his to stop him." His head lifts, his perfectly styled blonde hair a little mussed from running his shaky hands through it. "Double or nothing?"

"No time." I pick up my phone to check for messages. "I have somewhere to be." I don't but I'm not playing him again. I'm sure I could beat him, but taking his money isn't the point here.

"Listen I can't—"

"Can't what?" I ask, and take my coat off the back of my chair as I cast Andrew a glance, wondering if he's going to step in. Looks like he's going to let me handle things my way.

Cochrane leans in, and steals a glance around. "I can't get the money to you tonight."

I give a low, slow whistle. "That's against the rules, bro."

"Yeah, look, can you give me a week."

I click my lips, and give a slow shake of my head. "Don't think so. There's a new ride I've had my eyes on." I put my hands out, and mimic the action of revving a motorcycle. Yeah, he owes me a shitload of money. I lift my hand, like I'm about to gesture security over, and Cochrane pushes his chair back.

"Don't."

I drop my hand. "Don't what? Don't tell anyone you can't pay?"

"I can pay, it's just going to take me a while."

I shrug into my Falcon's coat, and fold my arms. "I'll wait why you call Daddy."

He curses under his breath, and pulls his phone from his pocket. He scrolls, but he's stalling.

"I want my money, Cochrane. Tonight." I bite back a chuckle, and decide to let him squirm just a little while longer. The truth is, I already won. I don't need his money, or a new motorcycle. My old one serves me well.

"Look." he leans closer, all conspiratorial like. "My girl..."

Okay, now he has my interest. "What about her?"

"You like her. I know you do."

I don't, and sure I was nice to her when I shared a room with Cochrane. Why wouldn't I be? But okay, let's see where he's going with this. "What does that have to do with any of this?" I wave my hand over the disarray of cards. "You want me to play her or something. I mean if you're desperate for me to take her money—"

"You can take *her*."

I sit there, my ears buzzing with the hum in the basement, positive I'm not hearing him correctly. Cochrane did not just offer his girlfriend up in exchange for money, right? No way, now how, did he mean that. If he did, I might just have to beat the shit out of him once and for all.

I stare at him, trying to regulate my breath, slow the pulse at the base of my neck as I wait for him to continue, and he finally does.

"I don't have the money right now," he lowers his voice and continues with, "Reagan, maybe you can...I don't know..."

"Fuck her?" I blurt out for shock value, and his nostrils flare as he scrubs his face.

He shakes his head. "No, I don't mean that." He tugs on his hair clearly digging himself in deeper and it's going to be fun to watch him try to come out of this with a shred of decency left. I mean who offers up their girlfriend? "I just, maybe you can hang out with her or something. I'm not suggesting sex. It's not on the table."

"Yeah, because that would make her a whore, Cochrane."

"She's not a whore. She's just the only thing I currently have of value."

Holy fuck.

My heart beats a little faster against my chest, and as my shock ebbs, rage takes its place. To think this guy would actually use his girlfriend for payment...I mean...I just can't even wrap my brain around that. I always knew he was a dick, I just never knew he was this big a one. Reagan docs not deserve a douche bag like this for a boyfriend, who is willing to basically trade her to cover his own ass.

Speaking of asses. Reagan has the sweetest ass I've ever set eyes on. The sweetest everything...but I am not going to take her in exchange of money. That is fucking ludicrous.

I crack my knuckles. "What the fuck would I want with Reagan?"

"She could maybe help you with your homework."

"I've got straight A's dude." I gesture to the cards. "I'm kind of good in math."

"Yeah, okay well. Maybe she could...cook for you. She's a great cook."

"Keep going?"

He sits up a little straighter. "You could—"

"Show her what a loser you really are? That she should be with a guy like me?" I'm just egging him on. Reagan is a nice looking princess, but a princess nonetheless, and we don't belong together. Not in this world or any other.

He snorts. "Yeah, like she's going to choose you over me, Rocco."

"You sure about that?"

"Yes."

"Maybe I'll prove you otherwise. Maybe I'll get sweet princess Reagan to fall for me just because I can. Just to prove you otherwise." I'm bluffing. I'm not an ass who goes around playing with other people's feelings.

"You can't."

He obviously wasn't worried about that when he put her name on the table. Now though, as he averts his gaze, I catch a small hint of worry. I can't help but think she should see what a disrespecting douche he really is, ready to hand her over to bail him out. Anything to save his own ass. first chance he could. Fight your own battles, dude. Christ, if I had a girl I loved—and I'm questioning Cochrane's love for Reagan—she'd be on a damn pedestal, and I'd fight tooth and nail to protect her.

"You can't touch her. She doesn't deserve that."

I snort. "She doesn't deserve any of this now, does she? But here's what I'll agree to. I won't touch her, unless she wants me to."

"She won't," he bites out harshly.

That's fine by me, I don't want to touch her either and I am one hundred percent sure Reagan is going to shut this shit down. Although there is another part of me, a small part that sees the obedient daughter, the doting girlfriend, the straight laced, albeit snooty college student who might, just maybe, just to save her boyfriend's balls, as little as they might be.

I crack my knuckles. "If she says no, we'll have to find another way to make you pay." I've been keeping score of all the cruel things he said to me, all the cruel pranks to make me look like a loser to his buddies at Wolf House Freshman year. Yeah, it was Cochrane who had a huge end of year bash at a posh downtown hotel and invited everyone from Wolf House—everyone but the loser from the wrong side of the tracks. He did love to flaunt his money, and drive home the fact that I didn't belong. I can't help but think there was more to it though, that there was other reasons he hated me. I'm not sure if I'll ever find out. I'm not sure I care.

He gulps. "She'll agree."

I tap my fingers on the table. "So if I agreed to this, we'd need to set rules."

"Yeah, of course," he says, a measure of relief registering on his face.

"You owe me a shit ton of money. Reagan is going to have to work that off for as long as it takes."

His throat gurgles as he swallows, hard, and tugs at the collar of his shirt as his gaze drops to my knuckles. What, is he suddenly realizing the error of his way, the precious cargo he's putting in the hands of a guy who was dragged up on the streets? Oh, what would senator daddy think of this? Yeah, like Reagan, he too is following in his father's footsteps.

"What other rules?" he asks.

"She's mine for one month," I say.

His body stiffens. "You...want her for one month."

"Yeah, I think that sounds about right. One month to work off *your* debt." I press my thumb into my bottom lip, like I'm considering what she might taste like."

"You can't touch her. It's not like that."

"Like I said, I won't, unless she wants me to."

"She won't." He shakes his phone. "Can you give me a minute to talk to her? I need to run the whole month thing by her."

I grin. I don't want Reagan—don't want to fuck her. I'm not into high maintenance princesses, but his comment about her never wanting me pissed me off enough to say, "Sure, but don't blame me if it's my dick she wants when the month is all over."

ALSO BY CATHRYN FOX

End Zone

Fair Play

Enemy Down

Keeping Score

All In

Blue Bay Crew

Demolished

Leveled

Hammered

Single Dad

Single Dad Next Door

Single Dad on Tap

Single Dad Burning Up

Players on Ice

The Playmaker

The Stick Handler

The Body Checker

The Hard Hitter

The Risk Taker

The Wing Man

The Puck Charmer

The Troublemaker

The Rule Breaker

In the Line of Duty

His Obsession Next Door

His Strings to Pull

His Trouble in Talulah

His Taste of Temptation

His Moment to Steal

His Best Friend's Girl

His Reason to Stay

Confessions

Confessions of a Bad Boy Professor

Confessions of a Bad Boy Officer

Confessions of a Bad Boy Fighter

Confessions of a Bad Boy Doctor

Confessions of a Bad Boy Gamer

Confessions of a Bad Boy Millionaire

Confessions of a Bad Boy Santa

Confessions of a Bad Boy CEO

Hands On

Hands On

Body Contact

Full Exposure

Dossier

Private Reserve

House Rules

Under Pressure

Big Catch

Brazilian Fantasy

Improper Proposal

Boys of Beachville

Good at Being Bad

Igniting the Bad Boy

Bad Girl Therapy

Stone Cliff Series:

Crashing Down

Wasted Summer

Love Lessons

Wrapped Up

Eternal Pleasure Series

Instinctive

Impulsive

Indulgent

Sun Stroked Series

Seaside Seduction

Deep Desire

Private Pleasure

Captured and Claimed Series:

Yours to Take

Yours to Teach

Yours to Keep

Firefighter Heat Series

Fever

Siren

Flash Fire

Playing For Keeps Series

Slow Ride

Wild Ride

Sweet Ride

Breaking the Rules:

Hold Me Down Hard

Pin Me Up Proper

Tie Me Down Tight

Stand Alone Title:

Hands on with the CEO

Torn Between Two Brothers

Holiday Spirit

Unleashed

Knocking on Demon's Door

Web of Desire

ABOUT CATHRYN

New York Times and *USA today* Bestselling author, Cathryn is a wife, mom, sister, daughter, and friend. She loves dogs, sunny weather, anything chocolate (she never says no to a brownie) pizza and red wine. She has two teenagers who keep her busy with their never ending activities, and a husband who is convinced he can turn her into a mixed martial arts fan. Cathryn can never find balance in her life, is always trying to find time to go to the gym, can never keep up with emails, Facebook or Twitter and tries to write page-turning books that her readers will love.

Connect with Cathryn:
Newsletter https://app.mailerlite.com/webforms/landing/c1f8n1
Twitter: https://twitter.com/writercatfox
Facebook: https://www.facebook.com/AuthorCathrynFox?ref=hl
Blog: http://cathrynfox.com/blog/
Goodreads: https://www.goodreads.com/author/show/91799.Cathryn_Fox

Pinterest http://www.pinterest.com/catkalen/